BREAL...........

CHRIS BARKER

First Edition

A CIP catalogue record for this book is available from the British Library.

ISBN (Paperback):   978-1-7398550-0-0

ISBN (eBook):   978-1-7398550-2-4

Published by Squid Ink Publishing

www.squidinkpublishing.co.uk

info@squidinkpublishing.co.uk

Squid Ink Publishing

Book cover design by Book Beaver

For LB,

Always

BREACHMAN

-How It Ends-

Volchak knew this was how he died.

An inevitable end to a violent life. This time it wouldn't matter how hard he fought, how stubborn he was, how many times he got up. This was just the one that got him. There was no help to come. No one even knew. He smiled to himself, resigned. What a suitable way for the great "Commander of the Breachmen" to go. No grand duel, no glorious battle, no damned breach... just propped against the cold, crumbled, stone wall with a bronze axe blade in his shoulder. The warm summer evening breeze licked his cheek as his life leeched away. He felt almost calm. About time.

Although he had not really expected to die by his own axe, he supposed it made sense. He was dead already, of course, bone and muscle crushed and torn where the gaping wound had been rent into his body. He was more or less held in place only by the weapon itself. A slow, but steady, pool of deep crimson blood trickled down the front of his blue wool uniform. Not his uniform. He hadn't ever been issued his own uniform. Volchak looked down at the axe head. He watched it with certainty. Each drop of his blood across the bronze head caught a glint in the sunset. After all the fights, the charges, the miles, the struggle, it had not lost its shine. Now it glistened, burgundy in the failing light. It'd been nearly fifteen years since the army drafted him. Ever since that day, it had drenched his world in sweat, grime, and blood. Some of it hadn't even been his.

'Don't die,' he croaked with a chuckle.

As he lay there, he realised it wasn't his shoulder that hurt, but everywhere else on his body. His tired aching neck burned from looking down at the wound, his back stabbed at him from slumping against the wall and his eyes stung from sweat, or blood, or maybe tears. At least he'd be closing them for good soon, they wouldn't hurt any more then.

Volchak supposed there was some rush that a person usually felt when agony overwhelmed them; it meant they couldn't feel the pain. In his second charge, he'd seen men with wooden arrows stuck clean through them keep running as if it was nothing at all. During his fourth, at the battle for Yrfrite, a pikeman had used his own severed arm to block the second swing of Volchak's axe, brown leather stained black with the man's own blood as he held it up like a shield. It hadn't ended well for the man. The second swing was as deadly as the first, more so, really. But Volchak doubted he would get the impulse to jump to his feet or make a last heroic stand against his killer; he just sat slumped with his heavy legs out before him and his lifeless left arm on the cold stone floor, and wished he didn't ache so much.

He thought about how one day he'd take this axe and trade it away. A life of peace, somewhere away and forgotten. Maybe wander into the Western Mountains and never come back, cross the sea or just head north until he passed out of memory. Somewhere to be left alone. But for now, it stubbornly refused to let him die, not straight away at least.

Volchak's vision was already blurring, through blood loss, or maybe the pain was deciding where it actually belonged. He looked up with misty grey eyes at the shape of his killer, slightly obscured in the shadow of the moss-covered parapet on the far side of the wall. He knew the shape, of course. Maybe he'd known for a while.

Like most fights Volchak had been in, which was a respectable number, it had been unceremonious, messy, and brief. More luck than skill, bad luck for Volchak. He had seen a fencing match performed as part of a festival once. More like a dance than a fight, all that spinning and thrusting and parrying with sparks flying. The bowing and the breaks in between rounds, and the drinking afterward. Well, that part was like a lot of his fights. But the rules, oh how he had marvelled at the rules. No one threw sand, they didn't kick out, hadn't spat in the face, punched at the crotch, gouged the eyes. It was all so... civilised. His own experience fighting in the breach had far more scratching, clawing, beating, shouting and spitting, until someone got lucky or someone else's luck ran out.

Volchak's long, lifeless, greying hair was soaked with blood, which made it stick to his brow, as he raised his head to look towards the man's face.

'Don't... die, eh?' Another cough, the gurgling in his throat more pronounced now, the sharp copper taste of blood.

The shape looked down at him. When Volchak met the eyes, there wasn't any hatred there, just indifference. This was just a natural end, the next step they both had to take. They both knew that it might have eventually ended up here, this was the only peace to be had for either of them. The person shrugged slightly as they turned away to walk down the wooden steps, back into the city below. Volchak swallowed another retching cough and watched the figure leave, without staying to see him die. Left him alone. Of all his wounds, it might be that was where the pain really belonged. His eyes stung as they teared up, before he leaned his head back and closed them.

Volchak knew this was how he died, and that he deserved it.

Chapter 1

'Perfection.'

Volchak's head snapped up from staring into the fog that hung lightly around the crest of the hill. He immediately knew to whom the nasal voice belonged; and importantly, he knew it was asking him for attention. Not a reply. His ribs, almost imperceptibly, stung a little just from the movement, one old wound or another tugging at the skin.

He breathed a grunt of acknowledgement. The sun had been shining all morning but was yet to clear the fog entirely. The hill he was standing on had a pleasant breeze, which made the grass sway in waves all around them and there was even a smell of cooked meat coming from somewhere nearby. On any other spring day, this would be an incredibly pleasing place to find yourself, although Volchak suspected this isn't what the High Commander meant.

'Your...' there was a pregnant pause, 'division... is prepared?' Smiele waved his hand. Indicating beyond the army gathered below the bluff in their neatly ordered rows - armor shining. He had clearly noticed the other group lazing just off the side, lightly armed, wood and stone weapons, more common folk than soldiers. The Breachmen were Volchak's command, and were a lot less grand than Smiele's own Royal Guard.

Smiele had always suited his name somehow, Volchak thought. High born, of course, of excellent stock.

Educated yet foolishly arrogant. He was a big man despite his voice, standing a head taller and broader than most in any gathering, causing those around to look up to him in not just a figurative sense. Smiele's plated mail, polished to a mirror shine, was expertly crafted to give an air of authority and opulence that the people would expect from the High Commander of the Royal Guard. At his hip, a long sword, as smart and wealthy as the man, more gold and more polish. Although Volchak had never actually seen it get dirty enough to warrant a good cleaning.

'Aye,' Volchak said again knowing he wasn't really being asked. He was being told they weren't.

Volchak looked over the Royal Guard regiment at the base of the hill, twelve neat rows of twelve men, glimmering halberds pointed to the sky. Their armour just as polished. Their formation just as sharp. Volchak admitted to himself this was an imposing force. Well-trained, well-armed, and well-drilled. And the armour... Volchak hadn't known for sure, but he suspected half the metal in the kingdom was on these men. The mine at the capital must have churned for years to deliver enough iron to put so many in such finery. Not a lot of good it did, standing in an empty field in the barren flats between the capital and Yrfrite, about to crush some of the city's people.

Not as handy up close, of course, but then wooden and bone weapons could barely scratch the armour, let alone the man beneath it. They had given each man a full-face helmet, complete protection in a melee, only a small slit to see through. Volchak scratched at the thick scar across his right cheek, the tough skin catching on his nails as it itched. They afforded him no such luxuries.

Even if you were to draw them out, try to get a short spear under the arm or in the visor, for that each soldier carried a short sword at their side. A good idea in theory, but in all that mail and tight quarters, Volchak doubted they could draw them, let alone fight; they'd probably never had to. Another tremendous waste of metal. But like Smiele, the Guard would crush those who got in their way under their plated boots.

'A fine field, Commander. Finally, a chance to break the back of this troublesome Duke Olaf and his paltry rabble.' Smiele was grinning. He hadn't heard him. Hadn't tried to.

'Those buildings will give the Guard some trouble.' Volchak nodded to the centre of the open flat ground in front of them. Beyond the Royal Guard stood a small collection of four farm buildings, a house and some barns, before more ground, that gave way to a solid mass of angry looking brown shapes. Each of those shapes was a citizen of the city of Yrfrite, a guard, a soldier, a mercenary... 'or a farmer, a shopkeeper or a clerk...' Volchak had heard Harkner say as they gathered earlier that morning.

'Nonsense.' Smiele was confidence embodied. 'It's closer to us than them by a third.' Volchak knew arrogance wouldn't make it true - likely he'd just have to run faster to stop the Duke's army getting to it first. 'We will have cleared those buildings before engaging, I am sure of it.'

On the outside, Volchak's face didn't move, but internally it wrenched every time Smiele said 'we'. *We* meant Volchak. He looked at the opposing army. Even at this distance, they clearly outnumbered the Royal Guard - even with the two supporting infantry units under the High Commander's control. But Volchak could tell the enemy lacked significant organisation or training. They were not as well-armed, and certainly not as well-drilled. They had their weapons, of course, maces and clubs made from heavy oak, pikes cut from long willow and short spears from birch. All quite effective at killing a man - unless that man was in plate mail surrounded by dozens more just like him. These were mostly just people who would fight for a cause they believed in, but the belief wasn't putting armour on their backs or swords in their hands.

Volchak watched, itching his face again. They were moving, but not advancing, a general thrum of activity with no particular direction, just pulsing in place. Duke Olaf had roused an impressive army in numbers and spirit, but they weren't soldiers, he thought. Volchak knew that Smiele was probably right, the Breachmen would cover the ground to the centre faster than that army would.

The rebel Duke walked back towards his force from the negotiations in the centre of the field, whilst the King's men headed for the bluff where Volchak stood. The Duke would have asked for terms, maybe some freedoms for the people of his city, self-government or something. Probably he had thought he had the numbers and might have believed he could get them. But the King's councillor would have waxed on about treason, duty and the birth right of the King to protect his citizens. He was more than happy to have a battle, especially one he wouldn't fight in. Volchak shrugged to himself. How better to control a city than to invite those who would stand against your rule out to a field and send others to kill them?

The councillor and two guards grew closer and each held up a plated hand towards the hill, a pre-agreed signal of sorts. Pre-agreed before the negotiations even started. Volchak barely noticed, he stood staring, entranced by the beast. The councillor's mount was the only horse Volchak had ever seen, more than most men ever would see. It had been said that many generations ago, the richest men of Tydrian had enough horses to race them, or even fight on them, but now they were unheard of. Gone, like so much of the glory of the past. Horses fascinated him. Large awkward beasts stomping around, occasionally shaking their massive heads or circling in place impatiently. Like riding an overly excitable bull. The reigns and saddle (he had heard these

4

terms around the camps leatherworkers) seemed so fragile and a primitive a way to control them, tugging on the face as you sat on its back. But then Volchak had seen the councillor flee from a negotiation turned sour, and then the horse had moved with such alarming grace and speed Volchak had thought it would be a terrifying thing to stay on, let alone stand in front of.

Smiele drew his long sword with a dramatic ring from the silver blade and turned to his military entourage, eager dogs that turned to their master for praise. Some still chewed on meat from their hearty breakfast, others appeared to have already started on the wine. Volchak wondered how many times that Smiele had drawn the sword for dramatic effect, then carefully, and quietly, sheathed it again within a matter of minutes. Smiele certainly wasn't about to start a duel with his own subordinates.

Volchak squeezed the worn leather grip of his axe, *just in case*, he chuckled to himself. It was a formidable, yet crude, weapon. Larger than was practical. And heavy. Volchak had used a stone hammer in the war with the Boatman. But during his fourth charge, outside the walls of Yrfrite, he'd taken it from a rebel infantry commander. Volchak had pushed an antler blade into the man's throat as he raised it, watched as the dying man dropped it, and then caught it himself before it hit the floor. Two large bronze blades held the solid bronze haft between, their weight and thickness meant to bludgeon as much as carve their targets. The sharp spike on the head made for thrusting, or to catch a sword. Not as well made as, say, the High Commander's sword. The axe was clumsier and the metal was of lower grade, mixed with weak tin and supple copper in Yrfrite when the mines still flowed there. It commanded an imposing presence, however, and was worth a small fortune in and of itself. Enough to leave this all behind, one day. It wasn't a delicate weapon and showed little grace, but it worked from the front, the side and the back, which suited Volchak fine where he was going.

'When you are quite ready, Commander Volchak?' the weasel-faced lieutenant sneered at him. He probably hadn't so much as looked down his nose at the battlefield. His nose was firmly occupied with pleasing Smiele. Volchak didn't know his name, didn't care to. He shot him a glare whilst gripping his axe, hands straining on the bronze haft. What little of the man's courage buckled, and he disappeared into the group behind him.

As Volchak turned and walked towards the gathering around the large map table, no gaps formed and no one else acknowledged him. He stood half a head shorter than most of them and several dozen heads lower in their minds. It was the axe, or rather how he had wielded it, that had earned him enough recognition, and even begrudging tolerance, from the officers to grant his place in the High Commander's personal entourage. Whilst the others in their small group had their high-names, estates on the outskirts of the capital and their own plate mail with their own golden inlays, Volchak had his axe and a soldier's reputation. Stocky and not handsome, his manner was serious and gruff, not full of snarky remarks like them. He muscled into the gaggle of officers, paying little heed to whose shoulder he knocked or toes he stepped on. It reminded him all too much of a battle, jostling and clawing for position. Except they used titles and words over axes and hammers. Volchak had a determination to not die, which had got him through some tough skirmishes, but here he was poorly armoured and poorly equipped.

Volchak had never really understood why he accepted it when they drafted him. They had come to his small homestead and rounded him up, alongside some of his friends from neighbouring farms. He had seen this happen twice before in his memory. He'd seen none of the last ones come back. Over the years, he understood how a draft worked, why they were, how they were, but not why the people accepted it. He supposed that when armed men, with their wooden spears and antler blades, dozens of them, demanded you fight for your king and do your duty – you just accepted it. It was robbery, but robbery of a man's life. They had taken him then. It was at the camp that they had brought him to Smiele. The man who would become High Commander was younger then, less experienced, but just as capable and just as ruthless. He had singled out Volchak from the other draftees. A man had tried to draw an antler blade on Volchak during a drill, a stabbing over some forgotten slight wasn't unheard of from draftees after a few months training. Volchak had beaten the man to the ground with his bare hands, all but killed him. Smiele had seen the whole thing. They took Volchak and rather than punish him, they had taught him to read, to think, to plan and to lead. He was to be a Commander; they had told him. He could choose a staff, and together they could command strength and glory for the King. Ever-since, Volchak had never met the King. He had seen the monarch once at a war council, but only from afar. If he had spoken to him then, Volchak would have asked him what was the difference between glory and punishment.

Despite his place on the High Commander's staff, surrounded by lieutenants, with their shining helmets and majors in their tight battle dress, Volchak was dressed little better than the peasants on the other side of the battlefield. He had a thick leather tabard, worn belt and creased trousers. His unkempt shoulder-length hair stuck to his face and neck and only partially hid the round, weathered face underneath. He clearly stood out amongst this crowd, and not only because no one would stand within arm's reach of him for fear of being associated with someone with as unpleasant a reputation as him. As he pushed through, Volchak soon found a corner of the table, which within moments he had to himself. Volchak was no stranger to having to jostle for his position. They had drilled him as a Breachman, assaulting the enemy to get behind their shield walls. Get up close and hit hard. Sometimes it was just as useful to push a man out the way as it was to kill him. But it was nice to not have to do either here. An axe could tear down barricades, chop at pike heads, smash shields and cause enough confusion that when the Royal Guard arrived, they would roll over the enemy's broken wall. But the axe also marked him out as a dangerous man to associate with, not just because of his reputation. When it was swung it wouldn't always hit the right person, too unwieldly.

His wasn't a glorious role. Few lived long enough to suffer much glory, but a drafted man owed the army twenty-five years - a Breachman was done in fifteen. Payment for the danger you were put in, reward for having lived that long fighting in the Breach. Volchak was the first person to come close to claim this reward. So, whilst the other officers might judge him, snipe at him, degrade his low birth and question his place here, they would think twice before telling him that to his face.

'Well met, Volchak,' Fedal offered an armoured gloved hand. Volchak gripped it and nodded to the man.

'Aye, Major Fedal.'

'Fine morning for it, Commander?' Fedal's manner was professional yet cordial, with the slightest hint of irony. The fact he would speak to Volchak directly was a minor act of defiance to most of the gathering. Major Fedal was a heavy set and serious man, one of the lowest high-born and the most sensible of the entourage. Apart from himself, Volchak thought, on both counts.

'Fine day to die?'

'S'pose not. Your men are prepared?'

'Aye. Breachmen are always ready for a fight.' He spoke with an air of authority, clear and confident, whilst looking over the table at the gaggle of officers. 'You'll be on the flanks with your divisions?'

'I expect so. And you the middle?'

'Aye, straight up the middle.'

Confidence had its uses in these circles, Volchak knew that, especially with his reputation for violence such as it was. Even if inside, his stomach was turning in circles with panic, just like it did during every charge.

Volchak glanced to Smiele, who had emerged from the command tent and was pacing in front of the table. No one shared his side either, but Volchak doubted for the same reason.

Through his dark hair he looked back to Smiele and held his gaze, sternly. His dull grey eyes did not blink, just peered above his crooked nose, from his weathered face. Whether Smiele respected him, Volchak didn't really know. Saw him as a blunt instrument to be wielded, most likely, to advance Smiele's own illustrious career. Five charges, two pitched battles, and all successful victories. Unfortunately, few of the Breachmen had lived through most of them to enjoy their success. Smiele had singled Volchak out from the training camps early as a Breachman. Smiele had used Volchak more and more over time as he came to see the effectiveness his heavy infantry had when coupled with Volchak's ferocious Breachmen.

'Good men and good ground.' Smiele repeated to himself. Loudly, proudly, to the rest.

'Fedal, have the infantry proceed half pace on each flank. Royal Guard slow and steady in the middle when they are engaged.' Smiele was confident and clear, convinced of his superiority of the force and his mastery of warfare as he pointed at the open ground in front of them with his long sword.

'Arrows sir?' Major Fedal replied. As a commander of the two infantry divisions, he was more aware of the potential casualties of his men. He had a more seasoned approach to war than the majority here, albeit always less pragmatic and therefore less successful than Smiele. He wasn't seeking glory, but it wasn't likely to find him either.

And besides, when it came to the charge, he'd be on the hill with the rest of this lot and not down there fighting with his men.

'No. This ragtag mob will scatter if we let them, killing a few of them from afar, so the rest run achieves us very little. Better to crush them now up close with the Guard whilst you keep them tied down.' Smiele didn't mention that there were barely twenty archers in the entire army he had with them. Nor that their bows and wooden arrows were more suited for rabbit and deer than the militia of Yrfrite. Bows had never been much used in combat, except perhaps by the more exotic tribes found many months journey north of Tydrian, where the game they hunted was bigger and had a thicker hide. Arrows were expensive when tipped with iron, and without that, they were of little use over long range. Besides, Volchak supposed that the Kings and High Commanders liked to get their men up close. Tear apart their enemies so they never came back to trouble them again. That's why they would rather equip dozens in steel armour so they could crush their enemies than try to risk wastefully shooting them from afar. A corpse cost nothing to make, even less if you didn't have to pay the one who made it.

'Aye.' Fedal stepped away and began marching down the bluff, relaying the orders to a gaggle of lesser officers to take to the two larger infantry divisions on either side.

'Volchak?' Smiele didn't even turn. 'Breachmen out front.'

Volchak's heart sunk and stomach churned. Not that this tactic was ever in doubt. Every time the Breachmen were out front of the Royal Guard. Every time the same. His men would hit the shield wall first, disrupting the lines to make sure nothing would disrupt theirs. Volchak thought by now someone would have caught on and tried some other way of fighting back, but it seemed the Duke's commanders were just as obstinate as the King's.

In that moment when he heard Smiele's command and he stepped back from the table, the same thought crossed Volchak's mind as it had before, and before that, each time a little louder. None of the other commanders were drawing weapons to go down to fight. As he marched down the hill towards his thirty grim fighters, the Majors and the Lieutenants would still be up on their hill with their eyeglasses and their cloaks, warm and safe. Volchak didn't understand why some men got to stand above a battle and decide who had to charge at what. Or maybe he understood, but hated how they decided who those men were. Or maybe that they decided it wasn't to be him.

These officers would live long lives. They'd have wives and families who'd grow up to become officers to have more wars over cities that did or didn't want to pay homage to their king. Then they'd get to tell more men to run at other men with spears.

He opened his mouth to protest the order.

'Aye, sir.'

Damn.

Chapter 2

Kaelith slouched in the uncomfortable chair at the grimy table and pretended to be less drunk than he was, and less like he cared about what happened one hour to the next. The tavern was noisy, hot, with flaking walls and splitting furniture, about as uncomfortable as the chair. Too many men were crammed into too small a place with too many drinks. It was simply a matter of time before it all boiled over. This suited Kaelith fine. If they involved him in the scrap, he'd pick a few of their pockets whilst fighting, maybe catch the eye of the guards who looked after this place to toss him out and he wouldn't even have to pay his tab. He was hardly helpless if it all got out of hand, even when as drunk as he was pretending not to be. If they did not involve him in the fight, then the picking the coin up afterwards was even easier. He smiled at the thought. A good lie was about telling as much truth as you could. He scratched at his stubbled chin and peered out from beneath his golden, greasy hair, most of which was in an untidy plait over his left shoulder.

His ornate breastplate was also uncomfortable when sitting, not much more comfortable when standing, but the heavy scratches and puncture marks across it proved that it was better to be alive and uncomfortable than the alternative. The rusting edges and flaking filigree suggested it had seen better days, rather like the man who wore it. At his side hung his cutlass. Long and arching, it almost touched the floor as he sat. Wholly impractical for fighting indoors, too long, although he supposed it was quite light. And he knew he could flourish it with enough panache that most people thought otherwise when it came to a fight. That's the trick to a good fight, he thought, don't be in it in the first place. He knew as he sat, though, if he moved, it'd jab him in the side at an uncomfortable angle, so he didn't move. All in all, this place wasn't that comfortable. Still, here he sat, cutting an imposing figure, the gentlemen mercenary, armoured and armed. Princely armour and with his glorious sword. Not spoiled by the fact he was a little overly liquored, chin stained with cheap wine and with a rather unwashed aroma that seemed to surround him.

He had spotted the woman against the far wall watching him from the moment he stepped in, of course. How could she not have been watching him? He'd always found it amusing when someone tried to look mysterious and covert by wearing black cloaks, hiding their faces. For one, it was far too hot in here for a cloak, so she stood out from the crowd, and second, they were ridiculous to fight in. You could grab a cloak, you can pull it, it'll get twisted round their legs or sword. Wear a cloak and you're as likely to stab yourself as get stabbed, although you might look dramatic whilst it happens, which is not saying nothing.

She walked over. Obviously, from her gait, she was confident but also wearing armour under that cloak. Weapons too, Kaelith wagered.

'You should take the cloak off before you stab me,' he said in a scratchy voice.

'What?' her voice was softer than expected, almost disarming his wit, almost.

'Cloaks can get grabbed, pulled, twisted round your legs or...' he started, before realising the absurdity of explaining this to her if he was going to have to grab it to save his own skin. His line of work meant he had made many enemies and no real friends. The enemies he made were, mostly, made unfairly. He was simply paid to fight them; it didn't mean he didn't like them. And it was rarely ever personal who he fought. The lack of friends was a professional hazard. When people stopped paying, you didn't keep fighting for them and when you didn't keep fighting, they were rarely still your friends. And when your enemies started paying you to fight your friends when you didn't have friends, then you just had enemies on both sides.

'Never mind. What do you want of Kaelith, a gentleman mercenary, famed swordsman and-' he grumbled slightly as a burp escaped his lips, he hadn't opened his mouth in a while other than to drink from the bottle nearby so it had caught him off guard '-tactical genius?'

The woman snorted with laughter and made no genuine attempt to hide it.

'You wound me, miss. Have you not come here based on my irrefutable reputation? Or was it my dashing good looks that wooed you to my table after an hour of looking? You'll only need *that* for one of these.' He nodded to the now visible hand bow hanging from her belt, as she swept aside her cloak to sit. Interesting, he thought. She obviously was from a very well-funded and well-equipped background to come after him with such a rare weapon. Bows of any kind were relatively rare and expensive, and the smaller ones more so, with their intricate metalwork mechanisms and refined design. A wooden bolt from a hand bow could kill a man sitting down at a table and people around wouldn't realise till he didn't raise his head to pay his tab. Could kill a man standing up too, but people usually noticed it when he fell over.

Huh, he'd always thought he'd go by having his head bashed in with a rock.

'I have a job for you.' Again, her disarming voice put him off his stride towards accepting his own murder.

'Ey?' His left hand released his cutlass grip, where it had silently strayed. He hadn't yet worked out how he would draw or whether he had room to swing it.

'We need a mercenary and yes, you do have a...' the woman glanced about at the unpleasant surroundings '... gentlemanly reputation.'

'Well then, you won't need to shoot me after all! Huzzah!' His hand emerged from under the table, seized the green glass and took a long drag on the wine bottle, choking slightly at the end and spilling some out onto his breastplate. The spill ran across one of the deeper grooves and onto his hair.

She took out a small bronze button, stamped with two hands on its back and placed it down in front of him.

'Ah, the good Duke. He's the one with the deep pockets then. And let me guess, his little rebellion isn't going as well as he'd liked and he's sought a famous warrior-' he paused, '-warrior-*poet* to turn the tide?' Kaelith chuckled, his bounding confidence showing in his pearly white smile.

'His struggle for the freedom of his people to govern themselves and not be beholden to a tyrant five hundred miles away continues, yes, and he is having his challenges with it. But he isn't interested in your strategic insights or your poetry.' *Damn but her voice, it almost sang.* 'He has a very specific job for you, and just over two weeks in which to be ready to do it.'

'... And he will pay...?' Kaelith said.

'Five hundred, and one hundred more if the job is complete and total.'

'And where is this small fortune? You don't have a small chest.'

That hung awkwardly for a moment.

'I have already delivered half to the men who guard your... equipment.' She couldn't stop one of her eyebrows from rising. 'You will receive the other half and the bonus when you have completed the task, and our problem taken care of.'

'*Your* problem.'

'You'll return after the battle, then back here to the city of Yrfrite and collect this from the Duke himself. Those are the terms.'

Kaelith leant back in his chair in a thoughtful and musing pose, or at least he hoped it seemed thoughtful, whilst he considered the proposition before him. It wasn't quite the offer she had first made it out to be. After all, he had to travel south first, fight, then back here. As he put on his most considered and business-like face, the chair slipped back slightly on the muddy floor and he kneed the underside of the table - knocking the small button and the bottle of wine into the air. He snapped back to seated and groaned as his cutlass dug him deep under the breastplate directly in his ribs.

'So, you've given me several hundred pieces,' he said, as if nothing had happened. 'It's with my men right now in the same place where we keep our most important belongings, well-guarded and well-equipped with some very burly and unpleasant chaps.' He paused as she regarded him with a blank stare.

'You are here alone in this tavern, with no guards, asking me to travel for two weeks to fight in a battle, possibly dying, or having many of my men die and losing all my most precious belongings in the meantime. Then travel several hundred miles back to pick up another similar number of pieces?'

She nodded slowly. He knew exactly where one of her hands was, and he could see the other.

He paused again, this time a glint in his eye gave away that he really was weighing up the options.

'Yerr… alright. We're in.' He smiled widely.

'You'll bring all of your equipment?' she asked, clearly pleased with the direction this was going.

'No. But some of it. Yes.' Kaelith only ever had so many eggs to put in a single basket. And what he kept back; he might need to get away after he finished the job if it didn't go the way they all wanted. Replacing his equipment was arduous at best, impossible at worst.

'Then we have a deal?' Her hand stretched out in front of her, the one not holding the hand-bow.

'My lady, we have an accord.'

The moment they shook hands, the noise in the tavern dulled considerably. The jostling, the drinking, the drunken singing dried up as most of the patrons looked over at the pair. Even the two brawny groups that had been eyeing each other from adjacent tables seemed to abandon their quarrel. Everyone looked over at Kaelith and his new employer, sat in the stuffy corner at the grimy table, hands grasped in a single shake. With a nod, Kaelith let go and stood up, and almost every other man there packed up their belongings to follow him. Kaelith smiled to himself. He knew his ruse had been impressive, of course. Each man in here carefully placed, acting their parts perfectly. The ale suitably watered down and the wine of suitably poor quality that it mattered not how much it flowed. Well, actually that was more because it was expensive and he found himself rather without a benefactor currently. It was a shame it hadn't come to one of the pre-agreed brawls to clear the place out a bit before she spoke to him, but no matter. He smiled at his own dashing brilliance as he strode past her, then tripped on her cloak.

Chapter 3

Flea watched the small, black-haired man make his way down the hill. She sat listening to the sounds of nervous men griping and joking to each other on the cold, damp grass. The fog hadn't lifted but she could see the small shape growing larger as he worked his way round the far division and towards her and the rest of the Breachmen. Some were sitting, some were standing and one was even sleeping on the dewy grass. Flea looked quizzically at the sleeping man, clad in his dirty stained leather armour with a serene look on his face, gripping his dirty stone warhammer to his chest like a statue of a forgotten king. She couldn't understand how Harkner could sleep. They sat here a mile or so from a thousand angry rebels on one side and a few dozen strides from the walking meat grinder that was the Royal Guard on the other. Fear hung in the air, as well as a certain grim acceptance from the others gathered in small groups on the surrounding grass. It was daytime, and they might all be dead by sunset. She wondered if maybe he was dead already. People died on campaigns all the time. They got sick; they fell over, they never got up. Or they got mad, hurt themselves, or they wandered off and the Ropers got them. Occasionally they even died in battles…

'I'm still here, Flea,' came his calm voice. Had she said something? She didn't think she'd said something.

Harkner propped himself up on his elbow and smiled at her, casually, as if he was a lazing in the meadow without a care in the world, enjoying a morning by the River Vioene.

Aside from his battered armour, tightly cropped hair and the large heavy looking warhammer now lying next to him in the dewy grass, he wouldn't have been out of place there at all. Confidently grinning at the courtiers who sidled past towards the palace as he carelessly wiled the day away.

'Not for long.' Flea nodded towards the Commander of the Breachmen who was chatting with a burly infantryman, a major by the look of his uniform. Flea smiled as he approached, as you would smile to an approaching monster when it is on your side. Mr. Volchak was a fighter too, like Harkner. He had been leading from the front on all three of the charges that Flea had suffered the unfortunate pleasure of having been part of over the past year with the Breachmen. But she knew that Volchak was a draftee, unlike Harkner who chose this life. He was stuck here and had been for fourteen years. Stuck with a very bloody reputation, along with that axe of his - both blades of it. That's why he spent his time with his high-born friends, the famous Commander Volchak, feared axeman of Tydrian. She raised her shoulders, paused, then breathed out. She'd seen what his success had cost, three times. Breachmen's blood had literally bought the Commander his seat at the head table with Smiele and his cronies.

'You have murder in mind, little sister?' Harkner chuckled as he saw her gathering all her things. She smiled back at him. He loved to joke about what happened. He wasn't even there when it did, she must have told him about it. She didn't tell many people. Mr. Volchak knew; she had to tell him when she agreed to sign up. He hadn't said a word when she told him though. He didn't seem to care about how she'd killed the slimy foreman. She had shoved the creepy man over a railing onto the track used to extract the precious metals. Squished him outright, in full view of the workers and the factory guardsmen. But now, whenever she was angry, Harkner would joke about not being near any long drops. He would tease her and say he'd get an army of Ropers after her again. She always shuddered at the thought of having them chase her down. When they had caught her and taken her to the prison, the army had come through a short while after and they had given her a choice - Breachmen or prison. And that wasn't really much of a choice at all.

Still, she'd lived through it so far though, despite her diminutive size. Two years' sentence done, six to go. Then she'd be free and maybe still young enough to do something with her life. She saw the irony of paying for having killed someone by being made to kill other people though.

Wait, was irony the right word?

'Daydreaming again?' Harkner got to his feet as his words snapped her back to focus on him again. He was the only other one there who'd been on the same three charges as her. She knew very little of what he was before all this. It wasn't something Breachmen discussed. Most were the worst sort of bastard she knew of. Murders, racketeers, traitors, or maybe those who didn't fit in with the King's rule quite as they should. Harkner had been there when she arrived at the Breachmen camp and seemed a decent enough type, so he had probably been the worst kind of bastard. Calm, cheery, completely unphased by the situation. He always seemed to stroll through life with a type of tranquillity that Flea envied, as jittery as she always was. He was a big man too, muscular and thick-set like a giant statue carved from something solid. The hammer he held likely weighed more than she did. Dark leather-wrapped wood with the lump of stone on the top, one edge beaten flat. A decent enough type, sure, but she never wanted to find out what happened when you got on his bad side, which, so far, she never had. Also, he'd made sure that none of the other Breachmen so much as glanced in Flea's direction. Something about his way, or his charming smile and tone maybe, meant no one would cross him when he said to leave his 'little sister' alone. *Probably the hammer helped.*

'Flea, Harkner, when you have a moment?' The Commander's serious voice and weathered face put an end to Harkner's smile, but not Flea's daydreaming. Volchak stood firmly planted to the ground in the centre of the thirty fighters, whilst she looked about at them, wandering what they had done before or how they'd got here. The jumble of criminals, draftees and the very occasional madman who'd volunteered to be here. Most of this group were first timers. Rounded up over the last few months by the Order from the prison, or straight from the towns and farms that surrounded the capital. There were a couple though who'd survived the last charge, probably more than there would have been if Volchak hadn't caused such a panic in the rebels when he lopped the shield wall commander's head clean off. They looked sad. Flea frowned.

Breachmen didn't live long. That was a given. It was a last roll of the dice for most of them, but most weren't planning on sticking around long enough to get in the real thick of the fighting. The scattering after the charge, that was the part that Flea was good at. Being barely five feet tall and slender as she was, with her short hair and simple tight armour. She left very little for the enemy to grab hold of when she danced away.

'Flea...'

She didn't hear. Kept looking back at the Royal Guard. Their halberds swayed slightly in the wind like trees. Long, big axes would crush you, cut you or simply push you over till they stamped on you.

'Flea!'

Harkner jabbed her in the side with his elbow, and she shuddered and shook her head, looking back at Volchak.

'Yes? What?' Her voice wasn't timid - but soft.

It was Volchak who'd given her the name, during her first charge. Or rather, he'd bellowed it at the top of his voice and she and Harkner were the only two left alive to hear it, it had been nearly two minutes of fighting in the breach.

'Flee!' Volchak had shouted towards the remaining Breachmen as he sprinted past. He had barrelled shoulder-first into three more rebels, who'd been rather better armoured, armed, and trained than there were expecting when they first charged the line. Flea, although that was before she called herself Flea, had seen the enormous axe take off the arm of one and then the spike pierce another just as the third shoved a broken spear haft under the Commander's arm, causing him to shout out in pain. She'd then ducked as someone swung something heavy and wooden near her head and made for the gap Volchak had created in the line, just as the Royal Guards reached them. Later that week Harkner had joked that it must have been her name Volchak was shouting. Because there was no way the Commander was talking to him. 'Volchak knows my name is Harkner,' he'd laughed. And it had stuck.

She shook her head again, tried to listen.

'Plan is simple. We'll charge the shield wall head on. Aim is to cause some mayhem, try to claw away some of their shields and create some holes. You'll get maybe ten or twenty seconds before you need to get out the way, the Guard will be close behind. They won't stop for a few of us still left brawling. For the first timers, this'll be the worst time.' Volchak was grim as usual.

'Aye, 'cause it'll be the only time' Harkner whispered to Flea, caring little for those others around who heard him but still swallowing nervously when he realised that the Commander had stopped and was looking at him with his sunken grey eyes.

'For you, Harkner, I can guarantee it - if you'd like.' Volchak almost cracked a smile, but his axe shifted ever so slightly in his hand, which kept Harkner's mouth firmly shut. He never found himself in a fight if he could avoid it.

'Remember, if you run the other way, or you don't run at all, Ropers will catch up to you. Then the breach will have seemed like child's play against what the Hermetic Order will have planned for you.' It wasn't a threat, a warning, the Commander looked over their shoulders towards the hill he had come down from. The air had turned chilly despite the morning sun. The fog was light enough to see the red tent set aside on the bluff above them, as threatening and mysterious as the robed figures they all knew were inside it.

'If you chose Breachman over the rope, you chose your chance to get back to your lives, if you live long enough. I'm offering you the chance to do just that. The Duke hasn't armed his men well or trained them much, but they believe they are right and that's dangerous. They'll hold their ground for the Guard, I'd wager, but by then you'll have finished your job. I'd make for the buildings in the middle of the field when you're done. At least you'll get to lie down somewhere dry till they find you to patch you up.'

'Now,' he said with a lingering finality, 'don't die.'

Flea watched Volchak take a moment to look at the fighters, each of them in turn. All of them were holding some variation of heavy wooden club, sharpened stake and even several antler blades - their prongs filed to sharp points. He stared down some of the burlier, mean looking types. Flea guessed many of them were already seasoned killers, criminals or cut-throats. Some though, he looked at with pity, those who weren't burly or mean looking but just terrified. They were the men and women who might not have chosen to be here at all. Draftees, forced from their farms or villages to do their duty. Probably assigned to this unit through sheer bad luck. They probably wouldn't live through this battle.

Well, thought Flea, *it's unlikely any of them would, except maybe Harkner.*

With a nod, Volchak strode through the group and stood alone about forty paces in front of the Royal Guard. They had remained disconcertingly still for the last fifteen minutes of facing the battlefield.

'Nothing like a pep talk before a fight,' Flea muttered under her breath, as she picked up her short wooden spear and strapped the tiny wooden buckler to her wrist. She'd seen men with bigger shields be too slow, or too easy to grab and pin down, which was a sure way to get stabbed by something sharp and nasty. She preferred to dance and dart around, using her buckler to push away any of the sharp nasties so she could jab the enemy a few times with her short spear - but be away before they realised.

Also, it wasn't as heavy when she eventually lived up to her name and needed to jump away. She'd have liked a metal buckler, but the chances of her ever getting her hands on one were low, and she knew it.

She stood next to Harkner, who was leaning on his hammer like a drunk would a bar, propped up on one elbow with his chin resting on his enormous hand. Had he fallen asleep again?

The others fell in around them, and Flea noticed for the third time that everyone stood at least an axe-length away from the Commander. She looked back up the hill, past the red tent to the much grander blue one and the armoured figures standing to its side, where the fog was now clearing. They shone in the sunlight.

'Don't die, little sister.' Harkner said, still leaning on that large stone hammer.

'Don't die.' Flea murmured.

Chapter 4

Volchak's chest heaved as he ran across the hard flat ground, not at fast as he could, since there wasn't much of a prize for getting there early other than having to fight harder to get out again. His heart was beating against his leather armour and his thick tan belt dug into his stomach as he ran. Glancing right and left, the other thirty Breachmen, had kicked up a small dust cloud in their wake as they crossed the barren gap. Volchak realised there were only twenty-eight with him, he had seen two of the petrified-looking scrawny men dart away as soon as he sounded the charge. Pity, they could have died quickly here, instead of suffering what waited for them when the Ropers found them. Ropers had a particular skill for finding deserters. Afterall it was deserters and criminals who were the primary source of the Hermetic Order's 'research subjects'. A man with no rights had little means to complain as they slowly dissected him to find out what made him tick.

There was a healthy sized gap on either side of him. Not for any tactical purposes, if anything, it made him stand out even more than his enormous axe already did. It was just there, like it always was. He knew it was a bad idea having the commander displayed as a prime target for stabbing when sprinting towards a line of angry militiamen. Yet he didn't really know what to do about it. They always stayed at least a few feet away from him for when the fighting got going. Shrugging to himself in his own mind, he kept running at a steady pace, boots pounding on the hard ground. Besides, he'd probably would get stuck with the first five spears and make a lovely gap for the rest of them to breach through. Might actually be the most useful he'd ever been.

Volchak knew the two infantry units would have circumvented the rustic farm buildings in the middle of the field, and would be engaging the flanks at about this moment. Major Fedal was an effective commander. He'd have timed it well, so that both engaged in their own small but certain fashion at almost the same time. Not the most imaginative of tactics, but it had proven effective the past five times and Smiele wanted a nice clean half-dozen. Volchak's Breachmen were well ahead of the Royal Guard and were about to clear the fence on the edge of the buildings. The Guard themselves had moved steadily and methodically behind, no doubt kicking up a much larger dust cloud. Possibly so much that the commanders on the hill would be unable to see their own troops. No doubt they would hear them though, causing quite the marching beat in their perfect unison.

On reaching the outer fence, Volchak knew it wouldn't slow down the Breachmen too much; the Breachmen would be up and over the fence quickly where the Guard would just trample it completely. Then, straight through the middle in the wide gap between what was now clearly the main house and the two large barns. When they reached the line, the peasants may try a counter charge, but Fedal would pin them in place in the flanks. The rebel commanders would know that if they got out of formation, they'd end up pushing into a wall of sharpened steel without their shields in the right direction. Volchak's aim was to get out the way before that happened. He would head for those buildings, as he said, which was a bit too much like running towards the Royal Guard, but there was nowhere else to go. Breathing heavily, Volchak didn't really think about the way those barns, and the dust, would block the view of the bluff where Smiele and Fedal stood. It didn't really matter.

His leather boots thudded on the bare ground as he moved through the farmyard itself. The ground wasn't as smooth here as he expected. Volchak had to slow slightly to stop from twisting an ankle and pitching onto his face, as he and his unit cleared past the first barn and advanced through the gap.

***

Flea had fallen to the back and the side again. Not that she wasn't fast, she was incredibly agile over short distances, and once they got into a fight. But in a long charge like this and with getting over the fence, her smaller strides simply meant she had a harder time keeping up with most of the Breachmen. Harkner was big, of course, but his hammer must have about doubled his weight and his red cheeks were already puffing and he sweated heavily despite the air still being clean and crisp. Flea felt she was probably the first girl in a long time to see that strained and sweaty face, and almost chuckled to herself. That was the thing about big men. They were usually not quick. Flea and Harkner hadn't fallen behind really, just to the back, and if it meant she wasn't the first one to run into what seemed a far more dangerous looking wall of shields and pokey spears now, compared to when it was a mile away, well Flea was willing to accept that. And if it was nearer being over by the time that she and Harkner got there, she could accept that too. This is something she'd learnt from Harkner. Never run too quickly towards a fight. If it's over when you get there well, then you've done well. Harkner would always rather talk his way out of a fight than put the effort into lifting that huge hammer.

They ran a few strides behind a first timer. He was a surprisingly well-dressed man for a Breachman. Flea wondered what cruel twist of fate had given him the choice of breach or noose. Or maybe he was a volunteer? Looking for glory? Most likely he was a criminal, maybe even a middle-born son who'd gone too far in a bar brawl, or took a liking to a servant, who hadn't been willing to succumb. Wait, that wasn't the right word, was it? She thought a moment whilst still running, slipped slightly in a semi-circular rut in the ground and swore under her breath. *Stop daydreaming.* The man wore a full faced wooden helmet and a rather fancy and expensive looking cloak that whipped dramatically in the wind as he ran. He was wielding a large stone axe over his shoulder and she'd already made a note to not be near him when he swung it. Flea was sure a lump of rock like that would have a habit of getting away from you and who knows who you'd hit.

Fancy-First-Timer had just cleared past the first barn's nearside corner when it appeared a sudden gust blew that fancy cloak against his back and tangled around his right leg. Maybe he had tripped on the ruts first and his leg had got caught in that cloak of his. She couldn't tell. It was all fluttering blue fabric and then suddenly the weighty axe shot away in front of him, head chipping as it bounced end over end on the uneven ground. The man spilled onto the floor and straight into the large heavy door of the second barn, splintering the weak planks and knocking a hole in them as his helmeted head punctured the door at the bottom.

He screamed for just a second before being suddenly completely silent, as his full-face helmet, along with the head inside it, was cut from his body with a sickening thud. Flea saw this through the gap in the barn, she was possibly the only one who did, and suddenly wondered what had happened to him. She looked up and her heart jumped into her throat as she saw what happened next.

Flea screamed.

Kaelith's men smelled just as unpleasant, unkempt and rough as they looked. It was stuffy despite the cold air with them all crammed into this barn. Of course, he looked fabulous in his polished breastplate and his white shirt with its glorious ruffles, a true blade master's outfit. He chose not to register the slight tarnish of rust and scratches, nor the smattering of mud across his shirt with one slightly torn sleeve. He was a noble gentleman after all, and such details were unbecoming. As a group of soldiers ran past, their shadows broke the light beams breaking through the slats in the barn door and created a dappled light that made it feel like the room was spinning - or maybe it was the wine he had drunk the night before.

The plan was solid, of course. All his plans were solid. The first group of ne'er-do-wells would soon reach the front line and shortly behind them would be the real soldiers in their neat straight lines. Kaelith wagered they couldn't see much out of their armoured helms with their tiny slits, and certainly couldn't see much to their sides. He knew that was the point of them, focus on what was in front and on trampling it - and that's what Kaelith was relying on. Once they were about to engage, then his dramatic entrance would occur. If he had more time he'd have thought of a witty line, or maybe a heroic quote, to shout. But he expected it would all be rather brief and chaotic once his men, and what they had brought with them, left the barn. So, a silent and stoic leader he would be. Straight into the enemies unguarded flank, overrunning them before they got to drawing their swords whilst in all that bulky armour.

It was a solid plan.

Kaelith had been looking around the barn, over his men and their wide assortment of arms and armour. Maces, spears, many with swords. He always spared no expense, or maybe the men were just good at robbing corpses. He was never quite sure where they got their weapons from, but there was a wide array here. A division he could be proud of. His eyes wandered to their surroundings. He looked up to the large hole in the roof, it would probably be a lot stuffier in here without it. Kaelith knew a great many things, but why a farmer had allowed a hole in his barn roof was not one of them.

Then, three strange things happened quickly and unexpectedly.

The head just appeared. Under the door. Well, more like through the bottom of the door, as it sent a small shower of splinters across the entranceway. It was a fully armoured head, and evidently quite a wealthy head, as was clear from the quality of the wooden helmet and the exquisite hem of the blue cloak wrapped around its neck.

Then, as quickly as it had appeared, Kaelith's cutlass had swung down and removed it from the body it had been attached to. His swing cut short the cry, although Kaelith couldn't be sure whether anyone had noticed it. He shrugged. It was evident that a headless body sticking out from underneath one barn may also be a dead giveaway that something was amiss whether it cried out or not.

However, it was the third thing that really puzzled Kaelith, despite having very little time to think about it. A woman's scream echoed out, clear as day, then just stopped short. 'What in the world?' Kaelith said to himself, just as his men flung open the doors and the thundering hooves and angry snorts of their twenty horses sounded as they stormed from the barn. It caught him unaware. *Damn.* He had been thinking about the woman screaming, not the first time in his life that this had been a problem. His horse, startled, reared and spun as his men shot past him. He squawked as it reared again and nearly threw him. Quickly, he was alone in the barn.

Volchak felt, more than heard, the scream and what sounded like the rumble of not-so-distant thunder from behind him. He knew they were some one hundred strides from the main line and the chances of the Duke's men possessing bows were even less likely than the chance of Smiele using his. He stole a glance over his right shoulder and almost fell over his own feet as he skidded to a halt mid-stride. Horses, dozens of them, from the barn. They came thundering out and had already kicked up more dust than his charge had several times over. But he could see them clearly, big bulking beasts with men atop them. Men. Volchak instinctively snapped out of his wonderment in the instant he realised what had happened. *Ambush.*

He turned his back on the army of rebels now, as had all the Breachmen, as the horsemen wheeled right towards them. The nearest men had no time to offer any resistance at all. One was crushed directly beneath the hooves of the large brown beast and the next man's head was split in two by a flashing swing of a sword. The same sword now bore down on Volchak and he raised his axe to block it but was knocked backwards onto the ground

By the time his head rattled off the hard ground, he'd seen two more men run down - one even valiantly trying to skewer a horse with his spear before the heavy hooves flattened him. Now the dust had really come up, blinding him, scratching at his throat and making him wretch. Volchak knew it was time to get out.

Rising quickly to his feet, he cursed. Not at the horsemen in particular. Not at the ground on which he had hit his head, or the warm wet trickle down the back of his neck which he thought probably meant he'd knocked out the last of any sense he had. But just at the world and his place in it at that particular moment. Volchak still vaguely knew from which direction he had come, despite the dust, and in which he had been going. He chose neither as the right one to run to. More hooves and more shapes had darted past as he was head-butting the ground. The Royal Guard would arrive shortly from where he had come from. They would spare him no mind if he was in their way.

So, he ran towards the back of the nearest barn and probably for as far as his legs would take him after that. As he started to flee, he saw the shape standing in the dust cloud motionless. In the same instant saw the white horse emerge from the barn at what seemed a slow walk, it turned, and headed directly for her. 'Dammit,' he shouted, as he sprinted towards Flea.

**

Flea froze. What seemed a tide of monstrous thunder had just emerged from nowhere and shot past her on all sides, as her eyes teared from the dry dust and her heart seemed to stop entirely. She had dropped her spear and, in shock, her arms hung limp beside her as she stared into the gaping mouth of the barn they'd emerged from. It seemed to her a portal to another place, from the world she knew and understood, to chaos. She snapped out of her daze with a jolt as she blinked and saw a single white horse with a man, not unlike the King's councillor she thought, except holding a large curved sword and coming directly towards her. She knew again she wasn't being given a choice. From fear or amazement or just pure disbelief, she wouldn't be getting out of the way and he would run right over her or sever her head from her neck, like Fancy-First-Timer at any moment.

Except his horse was slow, walking pace. And although he held his sword, it looked like he held his other gloved hand palm to her, as if trying to calm a startled dog. He was less than five strides away and suddenly she felt as if maybe the choice made for her was that he would not kill her where she stood, though she couldn't really understand why.

* * *

The strangest of sounds pricked Kaelith's ear, he realised that the best word for it was a repeating sound of rushing air, like a river tumbling over a cliff over and over. This was shortly before he was utterly and completely thrown from his horse and dumped onto the ground face down just two strides from the woman. Whatever she had done to dethrone him had been the single most impressive feat of battle he would ever come to know. He even thought it might be his last chance to tell her. When he looked up, he saw that the twisted corpse of his horse had an imposing and very heavy looking axe embedded in its neck. There was no hand attached to the axe, but Kaelith scrabbled backwards on the ground anyway, arms flailing for his own sword for when the hand that threw that bloody great thing arrived.

'Gargh!' A painful jab in his ribs and he knew at that moment that would be the end of him then. He could already feel a trickle of blood from under the breastplate and knew soon there'd be another and another and blood would pour out and he'd die in the dirt. At least his head not been bashed in with a rock. But none came, and he realised he'd crawled directly over a short, sharpened stick that was lying on the ground. It had caught him at a most unfortunate angle behind his breastplate, in the gap under his arm. He had half a mind to seize it and jump to his feet, brandishing it against his axe-throwing opponent in a last valiant effort at defending himself. But as he reached to grab it, not sure he had the wind left in him to get up, let alone defend himself, someone snatched the stick from his weakening grip and turned on him. Sure enough, the girl whose scream had caused all this drama was standing above him, with the stick pointed directly at his face. She was small, thin to the point of diminutive, with bedraggled hair and a slightly unwashed look to her. She had obviously noticed his glorious breastplate, but distinct lack of helmet – hence why she aimed at the head. He slumped onto his back and sighed.

A solid plan.

Chapter 5

Volchak arrived panting just moments after his axe had. The large white horse twitched slightly under the weight on its neck, but was completely and utterly dead. It amazed him that it had worked. Hefting a piece of bronze so far whilst winded, following a nasty blow to the head. It was a miracle it wasn't stuck in the of the barn door, maybe that's what he had been trying to hit?

After yanking the axe from the fountain of blood and split muscle tissue with a horrendous slurping noise, Volchak's eyes darted up and over the corpse. He saw Flea, standing above a man with plaited yellow hair and a fancy-looking steel chest plate. She seemed about to poke his face through with her spear. Neither one was moving though and just as Volchak went to speak, Flea spun and looked over her shoulder and then darted inside the barn as quick as a flash, almost in a leap. That girl suited her name, however she got it. Volchak looked through the space where she had been and saw why. Yards away was the drumming of the Royal Guard, their plate mail boots marching quickly up the gap between house and barn. Twelve abreast, they filled the space completely and halberds reached out ten feet in front of them, ready to skewer anything in their path. They rumbled like a never-ending wave, crashing as they marched in perfect unison. They would not be stopping for horse's corpse or the dandy lying next to it, nor for Volchak himself if he didn't get out of the way. His stomach lurched him towards the barn, refusing to die here. He hesitated briefly and stole one last glance at the wall of steel, ever so close now. He half-rolled and half-stumbled over the horse's nearly-headless corpse and seized the man under his arms, dragging his limp body into the barn. Volchak's arms ached at the weight of him. His tight grip tore the man's ridiculously puffy shirt under the arms as Volchak heaved the man backwards. Volchak's feet pushed against the ruts in the ground to gain purchase for one final surge backwards. The ruts made more sense now than they had the first time Volchak ran across them. Hauling the body over the threshold into the darkness, he fell backwards and was half crushed by the man's heavy form, the pock-marked breastplate scratching against stained leather armour.

As they both lay there breathing in what was actually becoming an almost awkward embrace, it dawned on Volchak; he had just saved the man from being pierced and trampled, but hadn't really known why. Especially given that it was thanks to considerable effort on Volchak's part that the man had ended up laying on the floor bleeding in the first place. Volchak rolled him off with a grunt and looked around for Flea as he stood up. She was several steps back into the barn with her spear still raised in his direction. Blood was starting to pool around the body on the barn floor.

'Easy, little sister… Best not skewer our Commander with so many witnesses.' Harkner's voice sung out the darkness, as he put his large hand on Flea's and lowered the spear for her. He seemed as cheery, chipper and relaxed as ever, despite a nasty looking cut above one eye and a reddening on his cheek that suggested heavy bruising. Seemed he'd actually listened and made for the buildings, despite none of them having made it to the Duke's line first.

'Still alive then?' Volchak half coughed. The rumbling of the guard now passed as they continued their march out of the farmyard. His vision was slightly blurry, and he put his hand to the back of his head, blood-matted hair hiding a sharp sting where he had absorbed the blow from the mounted ambusher.

'I'm still here,' Harkner smiled. 'Who's your friend?' He nodded over to the body, still lay on the floor. 'Hold up! He ain't quite dead!' Harkner released the spear and clapped Volchak on the shoulder, nearly knocking him down onto his back again, and stood above the bleeding man. Flea stood poised, not moving, eyes darting around as if ready to jump away again.

'Come, my friend, survived a tussle with the mighty Volchak, did we? You must be a hard fella indeed!' Harkner reached a hand out to him. The man lying on his back stirred and seemed to focus on Harkner, who had thumped his hammer down next to the man's head. Volchak wondered whether he had pulled him out of the way of being crushed once just to watch Harkner finish the job. But there was a jovial sound to the big man's words.

'I think I just might be.' The wounded man sputtered with a grin. Despite his expensive chest plate, his voice didn't carry the nasally high-born twang that his armour, hair and shirt suggested it might. He seized Harkner's hand and groaned, leaking from his side as he was. He stood unsteadily and clasped at the wound beneath his breastplate with his other hand as he looked over to Volchak.

Volchak's eyes darted to the ground and the walls of the barn, ready to find something to seize and defend against his enemy's attack. The man didn't have his sword, Volchak knew, but who knew what other tricks this man was hiding. Maybe a hand-bow? After all, he'd been riding an actual horse into a battle. The man clearly had some specialist equipment.

Harkner smiled, reading his leader well. 'You don't need your bronze chopper here, Commander. This man is clearly a gentleman.' Harkner laughed at his own reading of the situation... 'Also, he ain't got a weapon and he'll struggle to kill you with his pony-tail, I'd wager.'

The wounded man smiled awkwardly and almost bowed to Volchak, who stood rigid. Volchak was still confused as to why he wasn't currently rolling around in the mud wrestling and trying to bash the man's head in with a rock. Moments ago, this man was trying to skewer one of his Breachmen, after all. But it seemed Harkner was in control of the man for the time being, in his own casual way.

'This was of your making? How are you here? How did get men to fight on horseback? Or the horses themselves, for that matter?' Volchak's chest heaved as he tried to speak. The last few minutes caught up with him and the questions flooded from his mouth. His bloody, muddied leather tabard rose and fell as he came to his senses. His head throbbed and legs wobbled, but he figured he'd just about stay conscious for the time being. Shaking off the groggy feeling, he continued before he could get an answer. 'Harkner, bind the man. We will deliver him to the Order for questioning. He's one of the Duke's commanders. We will need to know what he knows and how he knows it.' He turned 'Flea?' She wasn't there. She'd got past him as he turned and was standing next to Harkner, peering quizzically at the man, seeming as likely to talk to him as to stab him with her spear.

'Flea, help Harkner. We will need to bring him back to the camp.' Flea hesitated and replied. 'He wasn't about to kill me, Commander. When you threw the axe, he'd said stop.'

'What?' Volchak's head was really hurting now.

'She's not wrong, Commander,' the man interjected. The prisoner's over familiar use of his title irked Volchak slightly. 'You weren't the contract. I've no interest in harming you or your...' he paused and eyed the group stood in the barn, 'men... folk... people.'

'So, you didn't just ambush us and run down the rest of the Breachmen? You're with the rebels and fighting the King's army. How are you going to do that without killing us?' Volchak retorted, as Harkner moved behind the prisoner, hefting his hammer with both hands.

'Well yes... but no.' He brushed the arms on his white shirt, which was now a nasty shade of brown from the dust, mud and filth in the barn. Both sleeves hung loose and torn around his wrists.

'I wasn't fighting your men, but Smiele's war machine. The Royal Guard. The Duke paid me to solve that little problem for him. He's lost too many waves of men crashing against that rock and he needed something extraordinary.' And he motioned to himself, unarmed and filthy.

'Kaelith, at your service.' The prisoner bowed with a flourish to Volchak.

'This is Smiele's army; my men are his men, the King's men.' Volchak's response felt a tad empty when his men comprised one small girl and one actual man.

'Are you sure?' That response irked Volchak again, but something unconsciously hung true in the back of his mind.

'Well, I have no personal quarrel with you. We were sent to do a job, which you can plainly see we have made an almighty cock-up of. I've lost my men; my weapons and I'd wager all of my horses. So, I shan't be of trouble to you again. I'll take my leave of your gentlemen... and lady.' Kaelith bowed again with a slight groan and turned to walk away.

Volchak was flabbergasted by the man's brashness. Kaelith swept across them with his bow, as if just wishing them all a fond farewell, and made to stroll off out the door without another thought of them all. When he deftly spun on the spot and took a step, he bounced straight off Harkner's bulking form, standing behind him.

'Ah. Bugger.' Kaelith looked up at the man with an almost pleading smile. 'My dear fellow...'

Harkner smiled, shook his head slowly and placed a large, friendly hand on Kaelith's shoulder. A friendly hand that gripped and guided him back to a seated position in front of Volchak. Flea removed some rope that was hanging on the wall of the barn. Convenient, thought Volchak, as she wound it round his wrists, then once around his body. It was apparent he wouldn't be bleeding to death from his poke with her spear anytime soon but Volchak knew a nasty wound when he saw one. He'd have to take this man to the physician and soon. Kaelith didn't struggle or make any genuine sound, which was a relief for Volchak. His head was still aching at the bizarre situation.

'Bring him, you two; we need to see Smiele.'

Chapter 6

Stirc hated this place.

Some dry barren piece of the middle of nowhere, far from the civilisation and culture of the capital. The people, what people there were, were dense. Simple. Thinking only of their next meal or their crops or their pathetic little livings scratched from the earth. There were no grand mysteries of the body to solve, no anatomical mazes to navigate, and no glorious recognition of secrets uncovered. Three months he'd been on this so-called campaign these plate-mailed buffoons had dreamt up, from one wretched place to another he had watched the last three major engagements as Smiele perfected his instrument of war, perfectly crushing one rag-tag bunch of peasants after another. It had bored Stirc, not because he had wanted the rebel army to put up more of a fight, but because none of them ever survived. There were so few left alive at the end on the other side and in such a terrible state he had barely got to operate on a living subject in the whole time he'd been with them. Of course, there were things to learn from a corpse and he had some intriguing notes to pore over in the quieter evenings from some of the more creatively killed. But after a while, the next dozen bodies, skewered by halberds, then crushed under plated boot into a bloody jellied mess, looked like the last.

The last battle had at least been different, although the result was largely the same from Stirc's perspective. From atop the bluff, he sat on the small wooden chair outside the red tent in his finest Order robes and watched the light-armed first wave, the 'Breachmen', set off across the barren ground. He had seen them disappear into the farmstead as the Royal Guard started their thundering rhythmic march. He watched with a slight sigh, knowing that more pointless tinkering with corpses would soon take up his time. At least it was practice. He wouldn't be learning a lot about the extremes that these men could survive when they'd all long since perished.

Thirty years in the Hermetic Order meant thirty years of study and experimentation in the safety and security of the monastery, of course. He had not travelled any further out than the mining district in the capital which was but a few miles from the monastery, which sat nestled on the opposite side of the city to the palace. Only the Ropers would leave the capital during times of peace. They would travel west into the farmlands, or into the hills to the north. There to seek escaped criminals, the homeless and the abandoned, for the Order physicians to study. And maybe the occasional other subjects as the High Registrar demanded. Stirc would be content to study in the library, watch demonstrations from his betters in large circular lecture theatre, craning his thin neck over the crowd of his peers to see what manner of wounds the registrars could inflict and restitch. It always amazed him just what they could remove and replace and have the subject still live. He was not shy about challenging his peers and furthering the Orders' teachings. A particular note of pride was his own demonstrations regarding the art of stabilising subjects after horrific injuries, enough that the otherwise uninjured parts of their bodies could still be of use. Stirc was becoming somewhat of a rising star on the fifth floor, working away in his chamber that doubled as his sleeping quarters. It is what has likely earned him this posting – a chance to prove himself.

However, none of his knowledge pertained to warfare or tactical subterfuge, so he had paid no mind to the fact that the Breachmen had become all but hidden by the two large barns and the cloud of dust around them.

Stirc had quickly taken much more of an interest though when the sounds of some beast screaming carried over the air from the sides of the derelict farmstead. A thundering noise which outmatched that of the Royal Guard's march. A series of majestic horses had emerged from the dust. Like everyone on the campaign, he'd seen exactly one horse in his life. The councillor rode it before each battle to the negotiations. It was then safely squared away the moment it returned, to be looked on only by the councillor's staff until next it was next needed. Within moments of losing sight of the Breachmen, Stirc had seen five more horses, maybe eight or could even be ten. They circled into view and then disappeared behind those barns again. A pang of curiosity had hit him. He wondered how different on the inside they would be when compared to a considerably smaller animal like a dog, or a pig - or a man for that matter. But he watched silently, and keenly, as the dust cloud became impenetrable. The Royal Guard arrived at the outer reaches of the farm and he saw the horsemen bolt for the horizon. He'd barely noticed how the rebel army had disengaged from that fat major's two heavily mauled divisions, and were also fleeing back north. They moved far faster than the Royal Guard had been able to march after them.

Several hours passed before they called Stirc to the High Commander's larger, much more impressive tent. His intrigue at the battle had waned in that time and he had been happy to retreat to his tent and spend the time in quiet contemplation over his books. Occasionally he had received some inane message meant to keep him updated as to the tactical situation, but he waved them away - he wasn't a tactician. The Order may have sent him on this expedition as their representative, but he didn't feel the need to represent them in person unless expressly asked. If they weren't delivering a body to him, he was content to be left alone.

When they called upon him, he had, of course, complied. He had donned his heavy ceremonial robes, and made for the High Commander's tent. The robes hung long onto the floor, and he carefully adjusted his belt so as not to trip but to allow them to remain long enough to give the appearance of gliding across the ground. Stirc kept his hood up, he found the less of his face he showed, the more ominous - and less approachable - he seemed. He had hoped to discourage either the messenger or any other witless soldier from engaging him in conversation unless absolutely necessary.

Upon entering the tent, with its high-pitched roof and solid upright beams, it felt almost like a feasting hall. The sickening smells of cooked meats laid out on the table to his right immediately hit him. As was the case for all those in the Order, once you understood the theory and had seen the practicalities of how bodies are made up, you tended to lose all taste for meat. Indeed, they generally rejected subjects that were delivered to them from house fires because of their adjacency to cooked animal flesh. Barbaric. Swallowing hard, he hid underneath his hood and floated into the tent. His small footsteps making no noise as he moved directly to the crowd of men around a table covered in little wooden models of armed men. It was clear Smiele was furious, and that the oaf Volchak was the subject of most of his fury.

'Well, if your unit had done their job we wouldn't have been in this mess!' Smiele's nasally voice raised in a rage as he spun angrily away from the crowd towards the large mahogany dresser at the rear of the tent. 'You... had a very simple task' his voice had slowed to a vicious rasp.

'Sir. With all due respect. We were ambushed at the...' Volchak was rubbing his eyes in frustration behind Smiele's turned back, but Smiele didn't notice nor care about what his trained attack-dog had to say.

'You were supposed to get your men to the front line, and tie them down. Instead, you got every damned man killed, and all you've got to show for it is that half-wit mercenary scum. Who, it would seem, hasn't said two damned words since you dragged him in!'

Stirc's ears pricked up, and he suddenly stirred from beneath his thick red robe. In his voice was a mixture of curiosity and offense.

'All prisoners are to be remitted to the Order.' he said, not so much demanding as stating a pure and irrevocable fact. His voice was cold and unwavering, and brought the tone in the room to a sudden sullen stop.

'Yes… well.' Smiele was put out yet polite. His face still burning red as he turned to the Order priest. 'Of course, this shall be done.' He nodded to an officer who scurried, somewhat clumsily in all that armour, out of the tent.

That was all that Stirc cared to hear. He turned on his foot without another thought and made for the door, floating over the rugs and throws that made up the floor of the opulent surroundings.

'Physician Stirc?' Smiele's voice was firm but with the faintest hint of subservience, maybe even pleading, Stirc didn't care. 'I would thoroughly appreciate if you would,' Stirc raised an eyebrow, not that anyone would have noticed, 'humbly, keep the man alive. Half-wit though he may well be, he may have some useful information to provide us on the war.'

Stirc looked back and smiled, his thin bony face now only half-hidden, revealing an expansive grin. Each of his thin teeth stood tall and perfectly straight as he faced the nobleman. Smiele had somewhat lost his shine as the light from behind Stirc reflected red from his robes as he stood in the doorway to the tent.

'The information the prisoner can provide shall be determined by the Order, and the Order will find it no doubt. Beneath the skin in the hidden depths of his mortal form, there will be your information, Commander.' Stirc turned back to the opening and the slightest pang of concern whether he might have gone too far here. The thought stabbed at his sharp mind and made his eye twitch. Smiele was no fool, for all his bluster and shining armour. He was well-connected back in the capital. The High Commander of the Royal Guard would have to be. Of both high birth and high value, as were so many of the most important men in the kingdom.

'But I shall endeavour to keep him in a state to allow you to extract the secrets in his mind, if that is what you would so wish.' Stirc was pleased with that. Respectful without over-promising. Well, promising nothing really. He walked out into the afternoon sun and headed back for his own tent, some distance from the others at the camp. As he walked away, he heard Smiele's tirade return to its previous level, and knew he aimed it at that savage axeman of his.

Upon entering his tent, he was met with the mix of sweat, fear and the incense he had left burning on the side table. He walked around the edge of the large wooden block in the centre, careful not to disturb the heavy ropes that emerged taut from either side of the block and now held in place his newest subject. He opened the drawer of his side table and from it took out a thick leather roll, his delicate apparatus of scalpels, tweezers, syringes and clamps. Pure steel glistened as it caught the thin ray of sunlight from the open tent flap. The eyes of the man on the table went wide, and wild, as he realised the gravity of the situation. The subject must have realised he would not be beaten, or hung. But instead, he was to serve a far greater cause - the furthering of Stirc's understanding of the human body. From the enormous chest at the base of the cot, Stirc retrieved, with some effort, a large rack of vials and herbs. He placed this carefully on the small table, which was held in place firmly by its weight. Some labels were peeling, a point of great personal frustration to Stirc, but he had no means of replacing them out here in this empty countryside. Glancing across at the man, Stirc's eyebrow twitched slightly as he pushed back his hood, revealing a bald, bony head and menacing grin. Stirc had already noticed the trickle of blood dribbling down the side of the block coming from the man's wound – an opportunity.

Sighing, Stirc adjusted one of the large dials at the head of the block with a heavy turn. The mechanism hidden inside the block adjusted the man's body with complete ease. The ropes bore his weight and forced him onto his side, each attachment point pulling the requisite body part with precision. It was clear the man had been wearing a breastplate during the battle; dirt caked his white frilled shirt on the arms, but on the torso, it was smattered only with the blood - which appeared to be oozing from a wound in his lower right side. Stirc watched the slow pump of blood without urgency. He made a minor note in his tome that he had placed next to his apparatus, the consistency and rate all recorded by his trained eye.

'It appears you are not long for this world, my unfortunate friend.' At the monastery, that would have earned him considerable reprimand. Taunting a subject was tantamount to admitting they are more than a subject and therefore worthy of conversation. Unacceptable, but he had to have his own little delights out here in the wilderness. 'Roughly half a quart of blood loss per hour, and that little messy battle of yours …' He worked in his head. 'A couple of hours ago… why any moment I'd have thought you would lose consciousness.' Stirc was actually a little surprised and made another notation. The man had showed surprising constitution to still be awake.

Taking a series of measuring spoons from his leather wrap with one hand and a large flask in another, he mixed several of his vials together with trained precision. Each drop well measured and stirred in at just the right moment. He soon had the thick white paste he had aimed for. Such perfect exactitude had always made Stirc happy, meticulousness had served him well over thirty years. Within a few minutes, he had perfected his concoction and turned back to the subject. The prisoner's eyes had rolled back and his head lolled against the block, whilst his body was held firmly in place on its side.

Another notation – unconscious; another minor victory in predicting the body's capabilities being granted to Stirc by his extensive training.

Applying the white paste now with care, just inside the wound, lifting the skin around before delving slightly deeper and plugging the hole in its entirety. Stirc nodded to himself at a perfectly sculpted application as he wiped away the last of the blood. He could see it had ceased leaking from the man's body. 'Can't disappoint the Commander. I never fail in my endeavours, my punctured companion. Besides, I would rather make use of you for some days yet.' Stirc chuckled at himself but the man wasn't awake to notice.

Taking his probe and adjusting the dials on the block once more, he moved the man onto his front, or rather the intricate set of whirring cogs held within did. Stirc made several more rounds of the body, occasionally prodding with one of his steel probes. He made several further annotations in his tome before declaring himself satisfied. The man would live until he awoke, not that it would be much comfort to him when he did. Sorry excuse for a man.

Stirc scolded himself for thinking of the subject as human again.

Chapter 7

Volchak trudged down the hill on the far side from yesterday's battlefield, his head aching under his bandage. He still hadn't come to terms with having seen so many horses, or that men had actually fought on their backs. Had he thought he'd have earned a reprieve this morning, having been on the wrong end of an ambush, he'd been very wrong. Smiele had been furious at his inability to repel the attackers, and that the Guard hadn't been able to catch the Duke's army when it retreated from the centre.

He stepped into the Breachmen barrack tent, heavy canvas drawn back to allow air to flow through past the two rows of cots and the cooking fire at the centre. The heavy leather binder he now carried, entwined in thick cord, held the next month of his life within. And the lives of several dozen more, most likely. The warm glow of the fire served as source of the smoky smell; several small gamey rabbits were roasting under some manner of herbs - no doubt Flea's contribution. She was useful to have around, knew things most of the men didn't think mattered, like how to get rabbits. She was good in a fight too, always dodging and weaving. She'd had to be, for when Harkner wasn't there to discourage the others from taking what they wanted from her. Although there was no 'they' left now… just the three of them.

The inside of the tent was sparse, but well-placed, on solid yet smooth ground with some shelter from the wind that often whipped round the hill.

Volchak stood a moment and looked at the cots, he counted thirty of them just as he had last night. Most were now empty, of course. Harkner was sat back on the one nearest the fire, large stone hammer propped against the end, as he whistled to himself cheerily. It was apparent he had picked up a few scratches and bruises yesterday but seemed all but recovered. That made Volchak's head ache even more. Flea was fussing over the rabbits, chattering away to herself, as she jumped from one side of the fire to the other making adjustments or sprinkling the herbs. Take away the cots, the canvas tent, the armour and the weapons and they were a merry little family enjoying their breakfast on a hunting trip.

'Ah Commander!' Harkner feigned reverence. 'Do step in. I will be your server this morning. Our chef has prepared for you a fine concoction of roasted rabbit with a sprinkled sage dusting. The talk of the capital she is!'

'Thyme.' Flea said. She didn't look up.

Volchak sighed, exasperated, then grinned slightly and shook his aching head as he approached. His grey eyes flickered in the firelight as he sat down on the opposite empty cot with a groan

'You came through more or less without a scratch again then Harkner?'

'Despite my best efforts, sir!' Harkner kept up his character. 'Why, I was on a pleasant stroll through the countryside and wouldn't you know it, I was accosted by none other than men on horses. Actual real live four-legged barrels, running circles around me!' He sat forward with his infectious grin. 'Why I was taken aback; was I in the distant far-away lands to the east across the Ruby Sea? No, of course it could not be; I had left the capital just months ago! And it was too damned cold! Needless to say, I did what any sensible man would do and found somewhere to collect my thoughts.'

Volchak raised an eyebrow in response.

'And wouldn't you know, whilst catching my breath, I stumbled across my little sister in a rather uncouth situation with two men nonetheless, Mother would be furious!' He snorted laughter, broke his façade and sat back.

Flea chuckled as well, sitting cross legged on the floor in front of the fire. When she spoke, there was no mock high-born accent.

'You've got a new recruit.' She said, smiling up at him sweetly.

Twenty-seven empty cots. Volchak had thirty soldiers and only these two had survived. There were supposed to be twenty-eight empty cots. There was someone asleep in the cot on the far side of Harkner, slightly obscured by the large man's body as he lounged.

Volchak stood back up, the ache in the back of his head abating with curiosity. He recognised the ruffled and stained shirt.

'They brought him in this morning. Harkner is watching him.' Flea said. Volchak was somewhat surprised that the prisoner was still in one piece; he had heard the order to carry him to the Hermetic physician's tent last night.

'We are to escort them both to the Monastery at the end of our journey.' Harkner nodded to the leather binder that sat on Volchak's lap. Clearly his talent for staying out of harm's way also extended to finding out when harm was coming his way. Volchak raised one scarred eyebrow and went to ask who 'both' was when he was interrupted from the tent entrance to his left.

'You will do as he says, Commander. This man is to be delivered to my superiors when you arrive back at the capital from your draft. He and I are to be given your personal protection, and guarantee, to arrive in one piece.' Stirc had donned a travellers cloak, red, although the hood was pulled back revealing his unnervingly gaunt bald head. 'I trust this will not be an inconvenience?'

Volchak knew full well the physician did not care, nor was he asking. No doubt any problems along the way would be Volchak's fault upon his eventual reunion with Smiele after this, so he saw no point in questioning.

'No problem, sir.' Volchak said.

'A member of the Order must be addressed as Physician. Nothing more.' The man was apparently done talking as he stepped back outside.

Volchak turned back to the prisoner. It was evident that his hands had been tied and a length of rope spanned the gap between the man and Harkner, who had tied it to his own wrist. Neither were going anywhere in a hurry without the other. The prisoner's shirt was dirty with a large blood stain on the lower half, no doubt where he was stuck with the spear the day before.

'Can he travel?' Volchak asked, practical, not concerned.

'Not a scratch on him. Honestly, I had a poke about and whatever that lunatic's done to him, he ain't got any holes where they shouldn't be.' Harkner grinned, shrugging his shoulders. Volchak knew about some of the more impressive feats the Hermetic Order had accomplished. The somewhat miraculous recoveries made by men of power with serious wounds. They were not the kingdom's healers. Their monastery was not for curing the sick. Although, over time, Volchak had noticed that Stirc had come to understand that patching a few soldiers up earned him additional gratitude from Smiele. The physician had twice worked on Volchak himself. Once on a puncture to the leg caused by the sharp end of a spear jutting out from the shield wall. Then again when an antler blade had got stuck in his shoulder, right up the hilt. Either could have been life threatening. But Volchak remembered the fear when he was strapped to that block, unable to move, thinking he was about to be the next experiment. The white paste had burned as Stirc had applied it and Volchak had eventually passed out from the pain. But by morning both were nothing less than red raw scarred flesh. He had tried not to focus too much on the various organs in jars sitting on the floor next to the block when the ropes pulled his head flat against it, he had just hoped that his innards wouldn't be next.

'The draft, then.' Volchak returned to a grim expression towards both Flea and Harkner. Both sighed and looked to each other worriedly, they had been through this once before and knew what they were about to do.

'We will travel east towards the coast, make our way through the farms in the flatlands before reaching the village of Brieth. South through three more villages, then turn towards the capital. We will need at least five more men before we hit the prison at the bridge where the remainders will join us. At the capital we will camp outside whilst I attend a war council. Each commander and his staff will be there.' Volchak parroted the orders from Smiele but without the disparaging tone.

'There's only three of us? That ain't much of a staff. Or much muscle to do a draft with neither?' Flea questioned.

'Four, with the physician, and his presence might actually make this a lot smoother. People in the villages fear the Order more than the army. Five, when we have the prisoner under control and in each farm as we gather more. We will find it easier once we reach Brieth, it's almost a town now. From there I foresee no further issues as our numbers will grow. The villages know they have to provide for the draft and they will do their duty, and the more men we get the easier it'll become to make them.' Volchak wasn't sure if he was trying to convince them or himself. He had seen a draft go bad before; the very three men they looked to recruit had been killed by the five guards Major Fedal had with him at the time. Two more by Volchak himself as they attacked him. Word of the recent defeat, or rather the stalemate and lack of a battle, that Smiele's famed Royal Guard had just fought would likely make this harder. Volchak hoped he would get out ahead of the news, at least at first.

'We will leave this afternoon. Have your packs ready and him ready to travel.' Volchak nodded to the prisoner. 'It is a week and a half's walk to Brieth, at least, and I do not trust the weather in the flatlands. An easy walk can turn nasty fast if we don't beat the rains.' He turned and headed back to the entrance of the tent himself, eager to secure what provisions he could for their journey.

Harkner raised his hand like a schoolboy.

'You mean we don't get horses?'

The man on the cot groaned slightly and groggily rolled onto his front.

Flea sprinkled more thyme on the rabbit.

Volchak shook his aching head and exited the tent.

II

Chapter 8

The rains started on the second day, several weeks earlier than usual in the flatlands. *Of course they had*, thought Volchak. *I'm walking through here*.

The small group departed Smiele's camp and headed east as planned, following the well-trodden wide dirt road which would carry them almost straight through to the village of Brieth near the eastern shore. Volchak knew that from there the same road curved south towards the only bridge over the River Vioene and to the prison fortress on its near bank. From there, it was a few more days to the capital and their journey's end. He had trudged the exact path in reverse a few months ago, although with close to five hundred men then.

He looked out across the flatlands, mentally shrugging at the aptness of the name. The hill where Smiele had commanded him to undertake another draft for more Breachmen was about the only terrain for as far as the eye could see. Volchak knew that there were impassable mountain peaks to the west, but they were too distant to be made out, even if the thick rain clouds hadn't shrouded the horizon. The land wasn't barren. Spinneys and thickets interspersed with large rocks jutting from the ground were spread across the plains in front of them. The story was that the stones were scattered by some unknown giant before time itself, thrown from the Western Mountains. But they did little to break the monotony. Volchak knew at Brieth they would have a sight of the river which ran alongside the coast from the Yrfrite hills in the North, through the city itself and down to the capital. Before the war, a small group such as theirs would have caught a trade barge and had a relatively relaxing last week on their journey back to the capital. The River Vioene had previously carried all trade goods, masonry and, most importantly, the metal from the mine in Yrfrite to the capital. But the river, like the trade, flowed in one direction. It was a long and dreary road north from the capital to the only other city in the kingdom and as the capital prospered and developed, its northern counterparty stagnated and rotted. Merchant caravans were constant, but the road was unpaved, wagons towed by cattle were slow and the journey was never a completely safe one, particularly north of Brieth. It had been many years since the Boatman invasion had been defeated, but still there were remnants of their enemy on the road, using the hills and woodlands to launch raids. Even the Order had a much lighter presence in Yrfrite, only a small temple no different to that in the much smaller town of Brieth. So it was of no surprise that when the Duke rose up against the King, he quickly took and sealed the city. There was little resistance other than that the King had sent to prevent the uprisings. Most of the infantrymen there were loyal to where they lived, where their families were, not to a faraway capital. The Yrfrite Guard, such as they had been, were the city's first army. Volchak pulled on the straps on his pack and felt the familiar weight of his axe wrapped in oil cloth and strapped beneath. It was the first commander of those infantrymen that he'd got it from.

Ahead of him, the prisoner Kaelith walked. He'd come to his senses a few hours before they left and had been quiet and inquisitive until they were out of sight of the camp, or maybe out of sight of the physician's red tent, perhaps. His hands were bound, but he was capable enough of walking. Between Stirc and Harkner, his rope was never unguarded and Volchak was fairly sure even that Flea could best him when he was unarmed and without his armour. Needless to say, Smiele had seen fit to keep the man's breastplate and sword.

'You see, my dear, the trick isn't to command it where to go but to coax it, gently, lead it and subtly convince it that it is best for both of you if it goes. A gentle nudge in the ribs and sway of the hips you see...' Kaelith's voice was confident, colourful, and his manner, even in his ripped shirt clinging tightly in the wet, gentlemanly. Volchak had to pretend not to be listening, but he had spent most of the walk so far hearing Kaelith explain the finer points of horsemanship, or swordsmanship, or 'courtmanship', to Flea. He had charmed her the moment he'd flashed her his pearl grin. She was captivated. Volchak had wondered whether this would irk Harkner, but although the big man had been cautious, he too had seemed to warm to the prisoner. Only Stirc treated him with utter contempt. He had asked why Volchak bothered to share food with his prisoner if his body wouldn't give out for weeks.

'A hungry man will soon become a weak man, sure enough. And weak men can't walk. Unless you want to carry him?' Volchak had told him around the fire last evening, as he handed a bowl of the rabbit stew Flea had concocted from yesterday's breakfast. Stirc had scowled but his intellectual mind couldn't refute the logic, and he certainly wouldn't carry the man.

'But what about when they get scared? Or hurt?' Flea had asked, clearly remembering back to the events just a few days before, but maybe not remembering that it was the horseman that did most of the hurting.

'Ah well, take your weathered friend here,' Kaelith motioned behind him to Volchak, walking at a steady pace. 'Will he not go where he is told? Be commanded and swayed? So when he gets hurt or scared, what does he do?'

'Usually kills someone,' Harkner tossed back over his shoulder.

'Not true! He kills our enemies and I don't think he enjoys it.' Flea protested, although the slightest twinge in her voice gave away that maybe she didn't completely convince herself.

Kaelith turned his head, hands still out in front, being guided by Harkner's rope.

'A ruthless killer, are we, Volchak?' He was overly familiar again. Volchak hadn't remembered telling Kaelith his name, but didn't pay it much mind.

'Never killed a man wasn't trying to kill me first,' Volchak replied, shrugging his pack on his shoulders again, battling against the rain that was trickling down his neck under his thick leather coat.

'What about a horse?' an awkward pause, the axe shifted in its oilskin, then Kaelith burst into raucous laughter. 'I kid, I kid my friend' giggling to himself merrily. 'I'm sure it'd have bitten your arm right off had it the chance.' Volchak wasn't completely sure he was joking; he didn't really know whether that was something a horse would do.

'And I've plenty more, do not worry! Why it wasn't even my favourite!'

'You have more?' Flea asked, glee in her voice.

'Enough!' Stirc had dropped back next to Kaelith and so had been listening to the conversation the entire time as well. 'The prisoner is to keep his tongue still or he will have it removed.'

'Right you are, not a word, silent as a...' Stirc stopped and shot a look at Kaelith that itself might have been sharp enough to remove a tongue.

Flea asked no more questions.

They spent the rest of the day in the grey, damp haze as the rain pattered off the road in front and behind them. Each had their own oilskins and leather coats and were well used to the harsh weather of the flatlands; each having crossed it at least twice, and Volchak twice more. In the early evening, they left the road and headed into one of the small woods that lay a few hundred meters from the side of the road. Its tall pine trees offered some protection from the drizzle, but the ground was wet and there was little chance of a fire. Volchak and Harkner hung a large tarpaulin from Harkner's pack, forming a tent under which they all huddled, with several oily skins from Volchak's packs forming a dry floor. It wasn't luxurious, but it warm enough as spring was slowly giving way to summer. Even with the rains, it wouldn't grow cold here for many months. The seasons were short and sharp, sometimes only a month separated by the snowfall and the harsh summer sun, but the army had grown accustomed to being too cold, too warm or too wet all within the course of one campaign.

The red robe had all but absorbed Stirc, curling it round his body and across his face. He wasn't moving. Whether asleep or merely listening, Volchak couldn't be sure, but he would likely stay that way till morning. Harkner tied the rope round Kaelith's ankles and then tucked in behind him as they lay on the damp forest floor, far too close for comfort of either man, but then Harkner promptly fell asleep. Guess not for him. Flea's back pushed up against Harkner's as she curled over the edge of the skin into a blanket and used some gathered ferns as a pillow. She looked completely comfortable.

Volchak lay a few feet from Kaelith, a tough root digging into his back. His head and neck still were still sore from the previous few days fighting and walking. And the previous few years years fighting and walking. His pack acted as his pillow and he propped one arm behind it, within inches of the haft of his axe.

'How did you know?' he asked.

'K-know w-wh-what?' Kaelith's teeth were chattering slightly as he lacked any real covering, just his soaked shirt.

Volchak frowned, front teeth pressing against his lower ones and hurting at the gum line as they always did when he thought. Leaning up on one elbow, he stripped the oilskin from around his axe. The inner lining was a thick fur from a cow. He handed it out to Kaelith without a word.

Kaelith took it with his bound hands, stretched the rope taught at its furthest point, but Harkner didn't stir despite it being bound to his wrist.

'Know w-what?' he replied again.

'My name. You knew my name.' The lined face of Volchak stared at him, with several dark scars around one eye and an angry pitted one on his cheek. 'Did the Duke send you to kill me? Or just all the Breachmen?' His voice was calm but cold. He couldn't bear the man any ill will. He'd simply been on the other side.

'Eh? The Breachmen?' Kaelith smiled his arrogant, knowing smile. As if he was privy to the juiciest of secrets and delighted in being the one to share them.

'She didn't pay me to care about Breachmen.' He laughed to himself softly, as if the concept itself was absurd. 'What's thirty fighters barely better equipped than the Duke's own army?' His voice lowered. 'She didn't pay me enough to keep it secret, either. I doubt I'll be getting the balance now, anyway.'

'She?'

'His sister. She's the brains of the operation. Well, he's actually also the brains too, but she handles the less heroic side of his war. We were after Smiele's Royal Guard. They were the key, Duke Olaf knew it. His men simply couldn't deal with them head on.'

Volchak thought about this for a moment.

'Why keep fighting then?' He asked.

'Wrong question. You should ask why they kept fighting the *way* they did?' Kaelith said. Volchak tilted his head. He wanted to know this secret. 'Every time your men charged, hit the shield wall, then the Royal Guard just rolled over them. Pinned in place and unable to mount a real defence, aye? So why didn't they change their tactics? Charge you back?'

This wasn't the first time Volchak had wondered about this.

'Well, the guard was just too well armoured, too well organised. He could send his men charging at them and no one could put a dent in that steel they wore. They couldn't hurt them. One hundred and forty-four men could have marched right up to the gates of his city and the Duke could barely make a dent in their metal heads.'

Kaelith wriggled across the ground, closer to Volchak, and whispered. Volchak's hand gripped his axe handle under his pack, but he didn't move away from the man. Something about Kaelith had shifted as he talked. His dashing bravado seemed to have drained from him. Without it, he seemed older, weaker. Somehow, Volchak saw himself in the man, weathered and beaten. But it disappeared in a flash of Kaelith's grin.

'So why did Smiele chase him round half the country? Go and take the city and be done with it.' Kaelith snorted. 'Why did Smiele not just do that? If it was about the metal?

Let the rebels starve out in the flatlands or the hills to the west? They wouldn't be able to hold a city, let alone take it back. It was never about the mine. It's something else.'

Volchak thought about this. Thought about what Smiele knew, what he planned, what he did. They'd been fighting this rebellion for several years now. The pace had quickened of late. Three major engagements in a year. The tide had been turning. Volchak had felt that as they advanced back towards the rebelling city. But they had always followed the Duke's army, always reacting and chasing. He never really thought about it, just did what he was told and went where they told him to go.

'Their mine ran dry about a year before the rebellion. When they first stopped sending shipments to the capital, it wasn't his greed or his revolution. They just ran out.' Kaelith's voice was low. 'It was the King that sent men to take the city in the first place. They thought the city was stockpiling weapons, readying an army. By doing so, the Duke reacted to defend himself, took what weapons they had and did just that.'

Volchak had been in the city when the rebellion began, a Breachman serving his time in the north of the kingdom, seeing out his days. No war. They had fed him, kept him warm and kept him busy drilling what few men he had. They were more for show, there to keep the peace instead of fight. The last war had ended, and he'd survived, done his time. It had been time to live out the last of his draft. He remembered hearing of production problems. Trouble at the Order temple. Then the two extra infantry divisions had arrived and garrisoned the city. He was put to work enforcing the curfew. He had known the reputation of their idiotic commander. A penny-pinching bureaucrat. Volchak remembers seeing him have his head caved in by a man with a builder's hammer. The riots afterwards. When the Order's physicians got themselves strung up to their blocks, the rioters burned the place down. He had thought the infantry were there to quell the rebellion, had always thought it. But he supposed they had arrived shortly before the fighting really started.

'This whole thing,' Kaelith's eyes motioned all about him. 'Some kind of big misunderstanding. Well, maybe anyways.'

Harkner grunted and rolled onto his back, snoring. In doing so, the force of his heavy weight tugged Kaelith back towards him, but not before he had caught Volchak's eye. Secret spilled; his roguish grin re-emerged as he rolled onto his back. And then Kaelith promptly fell asleep.

Chapter 9

Flea liked the road. She would sleep well, get to see new things, search for herbs and find small game. People would complement her cooking and she would sleep warmly under the cover of the thick skins they put down on the ground. She could chat with Harkner and he would tell her stories of Tydrian before the war. Tales of where the river starts, where it goes and why the boats always went in one direction on it and how they sailed back by sea.

But mostly, she liked the road because no one ever made her kill anyone, and no one tried to kill her.

She liked the prisoner too; he was funny and charming and told of far-off adventures. And horses! She'd only ever seen the councillor's, and only at a distance. Now Kaelith came along, and he had his very own, lots of them. Although she supposed he had one less now, since Volchak had beheaded one at the battle; that was a shame.

She trotted along next to him for four days, having jaunty conversations and giggling at his stories until that miserable physician had interrupted them. But even he had mellowed now, obviously realised there was no harm in her finding out more about the 'gentlemen' as he called himself and the fun adventures of a… what had he called them? His company?

She'd tried talking to Stirc as well. Most of the time he just scoffed and scorned her. One afternoon though, she'd asked about what a physician did and something lit up in his eyes. He told her of libraries, learning and hidden secrets. Of anatomy and the art of understanding the body. He made it sound almost... romantic. She guessed he chose to miss out the bit about chopping up people.

The small homestead came into view from behind the small wooded area off the right, and Flea's heart sank. She hated this bit.

As they made their way up to the small wooden house, she glanced a look at the large wooden barn, then to Kaelith, then to the barn again. This time the doors stood wide open and across the straw strewn doorway stood a large wooden rail which held back the several cattle inside. No men with swords riding them. Good.

'Cows.' Harkner said, nodding to the barn, as if knowing exactly what she was thinking. Kaelith stood beside him, the rope slack and almost imperceptible between them, held loosely in one of Harkner's hands.

'A fine observation by my travelling companion.' Kaelith said. He nodded at the farmer who was making towards them, a large wooden pitch fork held in one hand.

'What business have you? We've shelter, if you need it for the evening, but you will share with the herd.' His voice was gruff, common, just like many of the men in the mine. His manner didn't suggest he was welcoming them into his home, any more than the pitchfork did, but it seemed he knew there was little point in trying to send away Volchak, Harkner, and even Kaelith. Flea kept quiet as Volchak stepped forward from their group to speak. As he did the farmer caught sight of Stirc in his red cloak and the blood drained from his face. His voice shook as he spoke.

'You'd better move on to Brieth, only two day's walk there. Plenty of workers.' He was even less welcoming than the first time, but also more pleading.

'Friend, we come at the command of his Royal Highness and rightful ruler of Tydrian. Governor of the Capital and...' Volchak hadn't said the bit about the Duchy of Yrfrite, Flea guessed it made little sense given last week's escapades. He seemed to sigh his words, apologetic. She'd seen him say this before. 'We are commanded to request any able-bodied souls under twenty-two years of age from your homestead to accept the draft and accompany us to the capital there to serve one term under his Majesty's command.' Under Smiele's command, Flea thought.

The man's fork was now his crutch, as he wobbled in place, as pale as the straw on the ground beneath his feet.

'N-n-no you can't.' He whispered, tears welling in his eyes. This wasn't one of the brutal killers or criminals that made up most of the Breachmen. 'I, we, won't... No fighters here.'

'Training and equipment will be provided.' Volchak wasn't looking at the man. His head was almost bowed to him as he watched the pitchfork. To most, it would seem he was merely watching for any threat, but Flea thought he just didn't want to meet the man's eye. Flea had seen the Commander stare down a dozen murderers armed to the teeth, saw him charge a solid shield wall that was baying for his blood, but this, it seemed, was too much for him.

'They feed you too,' she chipped in, trying to be helpful.

No one even noticed.

The man hadn't moved, at first he said nothing, tears threatening to burst from him.

'You can't take them! I did my time in the infantry. That was goin' ter be the last draft. They promised. I was at the coast when we fought off the Boatmen. They promised me peace,' he was on the verge of exploding into tears. 'You were there.' He grabbed at Volchak's arm. 'You knew. On the beach. You charged that ship with your men. I saw it.' The farmer released the arm, panicked he turned to Harkner, then to Flea. He pleaded. 'We were supposed to go home, those that didn't die in the surf. You can't have them…'

'Them?' Stirc's high-pitched whine of a voice seemed to slither around Volchak as he did. 'May I remind you that refusal of the draft is forfeit to the Order, and if you have more than one subject here, we will gladly accept them all.' He smiled, his thin over crowded mouth nearly snarling.

The man collapsed, tears rolling from his eyes as he sobbed in the dirt at Volchak's feet.

'I can't lose no more sons; winter took two last year and…' His burly nature had imploded, and he was as a small child begging not to be punished. Two dark haired boys emerged from the barn, ducking beneath the rail and running over to their father. The vigour of their youth compelled them to brandish their two wood clubs.

'Easy, boys.' Harkner said, as if calming a frightened bull. He passed his hammer into his other hand, positioning it on the long grip. He let loose the rope attached to Kaelith. These bulls were still growing. But he wasn't looking at them. He was watching Volchak, who had brought his axe up as if ready to fight.

'This is the Commander of the Breachmen. Raise a weapon to him and you'll not see the sunset.' His voice was serious, more than Flea had ever heard outside of a fight.

At this, the farmer's sobs turned to a wail. 'Breachmen…' was all he had managed to say as the boys fell to his side, arms round their ailing father and tears of their own. He understood. Twenty-five years for each, they would not see him again.

'Listen friend,' Volchak knelt himself, placing the spike of his axe into the ground and putting one hand out in front of him. 'Your *only* son must come with us.'

The man looked up, confused, then to his two sons, then his tear swollen eyes back to Volchak. Flea realised right away, she'd been distracted looking at the barn but had been listening. The thing with barns is that she simply didn't trust them much these days. It took the farmer another few moments.

'But…' Realisation crossed his face; Flea had thought he would be happy. It was a kindness.

'Choose? No… How?' He looked back at his sons. The larger of the two stood up and turned to the unwelcome guests, wiping snot from his face.

'I'll come with you, and you'll leave them.' He couldn't have been more than a year or two older than Flea, better fed and stronger, but less bright. *Not bad looking*, she thought.

'Yes. Your family will have done their part.' Flea had almost added 'for now' but decided against it. 'And it ain't so bad. We had rabbit a few days ago.' She smiled.

'Unacceptable!' Stirc had turned his snarl to the Commander, his back to the farmer. Flea had hoped at that moment the farmer got some courage and jabbed him with the fork. No such luck.

'The law is clear, each able soul of the requisite age must submit to the draft, otherwise you are to the rope!'

Volchak stood slowly and turned to Stirc. To Flea, he had suddenly grown to rival Harkner in size, but that was just a trick of the light reflecting from his axe.

'As Commander of the Breachmen,' his voice slowed, and the air seemed still. 'I see one person here who is to be drafted and only one. And I remind the physician that the draft is the responsibility of the army. His services are only needed when I say someone has resisted.' Volchak had a point. And he had his axe in both hands and was rolling it the way he did before a charge.

Stirc had held his stare for a few seconds. Flea wondered whether he had any weapons. She'd never seen any, just that bag of his. He lingered a moment before huffing loudly and pushing past Harkner to seize Kaelith's rope and drag the prisoner several paces away from where they stood. Kaelith winked at Harkner, who chuckled as he feigned subservience and tripped under what was clearly not enough strength to actually move the man.

Volchak turned back to the farmer on the ground and his son standing next to him. 'I will do what I can for the boy. I will see if a place as a guardsman on the eastern shore might be possible. He is of no use to me as a Breachman.'

The farmer didn't stop crying for the next hour, nor did younger boy. Whilst the group of them entered the house, and waited for the son to gather his belongings and say his goodbyes. The older boy's eyes just remained wide and his face blank. Sometimes they would run at this point, or attack the Commander. It would always end the same, an axe in the skull, or back, or face. Flea had watched one who had run. Escaped out a window and covered some distance before Harkner chased him down. Harkner had spent the next week complaining about having to chase after the draftee. The draftee hadn't complained though. Volchak had killed him for running. Flea never knew why they ran; the draft was just part of life. The King decided he needed fighters, and he sent other fighters to go and get them. Eventually, those fighters would go get other ones, or they'd die fighting. Just the way it worked. Except for her, and the other criminals - they had a choice. They could stay in prison if they didn't want to fight for the Breachmen. *Not much of a choice though.* She shrugged.

They left the farm. The boy was wrapped in a rough leather coat and carried a club in his hands. As the farm faded over the horizon, Harkner walked next to the boy. Flea noticed Harkner had been strangely contemplative throughout the entire experience.

'They with you?' Harkner peered off into the distance, where the faintest blurred outline was visible on the horizon from the direction they had come. Flea couldn't make it out but there was something on the road. You could see a long way on the flats when it was clear. The boy didn't respond as much as let out a small whelp, and started to cry.

'Volchak, we seem to have picked up some hangers-on along the way,' Harkner said. Back to his cheery normal self, as carefree as if describing some unwanted guests at an otherwise private party.

'We need to move. Bring him.' Volchak hadn't indicated whether he meant the boy or Kaelith. Harkner shrugged and grabbed both by the shoulders, and nudged them along. Their pace now a steady march back along the road, Stirc remained at the back of the group, still holding Kaelith's rope although the prisoner was out in front. From where Flea looked it was Kaelith leading Stirc.

Flea peered over her shoulder at the distant blur and shrugged. *Maybe it was more men with horses?*

Chapter 10

Volchak knew within hours that their pursuers, whoever they were, would be catching up with his group at some point the following morning. He would push the others hard, but they weren't going be able to keep ahead, laden with packs as they were. If their pursuers had enough men, or if they had a base nearby, then they would be travelling lighter and probably be fresher. He had no way of knowing, but he doubted they'd had to fight in a battle and then walked for five days either.

They walked long into the night. The rains had abated the day before they reached the small farm and the sky remained clear. At sunset he halted the troop for several minutes, he knelt and watched the sun disappear. Harkner and Flea did the same. Volchak rose to his feet - back aching and legs threatening to cramp, and continued the march. The night stayed pleasantly warm as summer fast approached and they had not needed shelter, so they made no attempt to get off the road when they finally stopped. The farm boy was sullen, not making eye contact with his companions or responding to their attempts at conversation. After several hours Harkner had stopped trying and had trotted on merrily enough, Flea was silent but struggling with the pace. Volchak knew that she had started to dictate their speed as Harkner had slowed to match her without a word. In the end it was Stirc who had eventually caved in and been unable to carry on - too bookish for running from bandits. Volchak considered leaving him, but Smiele and the whole army knew he'd left with the physician under his guard, alongside the prisoner. Both the army and the Order would be after him if he didn't arrive with them both at the capital. Not that it mattered much, it was unlikely he'd see the sunset tomorrow.

After a few brief hours of uncomfortable half-sleep, they rose, taking what dried meats and rations they had left and sharing them all out as they started to march. It seemed they were walking at an even slower pace than the day before, energy almost spent. Volchak trudged the first hour of their march with his eyes fixed ahead of them, searching for any advantage for when the men behind caught up. Last night he had seen the fires they lit next to the road, apparently taking their rest maybe an hour before he had stopped his own march. The boy had spotted them too and suggested they stop. However, Volchak told him that if it was him chasing them, he'd have lit the fires and feigned stopping, then carried on another hour at least to see if he could catch his quarry napping. When they awoke, and found they hadn't been stabbed in their sleep, he thought maybe he had been wrong. But as the light came up the next morning it was clear the pursuers had made ground during the night. They were only an hour or so behind now.

Volchak saw what he thought was their best chance. As chances went, it was not a lot to go on - one of the large flatland stones stood upright, adjacent to the road with a small spinney less than ten strides behind it. He stopped the others and looked back, clearly able to see the men now only a few miles away and trotting fast. Volchak was right. They didn't seem heavily laden but they moved with a definite vigour of pursuit. He could count seven. *Damn. Seven was too many.*

'Listen, this is our chance. The rock will give us some element of protection to one side, stop them getting round us as easy.' Unless someone just took the few minutes to run the whole way round it, but he never said it was a great plan. 'You, boy...' he hadn't bothered with his name, and the boy hadn't offered yet. Once he learned who the boy was, it'd be one more sleepless night trying to forget him when he died. 'Take the prisoner into the woods there, try and find somewhere quiet to hide.'

'My dear Commander, I daresay you could use an extra hand in this?' Kaelith said. He seemed genuine enough, but Volchak shook his head.

'I'm sure you would swear fealty on your life's honour to defend me to your dying breath… But I'm not sure I'm ready to trust someone who so recently killed so many of my men, and nearly me.' Kaelith hadn't argued. That was one last little joy that Volchak was grateful for.

'Stirc, am I to assume you are no fighter?'

'A physician studies the body Commander. I am of rather more use in keeping them alive than in ending them.' Volchak didn't have time to argue the ridiculousness of this with a man who had probably spent his formative years cutting open live subjects to see what he could find inside. 'That's a no then.'

'Fine, then you take Kaelith. Boy. You wait behind the rock and if one tries to get around the side, you deal with them.' Volchak looked at the newest recruit, hands shaking and a scared looked on his face. It was clear he wouldn't be dealing with anyone but at least he might slow them down.

The three of them hurried off, having dumped their packs in the middle of the road at Volchak's order - as did Harkner and Flea.

The three Breachmen now stood in a line across the road. It wasn't lost on Volchak that the other two still stood an extra step away from him but close to each other. That was not part of the plan. Flea had the large rock on one side and Harkner on the other, holding his oversized rock of a hammer. Volchak had nothing but empty space keeping his flank safe.

The pursuers slowed to an almost meandering pace as they had approached the group, clearly catching their breath and making use of the time now they realised their prey was no longer running. They were an unpleasant crowd even by the Breachmen's low standards. Each of the six… W*ait six? Where was the seventh*? Each of the six was distinctly similar. Clearly these were seasoned killers. They were grizzled, rugged types, definitely not strangers to the road. Each had heavy cloth, or leather, armour in various mismatched guises. Most had large thickets for beards that covered their faces, and they each carried all manner of savage clubs and stone axes. Volchak would bet good money that most of their gear had been retrieved from the corpses of people on the road. The one who strode forward and spoke carried a rusted, but real, iron sword. That in itself would have made him the leader. He stepped several paces ahead of his men and stood above the packs that had been piled on the floor. He cleared his throat, signalling he was ready to talk. Volchak had no intention of doing the same. Why single himself out when he knew there were no terms that he could offer short of what these men wanted?

The raider stood a moment, spinning his sword point into the ground and looking at the three of them stood next to him. Volchak still only counted six.

'We, the Boatmen of Nakor, do inform you that there is a tax to travel on this road.'

He had directed his comments to Harkner, who stood stoically in the centre and clearly the biggest of the three.

'Listen, friend.' Volchak's voice was resolute, but not confrontational. 'What we have is there. Take what you think is fair and we will all get to live to see the sunset this evening.'

The man turned to him, his face half covered with what looked like an angry flaking rash and grinned, showing his mottled brown teeth. Sadly, this wasn't a beauty contest.

'We want taxes.' No surprise that this was the way it was going. Volchak tried once more.

'We are Breachmen from the King's army, travelling ahead of the army from the battle five days west of here to report to the capital. Our arrival is expected and our route known; our delay or disappearance will bring an infantry division down this road looking for answers. And they might not look too kindly to find army supplies with you and your men.' This would of course only rile him up, especially in front of the other five. Volchak stared at the leader with a blank expression.

'You think we are afraid of the King's army? They are too slow to catch us. Old men and the draftees, never held a sword. No match for my crew.' Of course, Volchak hadn't seen them when he had marched this road months ago with said army.

'The Boatmen were sent back to their ships way I heard it,' Harkner said, a vague threat sitting behind the comment.

'I know this one, Cap'n.' A man from the line behind the leader chirped up. He was tall, thin, carried a tall thin spear and spoke with a shallow breathy voice. 'He's that one that butchered so many of our men on the landing grounds. Dangerous fella. I 'eard that axe has split hundreds of skulls.' The tall man paused and lowed his voice slightly. 'Maybe we let this one go?'

'That's right, friend.' Volchak spun the axe in his hands, its large head swishing through the air. 'Hundreds. At worst odds than these. Take what you want from the bags and be on your way. I won't add to its tally.' Volchak tried to pour spite and malice into his voice, to sound like he had enjoyed splitting those heads. He hoped the man couldn't tell he tossed and turned at night, unable to sleep for the memory of them.

The man at the front considered the three Breachmen.

'Nah... rubbish. He ain't even the big one.' The leader was looking at Harkner with his brow furrowed. 'Now your contribution, we want that.' He nodded at the axe in Volchak's hands - no surprise, it was a princely sum of metal to be carrying and no doubt they could make use of it. 'And we want *that*.' The man grinned his foul grin over towards Flea. She stood unmoving, with a dead-eye stare.

'Not going to happen, boat-scum.' Harkner stepped forward and held his hammer over his shoulder, ready to swing, as he spat the words. Despite being two or three paces out of reach the man still took the smallest step back from the intimidating presence. Harkner didn't charge forward and swing it, although Volchak had thought for a moment he might.

'And how, tell me, do you think you will stop us, big man? Three against six.' The man pointed at each with his rusted short sword, bouncing the blade in the air as he counted them off.

'Three against seven.' Volchak interrupted. The man turned to face him.

'You're a bright one, aren't you?'

'Might only be five. When I kill you, maybe one will run? Sometimes someone runs.' Volchak sighed, talking more to himself now than to the man. For a moment his shoulders sank. He felt the exhaustion of the last week, the last year, the last fifteen, creep up from his hips into his back. He felt as if he could barely stand as his legs cramped and neck seized, a slight breeze would have had him in the dirt. And as quick as the feeling hit him, it left.

Chapter 11

Volchak surged forward. Rash-face had caught the movement and raised his sword to meet the axe swing, but the weight of the heavy bronze blade knocked it down as Harkner's hammer smashed into his chest. The hammer crushed the leader's chest and forced him to collapse backwards. Dead.

The other men charged forward -all but one who held the spear. He hesitated, watching his leader's body hit the ground.

Three ran straight at Volchak, swinging their clumsy clubs. He lurched sideways to avoid one, and then leapt at the second man. Volchak got in so close to the man's face, that his beard scratched at Volchak's eyes as he was now inside the swing of the club. Volchak drove the spike on the axe head deep into that beard, the force of the man's arms coming down with the club drove it deep into his neck. The third man caught Volchak with a glancing blow on his left shoulder, the strength of it knocking Volchak bouncing off of the second man and careening into the dirt. He scrambled up, one hand somehow still clutching the now blood-soaked handle of the axe. He raised its head to catch another swing from the first man's club. Volchak's arm reverberated as they connected. The weight of the club striking his axe drove the head down, sharp blade slicing against his own leg, cutting a red gash through his leather trousers. Volchak pushed the man back with his shoulder and then squared off against the two remaining assailants. Axe now held in both hands, leg burning, he circled around the fallen man's body, keeping it between them and him.

***

Flea darted, quickly and nimbly, round the tip of the spear. The man holding it hesitated upon seeing the small girl coming at him. By the time he had regained his senses and lowered it towards her, she was already skirting up the side of the long haft, using one arm to press it down and away from her. She went to drive one of her antler blades into the man's face, but he caught her arm with his empty hand and twisted her back towards him, wrapping one of his muscular arms around her waist. She butted his face with the back of her head, which snapped his head back, but he held firm. He dropped the spear and engulfed her with his other arm in a tight hug. He lifted her entirely off the ground, leaning back in a monstrous embrace and made to dump her body on the ground. But at that moment, the tremendous hammer shattered his right leg with a sickening crack. It continued to sweep the man's other leg off the ground entirely and dumped him sideways, releasing Flea - who rolled away the moment she hit the dirt. As she did, the hammer circled round vertically and crushed the man's head. It splattered gore and bone across the dusty road and his body twitched and danced from the moment of impact. Flea came to her feet and jumped onto the other man with a stone axe who had run towards Harkner's exposed back. She caught him in the side with her blade which snapped as it struck one of his ribs. He dropped his axe as he drew back the blade - splintered bone poked through the skin. She drove the antler up into his chin and pinned him as he fell onto his face.

***

Whilst Flea and Harkner dealt with their two assailants, Volchak swung his axe at one of his - only to have it meet nothing but air as the man sidestepped, then kicked out into the side of Volchak's knee. Volchak's leg gave way and he fell into a kneeling position, as the club swung straight for his head. Volchak saw this and released his axe handle and aimed a punch directly between the man's legs. The man doubled over, club-swing forgotten with the pain. The second man emerged like a shadow from behind him as the first fell to the side, swinging his own club. Volchak dove forward onto the attacker and knocked him over onto his back with the bloodied Breachman on top of him, straddling his chest. Rather than reach for the axe that lay on the ground next to them both, Volchak grabbed the man's fat face and jammed his thumbs directly into the eye sockets. He pressed with all his might, felt the warm blood spill out as the man screamed. Volchak gritted his teeth hard, spitting through them as he shouted in rage and pressed harder and harder until his soaked hands felt something sharp give in the man's skull and he went limp. A beat passed. The second man was starting to recover from the punch and started to stir. Volchak seized his axe that lay next to the corpse beneath him, and still kneeling, swung it sideways to where the punched man had just stopped rolling around in pain. It made a solid thud as it passed through his neck and lodged firmly in the ground.

A hand grabbed the back of Volchak's collar and threw him backwards, unarmed and scrambling. Volchak did not know where he had come from, but evidently the seventh man had gone around the rock, just as he'd feared. He readied himself for short sharp stabs in the stomach or neck from an antler blade, or perhaps for his head to be smashed in with an axe or club. As he fell back, he saw it was to be a stone hammer, smaller than Harkner's, one-handed. Well, he supposed that was one way to go, head bashed in with a rock.

***

Kaelith had seen the farm boy stand his ground. Brave lad. Foolish though. The man was clearly a killer. You could tell from how untidy his beard was, probably smelled awful too. Kaelith strained against the rope and grimaced to Stirc, nodding his head wildly in the direction of the boy. From their hollow in the thick undergrowth, they had a solid view of both fights, but Stirc had no intentions of intervening in either. He had wound the rope up tight, pressing Kaelith up close to him.

'Help him.' Kaelith whispered angrily into Stirc's ear.

But Stirc froze, cowered, and watched with a pale horror in his face. As if this was something entirely different to watching a body cut up on one of his blocks. Kaelith turned back and saw the boy try to swing the club at his opponent. The attacker just held out a hand and grabbed it mid-air and tossed it down at his boots. The boy turned to run, but the axe split his head and he collapsed in a heap to the ground. It had lasted but seconds.

Looking to the other fight, Kaelith watched Volchak stab the man through the throat with the spike on his axe and then a man raising his club blocked his view. The man had crumpled to the floor just as Volchak launched himself on top of the third man and seemed to crush his skull with his bare hands. *Dangerous, that one.*

But Volchak apparently hadn't realised the seventh man had got around behind him. Or maybe just had his hands full at the moment. Having killed the boy, the man came round the rock behind Volchak, wielding his blood covered stone axe. Kaelith couldn't tell for sure, but he imagined that Harkner and Flea were tied up elsewhere, fighting the others.

It was now or never. This was Kaelith's only chance. No one was paying attention to him, Stirc was clearly horrified that his protector was about to have his head split open by the remnants of invaders defeated years ago.

Kaelith head-butted Stirc hard on the bridge of his nose and took off running, hands bound but the rope dangling behind him like a dog off its leash making it's run for freedom. He sprinted as fast as he could. Fast and light. No armour or weapons weighing him down. He made it about fifteen strides and then tripped and launched himself into the air.

***

Volchak saw the man raise the stone axe and couldn't take his eyes off it as it fell. It was bloody and worn, like him. Suitable. The man grunted as he swung it downwards towards Volchak's head in what seemed like slow motion. That would be it then. In the moment, he didn't even feel angry, was it relief? Finally, it'd be over. No more fighting.

Suddenly, a blurry mass impacted the man, sending him sprawling. It was a dirty white mass of frills and rope and swearing and flailing. Kaelith barrelled into the man, apparently head first, in a full-on dive. He caught the attacker completely unaware and the stone axe spiralled off across the floor as Kaelith's flying body dumped the man unceremoniously onto his back. By the time they untangled themselves, the Boatman's skull was crushed under Harkner's hammer.

Volchak stood, wavering. His bloody hands dripping onto the dirt road beneath him, and he peered around. Seven men lay dead, dismembered and crushed. But his companions were all still, apparently, in one piece. Harkner and Flea were dishevelled but unharmed. Both were spattered with the blood of the men they'd fought. Kaelith was rolling around trying to reach his feet, hands still bound and trailing the rope that was now tangled around both his legs. Flea moved over to help him. Volchak was the only one who emerged from the fight completely covered in blood, although only a little of it was his own. The scratch on his leg burned, but he had no time to worry about it now. Eventually, it would be one more scar to remind him of one more fight.

Volchak knelt and picked up his axe. It had lodged into the ground and stood like a small shrine to where it had decapitated the man, moments before. Stirc emerged from the woods, his face covered in blood. It streamed crimson from his nose to match his red travel cloak.

'Seize him!' Stirc shouted as he stepped over the crushed body of the leader of the bandits, pointing his bony finger at Kaelith. 'He attacked me and escaped.'

Harkner snorted, looking at Kaelith kneeling on the dirt road next to the man with the caved in skull. 'He ain't done an outstanding job of escaping has he?'

Flea chipped in. 'He just saved the Commander's life! Dove across the battlefield, even tied up, and took out one of them!' Kaelith did not point out that it was Harkner who took the man out. Kaelith had just knocked him over.

Kaelith stood, breathing heavily, apparently with nothing to say. Stirc, twelve strides away, looked from Kaelith to Volchak.

Volchak sighed, limping slightly on his cut leg. He bent over and took up the loose end of the rope and held it in his hand, looking at it.

'Where's the boy, Stirc?' The accusation hung beneath the question.

'Dead. We watched. The brigand came around the rock and killed him, split his head with an axe.' Stirc replied, heartlessly.

'You watched?'

'Well… yes. These were trained killers. There wasn't anything I could have done. People die in a fight. It was a mess.'

'People die in a fight…' Volchak trailed off, as if lost in his own thoughts. Stirc seemed uncomfortable, as if he realised was in a more precarious situation than he'd expected.

'Yes. They were killers.' Volchak spun the axe in his bloodied hands and looked at Stirc, who took a step back and shrank into his red robe.

Volchak followed the rope back to Kaelith and looked him squarely in the eye, standing uncomfortably close. He took the axe and lowered it on to the ground, resting against his own wounded leg. With two bloodied hands, he untied the knot around Kaelith's wrists and dumped the rope to the ground.

'Stirc. They killed the prisoner in the battle. Nasty business. Head split with an axe, there was nothing but to bury him.' Volchak's eyes didn't leave Kaelith's. He saw the mercenary give the most imperceptible of nods.

'We were lucky the recruit we got from that farm was there to help. We'd have struggled if it was just three of us against seven.'

'He's a useful lad, that boy. Bit of a mouth on him, but he did well in a fight. Think he's called Kaelith. Shame, though, can't remember what that prisoner's name was.' Harkner stated, a simple matter of fact.

'I don't think we ever asked.' Flea was smiling.

Volchak turned and looked at Stirc, across the bodies and blood strewn about.

'Yes,' Stirc replied. 'A shame.' He wiped the blood from his nose on his robe sleeve and turned to the pile of bags to retrieve his own.

Volchak stepped forward to the body of the leader and picked up the rusted short sword. He looked it over once, spun it in his hands and looked down the blade. It was straight, sharp, in dire need of some care and attention, but effective enough.

With a nod, he tossed the sword to Kaelith. A tiny trail of blood remained on the handle when he threw it and it streaked in the air between the two of them. Kaelith caught the grip, fumbled it and nearly dropped it back on the ground, recovered, coughed, then nodded back to Volchak.

Chapter 12

Stirc trailed behind the other four. Pride, and face, hurting in equal measures. His mind turned over the events and how he would report them to the Registrars back at the capital. He would need some creative license, of course, some minor amendments to the details that would reflect more positively on him and his attempts to prevent the prisoner's death. He had already accepted that he would have to agree to Volchak's version of events. Four Breachmen, including their commander, made for compelling witnesses. And even if the Ropers had journeyed to talk to the farmer, he would confirm that his boy had indeed gone with them. The man would probably have heard there was a fight before the day was out, what with the mess that was left on the road. Maybe even hearing that a prisoner had died and his boy had lived. It was not like the Order would waste resources on all that, let alone making sure they got who was whom correct. Stirc's swollen face from the headbutt would likely be long gone by the time they reached the capital, and any evidence with it. It may be that the remnants of his soon to be black eyes would lend some colour to his story of valiant courage. Once he was being suitably ignored by the others, he had taken some of his white paste from inside his satchel under his robe and applied it to the bridge of his nose and a further dab where he was bleeding from. He was confident that, within an hour, the wound would be an unpleasant memory; he had quietly hoped no one else in their little troop would notice.

Stirc was still trying to fathom the logic of having the man brought to the capital at all. The Order lost its eyes on Smiele's army and there was nothing extraordinary about him. Stirc had rolled this over in his mind and decided that it was the horses they must have wanted. But would a foot-soldier, well, *horse*-soldier, know of their origin? The others appeared to have scattered after the battle, no leader was ever captured and the rebel army had escaped. *What then?* It was a mystery to Stirc. Maybe they'd have brought horses across the Ruby Sea into Yrfrite over the last few years from the lands to the far East or South? It would have taken a very long time to find so many. Any other way was impossible - across the mountain ranges to the West or from the freezing far North? The details of how they'd been kept secret so long was of interest to Stirc; they hadn't exactly appeared easy to hide. Any area of population would have erupted with rumours if twenty of the beasts had ridden into a town. So, he figured it was unlikely anyone had more stashed anywhere. Even if they did, how would this be of use to the Order? Maybe they wanted to understand the anatomy of how one rode them? Stirc knew the strict hierarchy of the Order well and was confident in his ability to navigate it in normal times. But this report would be one he'd have to be careful with, or he could end up posted on some long missionary posting, maybe even on an expedition to try and circle the Western mountains by sea, and no one ever returned from those.

They'd swept the bodies and found little of interest. Some silver that was pocketed by the girl and that sword that the prisoner Kaelith had taken. Stirc was pleased to see his small pack was undisturbed, the familiar clink of glass as he gingerly hooked the straps back over his shoulders. He'd kept his personal effects close to him under his cloak, of course, in his personal satchel. He wasn't about to surrender his valuables for the sake of these people.

The village of Brieth had been in view for some hours now. As they approached, he saw the mix of stone and wooden houses on the horizon steadily growing ever closer. The River Vioene had appeared to their left just after they had resumed their march. Stirc wondered if that would have not been a better place to take a stand, but hadn't asked. The fast-flowing waters were close to the road as it now ran alongside them directly towards the village. It was wide, fast flowing, but steady. Stirc had read many volumes on placing settlements along the banks, allowing trade goods to flow easily and simply towards the capital. Granted most of his study had focussed more on the effects the water would have on a corpse left to float down it to be retrieved by one of those settlements, but he was nothing if not thorough in his research. The Order had built a small temple at each of these major settlements to scoop up these finds and study them, although it was not a coveted position for a physician to take.

Up ahead, he could see how the river curved round to the right, with the village on the near shore. He knew the only bridge over it was a week's travel south. The docks would jut out into it and act as launches for crossings, but only the capital lay on the far shore down near where it began to estuary out into the Ruby Sea. On the outskirts of the village, before the buildings had changed to a more permanent construction of stone and masonry, was a large wooden stable for the cattle carts. These were slower than travelling by water but also far more common, now the trade from Yrfrite in the North had ceased. Stirc didn't know whether Volchak's plans included loading onto one of these, but he had mixed feelings. Whilst not marching would be a welcome change, cattle carts were not known for their comfort or ample personal space. They walked past the stables and Stirc closed the gap on his companions. They saw people working in the fields either side of the road and a couple on the road, but they did not appear too friendly. Mostly thickly accented country folks in simple brown clothes with simple wooden tools. As the group continued further into the village, there were ramshackle wooden houses, dozens lining the road, and none looking too permanent, as if they simply had sprung up in the last year from the ground itself. Several of the villagers that had been in the street quickly disappeared into buildings upon seeing the new arrivals. Stirc suspected they had been through a draft enough times to know to be wary of armed groups like this. Or maybe that group of Boatmen were well-known to the village.

'We don't draft in the villages.' Under his cloak Stirc all but jumped out of his skin. He hadn't noticed the girl drop back, and she had given him a fright.

'I beg your pardon?' he said.

'You were looking at them, wondering why they hide inside, weren't you? It is not because of us drafting them. You can't draft when there are so many people here, unless you have an army yourself. They could fight back and then where would you be?' She smiled at one of the passers-by who glanced up then hurried on, head down and eyes fixed on the road.

'Then why are they afraid?' Stirc was genuinely interested. This hadn't been in any of his books.

'It's you; they are afraid of the Order. Might come and take them away, cut them open.' Stirc raised a thin eyebrow at that, looking to make eye contact with a man leaning against an open door to his right. As he did, the man spat to his side, then walked back into his house. It was the first acknowledgement of their presence that Stirc had seen.

'But the Order keeps a temple here? Surely they see the physicians from there.'

'They ain't even there. We came through here several months ago and I saw it, boarded up and empty, might have even been burnt out.' Flea was looking him straight in the eye, as if worried it would upset him. Stirc had been with the same group, but had travelled by covered cart and had not sought to leave until they had arrived. The army hadn't stopped here long, and he had taken no interest in these common folk.

'What of the physicians who manned it?'

Flea shrugged, her face innocent but a slight twinge in her smile.

'Then I will report this back to the capital. They will have to send replacements. The people will need to understand the work the Order does and its importance to the kingdom.'

'Other than his army coming through and taking all their food, don't think they know much about the kingdom. I'd betcha that they wouldn't know a king if he kicked 'em in the shin!' She said with a chuckle, and skipped ahead to walk with Harkner and Kaelith.

Stirc contemplated that whilst they continued their walk towards the centre of town.

Chapter 13

Flea laughed as Harkner belched across the tavern, to the cheers of the small gathering that had sprung up around the group. Shortly after they arrived, Volchak had spoken to the innkeeper, parted with some of the silver they had taken from the men on the road and arranged lodgings and a desk in the side room. Volchak had put the word out that the Breachmen were recruiting and volunteers were welcome. They would give a volunteer a weapon and several years of training before they faced a charge. They'd be fed and housed, and given a chance to win glory for their families. A volunteer only had to serve eight years, like she would, but they would get paid at the end, like she wouldn't. Seeing the Commander, his scary bronze axe propped against the grimy table leg, and old weathered face smiling, gave many of them confidence that this was a professional and glorious lifestyle. But it was Harkner who had proved the real draw for the men of Brieth. He had paid handsomely for drinks across the tavern and had regaled them with tales, some quite tall, of the glorious battles in which he had fought. Flea was as captivated as the audience by her friend, who smiled and laughed with them as they drank. She hadn't really paid much mind to the silver coins he used. They had only got them the day before from a corpse; after all neither of them had ever actually received any pay, so a corpse was as good a source as any. But she supposed someone had given him that hammer that made the corpse, so that was something. He kept slapping it with an open palm as he reached the crescendo of one of his tales, using his hand in place of the man's head he was describing.

Kaelith too, had been merrymaking. But he was clearly content to be the side act to Harkner's show. He made no tell of horses, or mercenaries, or ambushes, but of the glorious charge he had witnessed the Breachmen fight in. Not mentioning he had actually been on the other side at the time and had all but wiped the 'glorious Breachmen' out. Volchak sat alone at the table at the side, and throughout the evening noted down three more names who had volunteered to join. Nearly doubling their force with the stroke of a quill. Arrangements were made and even some silver changed hands with the innkeeper towards the height of the evening.

But mostly, the evening was for being happy. Flea drank and laughed, although not half as much of either as Harkner. She tried to memorise each face of the men who had signed up. Most of them wouldn't live through their first charge. She had hoped to learn some of their stories before they went. Who they were, where'd they been and why they'd volunteered. People didn't usually volunteer without a story, usually they wanted to tell someone. Maybe they volunteered so they could tell someone? Or did the story come first...? She daydreamed as she watched the men merrymaking.

'Flea?' Volchak had the slightest hesitant slur in his voice - seemed even he had enjoyed some of the spoils of their recent fight, or maybe he was just drinking to the fact he was alive.

She sauntered over to him at the desk, alone to one side, with a smile on her face. She was warm, well-fed and well-liquored, and that was to be enjoyed.

'We've got all we can here. Retrieve Harkner and find Stirc, let him know we will be leaving in the morning. I've got us provisions from the innkeeper here and I want us to start marching just after dawn. We can make the prison in a week and then the capital in two, might give us a chance to train some of these men before the next fight.' His tone was business, but his eyes were soft and he had a relieved smile at the thought of ending this journey. He knocked his axe with his leg as he stood, it made a loud clang on the wooden floor before he picked it up and walked back towards the bar. A gap appeared from nowhere as people stood aside.

More walking. She frowned at the thought of their next destination. She'd been there before.

Flea returned to the main group and tugged at Harkner's arm – mid-story about the twelve men he'd killed on the road just to get to Brieth. Flea had only counted seven but then Harkner had drunk so much he probably was seeing double. She was sure he'd told this story earlier and it was nine then.

'Come on!' She tugged hard at his arm again, not moving it an inch, as he smiled at her and looked with bleary eyes.

'Little sister! Listen… sister…' He seemed slightly confused then shook the fog from his head. 'Little sister, don't interrupt a man whilst he tells of battles won!' The group around him cheered again and clinked flagons. She wouldn't have called it a battle. More of a scrap.

'We need to find Stirc!'

Kaelith interrupted, 'Stirc… There's a fine fellow. Bit up tight and his nose hurts my head…' He was lolling in his chair, threatening to pitch backwards from it.

'Yes, but he wears red you see… you see… red… makes it can't see it when his blood, his bleeds… when his nose…' Harkner giggled and made a motion as if his nose was pouring towards Kaelith and thumped his shoulder, throwing his head back laughing as if his own comedic genius needed no explaining.

'Urgh!'

They exasperated Flea, the two drunken fools. Although that maybe wasn't what she meant, she thought, but it sounded right. *Exasperated.* She looked back for Volchak at the bar. Maybe he could thump some sense into them, but he wasn't there. Must have gone to rest.

'Fine! Hope you both bloody drown!' Flea stropped and stood and walked back towards the bar, Harkner guffawing behind her and then turning back, laughing at his adoring fans as he told his story again, this time there were fourteen assailants on the road.

She didn't go to the bar, but moved past it and out the side door into the alley beyond. Flea looked up and down it before turning right to the main street. A couple at the far end were midst way through a tryst, holding each other's arms, about to embrace. She frowned and wrapped her arms around herself and walked off.

As she made her way down the street through the darkness, it was quiet. The occasional passer-by hurrying to get home, a bark of a dog somewhere in the distance. Her footsteps were light on the stone as she crossed the square in front of the village's main hall. She wasn't trying to be but she always stepped lightly. Habit. Lights shone in most windows and a few people milled around, returning from workplaces or running last errands before retiring for the night. As she reached the far side of the square, a small stone building with two columns out front stood from the street behind a wooden fence. She snuck through the open gate and towards the door, which had apparently been pried open. When she had been in the village last time, it had been empty and the windows were boarded up. Now, it seemed someone was inside. A single light. Stirc.

Flea had never been inside an Order temple, but it was blander than she expected. As she tip-toed down the hall in the low light, there were paintings on the walls of serious looking folk in white robes but no displays of half splayed corpses or organs in jars. She'd half expected bits of bodies attached to strange contraptions and little flasks bubbling away. But maybe that's just because the village folk had long since run the physicians out of town and Stirc hadn't had time to set it all up again.

She peered in the murk at the plaques and read each of them in her head

Bone, re-assembled.

Bedlam, a mind found.

Body, power beneath.

Brain, the source.

She looked at each of the figures. They all seemed somehow to resemble their titles. Bone looked, well, bony. Skin stretched too thin over her angular frame. Bedlam smiled, eyes empty as maybe a mad man's would be. Body was an enormous man; the painting actually looked like it hadn't been framed correctly. The top of his head seemed to touch the top of the frame. He would be taller than Harkner, and Flea hadn't thought that possible. Brain seemed... ordinary. Maybe a bit miserable? His face showed no emotion. Just stared out of the canvas. Flea shivered, and continued down the hall.

What struck her, was what else was missing. There were four paintings, two on each wall, but clearly space for more. She could see how the dust and grime on the walls wasn't as thick in patches where other paintings had once had hung.

There were raised voices down the hall - men. Angry voices. Flea's hairs on her neck stood up slightly, and she thought of running. Suddenly, the bland hall seemed a little more intimidating. But she had her antler blades, one slightly snapped but still sharp, and the villagers knew they were Breachmen. She wasn't afraid. Volchak had told her to go get Stirc. Volchak wouldn't have been afraid... Would just go get it done. The men would know Volchak was in the village, and that he was on her side.

She trod on the thin carpet, not making a sound in her soft leather boots, as she peered around the door. There were three of them, and they seemed to be angrily arguing with a wardrobe. Flea tilted her head and listened, hoping to find out what the wardrobe had done.

'Get yerrself out of there Orderman!' They had thick local accents, angry. Flea was sure one of them had been at the inn earlier, and had signed up - she remembered his face. They were simply dressed, plain leather and cotton. Two of them carried heavy wooden clubs, one appeared to have the haft of a wooden spear that was split, leaving just the jagged splintered edges about half his height.

'We kicked yur kind out before! Yur not welcome!' One of the men struck the wardrobe with the club, causing it to rock and strain against its frame.

'You took my boy!' Shouted the man with the broken spear. It was the farmer. Maybe he had arrived whilst they had been drinking in the tavern. The spear he held was probably the one that Harkner broke when he crushed the Boatman on the road.

'Aye! What of Crow's son, ya dog?!' The man struck the wardrobe again, then wrenched the door, which actually opened a fraction before being slammed from within. A final blow caved the door inwards and Stirc fell out, flat onto his face on the ground in front of them.

'Y-your son... I tried to help him... he... we buried him,' Stirc stuttered. His bald head had a nasty-looking cut on it and his robe was torn at the shoulder. Flea saw he had tried to lock himself away as a last attempt to save his own life.

The man with the spear howled, collapsing backwards as if struck by one of the other men's heavy clubs. Stirc's words had hit him hard. The other two seized Stirc by his cloak and dragged him out of the wardrobe completely. They held him firmly to the ground, one on each arm, as each of them looked to the farmer Crow.

'Skewer this pig Crow. Fer yer boy.' There was nothing but hatred in the voice. Crow had tears streaming down his face as he knelt back on the ground, lost in his own personal horror.

'Leave him alone!' Flea had meant to sound dark, violent, the way Volchak would when someone threatened him. Instead, her high-pitched, soft voice sounded tiny in the room as she stepped into it.

The two men turned, surprised, and eyed her up and down. Crow didn't move.

'Get gone, girl. The Order will pay for what their kind do.' They pressed down on Stirc's arms, although he had lost the will to struggle.

'Leave him alone, or I'll kill you.' This time she managed dark a little better. She held each of her antler blades firmly against her wrists as she took another step forward, creating space on either side of her.

'What do you care?' The other man slapped Stirc's raised head back to the ground, cutting his cheek, and looked back at her, full of challenge.

'He is with me.' *No wait,* she thought, 'With us.'

'Ain't no us, I see. Hold him.' The man stood as the other seized Stirc's shoulders and kept him pinned on the floor. The nearest man took several menacing steps towards Flea, stepping round Crow, who sat on his knees in a daze.

'If he's with you, then you'll join him.' The man pounced forward to seize her with his empty hand. She darted, jumped, danced, pushed aside his outstretched arm with one of hers and driving the antler blade up under it into his armpit. He squawked as he fell back with it buried up to the hilt. He crashed into the broken wardrobe, head disappearing into the dark clump of red robes.

'You scum!' The second man stood, releasing Stirc – who didn't move, and swung his club as he ran towards her, snarling. This time she sprang backwards and it connected with empty air where she had just stood. Suddenly, Flea was struck hard on her shoulder, batting her aside into the wall. There was a bronze flash as an axe head emerged from the darkness behind her and split the man's skull down to his chin. He collapsed into a crumpled pile of blood and bone.

Volchak reached out and pulled her to her feet. Her two attackers were dead. Stirc still lay splayed out on the floor beneath the legs of the skewered man who had fallen into the wardrobe.

'Are you hurt?' Volchak's voice was grim, but concerned.

'I'm fine they jus...' Her face suddenly, involuntarily, widened with a terrified silent scream. She looked down to see the jagged end of a spear jutting from her stomach. There was no pain yet, as her eyes met Volchak's, screaming at him for help. But no sound came from her. He stood as still as a statue, face sprayed with her blood, plastered across his chest, as he held her shoulders in his firm grip. The colour drained from his cheeks.

From behind him Kaelith moved like an arrow, straight into the farmer Crow, skewering him with the rusty sword. He caused the farmer to release the other end of the spear he had stuck through Flea's back. No one moved or made a sound for two breaths.

Then Harkner screamed.

Chapter 14

Volchak and Kaelith were barrelled over by the big man as he seized Flea from Volchak's limp grip.

She started choking sobs to him,

'Harkn...er.' Her face was turning deathly pale as her blood dripped down from both ends of the spear that protruded from her, having pierced both leather armour and flesh.

'No no no... shh shhh... Everything's okay...' Terrified and sobbing, he tried to comfort the girl with his arms, his eyes, his smile. No traces of the revelry from just a few minutes ago remained. Each of them was now sober with the sight before them.

How had he not seen it? Into the room, axe through the face, one dead; second, body in the wardrobe; third the man on his knee's - wasn't moving, no weapon. He'd slain the man who was attacking her with his axe, and she had seemed safe for a moment. Stirc was lying on the ground on his back several steps away, shuddering.

Stirc.

Volchak scrambled to his feet and rushed over to the physician, seizing his shoulders and rocking him violently.

'What happened? Are you hurt?'

Stirc looked at him, still in shock. Volchak shook him again.

'No… No… Thank you. She... saved me. They were going…'

'Save her.' Volchak cut him off. He was staring at the bald man on the floor, slick red hands gripping the thick red robe, as if the intensity of his look would snap the man to his senses.

Volchak shook the physician's shoulders again and threw the man up to his feet, facing where Harkner was cradling her little body.

'Save her.' Volchak repeated. It was all he said, but in his mind, he had already decided. He had already added the 'or else'. He bound this man's fate to hers now. Order, Army, Smiele, the King… all of them be damned.

He saw the moment Stirc's daze broke. The man shuddered, as if a wave had overcome him and he had lived through it. His brow dropped and his mouth closed.

Volchak saw the purpose return to his eyes.

'Bring her. Now.'

Harkner scooped up Flea, who moaned in her semi-conscious state, leaving a trail of blood behind as he ran across the hall to the other side. Stirc opened the door ahead of them and swept out the room as Harkner crashed through Volchak behind. Kaelith had stayed in the other room.

'On the block.'

In the centre of the room was the large wooden block, about table-sized but solid, protruding from the floor. All around the floor tapered slightly towards it, Volchak could see drains where Flea's blood had already started seeping.

There were ragged ropes on the floor that led back into holes cut in the side of the block.

Stirc moved with impressive speed, his deft hands drawing out a small satchel from under his stained travel cloak and whipping out several small vials - and a larger flask filled with a thick white fluid.

Harkner was still cradling her, even after having laid her down on the block. The spear skewering her causing her body to be propped up on her side.

'Hold her.'

Volchak moved to grab her legs, Harkner was still cradling her head. Volchak kicked him in the side of his leg hard and his head snapped to him, eyes bloodshot and full of tears.

'Hold her, Harkner. This is how she lives.' Volchak's stern order snapped the giant man back to himself.

They held her body still as the physician unravelled a small leather roll full of shining metal. Volchak had not known he carried such wealth, or he might have handled that business on the road a lot differently.

'Puncture wound, to the left lower quadrant. Object blocking wound. Blood loss currently minimal. Likely secondary infection from splintering. Exit wound on front smaller. Unlikely to survive extraction without suitable clotting application.' Stirc was chattering to himself in an almost excitable fashion. Volchak stared at him as his head bobbed like a curious bird at, and around, the two wounds. He said nothing.

Kaelith emerged in the doorway.

'Kaelith, take over from the Commander.' The quickest of glances around and the man needed no more encouragement. He had tied back the ripped arms of his shirt some time ago, and his bare arms strained to hold Flea's legs still as she seized and kicked. Bloody spittle began to drain from her mouth.

'Commander, upon my signal you take the spear and you pull. Hard and fast and then step out of the way. You two hold her completely still. We haven't time for the ropes.'

'You'll kill her!' Harkner spat at Stirc.

'Shut up, Harkner! Do it or she's dead.' Volchak spat back at him, his voice raised in directionless anger.

He stepped around the block and placed his hand above the haft of the spear and looked at Stirc. The physician had removed the stopper from the white-fluid flask and dipped the metal probe it in with one hand. In his other hand, he held what seemed to be a small metal pair of shears but with two flat ends.

'She lives, Stirc.' Volchak looked at him, without malice or threat. As if stating an indisputable fact.

The gaunt face peered back at him, the cut over one eye reddening but having stopped bleeding and the one on his cheek dripping slowly. The bruised eyes from the day before were still slightly swollen as he nodded, almost imperceptibly.

'Now.'

Faster than he had ever moved during the most vicious of fights, Volchak's hand gripped the jagged end of the spear, cracked it slightly in his vice-like hold, and pulled with all his might. Harkner held her body almost completely still, arms bulging. Kaelith had laid his weight across her legs, in doing so gave purchase enough for the spear to pull free.

The amount of blood that poured was immense, and instantaneous. It had clearly been pooling behind the spear haft and seemed to dump all at once in a rushing torrent.

But as Volchak watched, Stirc was a blur.

One hand shot metal shears straight into the wound, snipped, twisted, securing in place then releasing them. They held in place somehow with the twist. Stirc's left hand darted in with the white fluid - coating and moving, coating and moving. Without looking, the physician's right hand sought another probe, adding further fluid and then repeated from the other side, both hands mirroring each other. The man's bald head remained almost still as the hands worked in unison, operating as if from memory. Back and forward applying and retracting, twisting clamps then removing and spinning. Within moments, he had released both probes down onto the block and taken up the shears again, twisting them with his wrist as he took up some clean white linen and packed over the top of the wounds. The blood flow had stemmed. He took what appeared to be a metal fish hook with line still attached and sewed, as if stitching thin leather. In a constant and precise movement, he had pulled the circular wound into a tight spiral of metal thread on the front whilst the shears held tight the wound on her back. As he pulled tight, he bit through the metal cord. Volchak was surprised how thin it was. Stirc repeated this movement in reverse for the wound on her back, releasing the metal shears at the same time. As he stitched her, his other hand held a pair of fine tweezers which pulled out splinters as they presented themselves, and dropped them on the floor. They floated in the stream of blood that washed them into the drain below.

The whole thing had taken less than a minute, less time than Flea had fought in the breach her first time.

When he dropped his tools, Stirc seized up a vial from his satchel behind him and poured a sweet-smelling liquid over both wounds. It stained a dark brown against her skin.

'She… lives.' Stirc breathed, his eyes meeting Volchak's. He held that stare.

For a moment, nothing moved but the steady stream of blood running down the block into the drains below. Crimson swirls mixing with the thick layer of dust on the ground as they trickled away.

Chapter 15

Kaelith had a talent for knowing when a fight was about to start. It was one of his many talents. One that he had called on more and more in recent years. As he released the girl's legs, still in some awe over the bloody spectacle he had just witnessed, he turned to Volchak.

'The braggart who did…. This,' he waved over the girl's motionless body. 'Well, I skewered the dog, of course, but seems not materially fatal. That is to say… he's rather on this side of dead.'

Their eyes met for a moment. Kaelith stared at the two grey circles as the rest of the face seemed to age in front of him. Both their bodies were tense, coiled, poised for a sudden move. Volchak's grim face frozen. He knew what was about to happen. The Commander's eye twitched slightly. An itch started to emerge at the back of Kaelith's throat, he strained against it, eyes bulging.

He coughed.

Harkner shot out of the room, knocking Kaelith back against the block and causing Stirc to snarl a warning to be careful of his vials. Volchak scrambled after him, trying to grab the man's shoulder as he disappeared out the door.

'Ah,' was all Kaelith could manage, before slipping on the slick floor and colliding with the doorframe as he followed them.

Upon arriving in the first room, he saw the legs poking from the wardrobe, right where'd left them. But the farmer from a few days ago had dragged himself to lean against it, the rusted iron sword still poking out from his shoulder. Kaelith couldn't see the man's face, although he imagined it reddening with bulging eyes and open mouth. Harkner's colossal form blocked the view. As Volchak moved round one side so Kaelith did the other, tentatively, as the Commander spoke.

'Let the man go....' Volchak feigned calmness in his voice, talking down the bull. 'She's alive Harkner, the man didn't kill her.' He edged closer. Harkner's head shot round.

'Tried to. Would have.' Harkner said.

Kaelith could see the tears still rolling down his face, tried to place them. Anger, certainly. Beer, probably. Guilt?

'Easy, my oversized friend,' Kaelith said in his best charming voice. 'Our resident saw-bones has her nicely tucked up. No harm done.' His foot knocked the overturned table in the centre of the room and caused a loud bang that made them all jump.

'This village'll blow up when they find out we killed three of theirs.'

Harkner had both hands on the man's neck, cutting off the air, the man's eyes bulging. Kaelith didn't really know what his own plan was, stepping gently round the table this time to within a few strides of the man.

'We keep him alive. He can tell the others, saved him here we did. Flea most of all. A hero. Probably a grand parade in the square,' Kaelith continued. Harkner's grip slackened ever so slightly. He was no fool.

'Isn't that right, my fine fellow...?' To the farmer now, seemed the man could just about suck in enough air to keep himself alive, 'a hero. You'll want to let the others know, of course. After we've patched up that minor mishap there. Just in time she was, lucky thing. All friends here. One happy family…'

The farmer's eyes shot to Kaelith. Anger. Kaelith slammed his mouth shut.

'You… He… killed… my son,' the wounded man coughed out.

Harkner snapped the man's neck clean, twisting his head almost completely around with his huge, powerful hands. A sickening crack and he slumped down onto his side next to the wardrobe, back of his head staring at Kaelith. Volchak grabbed the big man's shoulder a fraction too late.

Volchak thrust Harkner backwards, pitching him over the body of the third man as he lost his footing and landing on top of him.

'You didn't have to kill him!' Volchak shouted into his face. A rage Kaelith had only seen when he was thumb-deep in that man's skull on the road, before he had decapitated the other whilst still on his knees.

'He hurt Flea!' Harkner roared back in his face, spittle and sweat splashing onto the man's weathered face.

'He wasn't a threat!'

'Like that's ever stopped you!' Harkner flung the smaller man off him. Volchak stumbled backwards but strangely didn't fall. Landing upright and recovering after a step. *Nimbler than he looks that one*, Kaelith thought.

'I've seen you carve a man's skull after he surrendered. Throw that blade of yours into a man's back as he ran. You killed the boy on the road, Volchak! Maybe didn't swing the axe, but he's dead by you. Could have left that house alone. Got them that chose the breach here, or at the prison!' Harkner stood as he spoke, vicious and loud.

Volchak broke, sighing as his shoulders dropped.

'Aye. I know.' The heat from the room disappeared in an instant. Kaelith saw the spring in Volchak's step leave it, flat footed on the bare stone. His was head down, voice soft.

'She lived though, Harkner.' It wasn't much of a defence.

'Yeah. This time.' Harkner barged past the Commander, who offered little resistance.

Kaelith smiled at him.

'Not sure about this little outfit I've joined. Seems all a tad dramatic for me.'

'Kaelith?' Volchak looked like he was about to turn his rage to him, then sighed and chuckled to himself, rubbing his eyes.

'Get us a place on a cattle cart. It needs to leave tonight. Pay them well.' He tossed a small leather bag that Kaelith caught. 'Get to the inn and pick up the provisions. Don't tell them we are here or that we are leaving.'

'Your wish is my command' Kaelith said, with a flourish he bowed - his face nearly touching the legs of the corpse in the wardrobe.

'Quietly Kaelith…' A question? Order? Command? No one could be certain.

***

The cart man had been far too eager to deal, and Kaelith walked confidently back towards the inn with a heavier purse than he had expected. They'd leave in a couple of hours and the man would collect their bags from the inn. This was enough time for maybe a quick bottle before he let the others know. He certainly would not spend it back at the abandoned Order temple. He wouldn't be going there sober anytime this evening.

The evening was very late now, and the tavern had largely spilled out into the street. There was bitter arguing, men jostling and drunkenly singing. One had slouched down across the mouth of the alley to the side where he had seen Flea disappear off to from the tavern, shortly before Volchak had retrieved him and Harkner. These villagers seemed to have gathered some weapons too. Clubs hung at sides, propped up against walls and a spear had fallen over into the street. Kaelith always knew when a fight was brewing, had a knack for it, and this whole place had the feel of boiling up, about to bubble over. Maybe they had stirred a little too much fervour with their talk of battles and glorious victory, or maybe it was something else. Kaelith couldn't shake the feeling the whole place seemed awfully riled up this evening. Now he'd seen the abandoned Order temple, he wasn't completely sure which direction that fervour was likely to be pointed, but he didn't doubt three of their own dead would make all those involved a fine target.

He entered the now nearly empty tavern, the only other patron evidently also having secured rooms and therefore allowed through by the bulky barmaid and her two solid looking staff. As Kaelith walked towards the bar, around half way across the room, he stopped his foot mid step. Hovering it in the air, he spun on his other one towards the right side where that patron stood.

She was wearing a cloak. A black one.

He slid into the chair opposite where she stood. Despite his wounding less than a week ago with Flea's spear, the pang of pain he expected did not jump up and bite him, just a dull ache from his side.

'There are soldiers about, my dear. Breachmen. Loathsome looking bunch too, a couple dozen of them if my exceptional mathematical ability doesn't fail me. Might not be best place for such a… connected… fine lady such as yourself.'

'I'm not worried. There'll be soldiers a plenty in these parts within a few days, I'll warrant. Besides, I only counted three.'

Her voice was still disarming, soft and refreshing against the backdrop of the grubby tavern walls.

'Then, maybe it is I who should find myself a better place to rest my incredibly handsome head.' He flicked his golden pony tail to his back, the layer of caked sweat and grease giving it a satisfying amount of weight as it thudded against him.

'My brother's not thrilled with you. You went too early; you dealt with that troublemaker and his merry band of delinquents, but you missed the major prize.' She said.

'We had complications, unfortunate and unintentional. Did I not, though, cut the head off the snake? Or maybe just poke it in the eye a bit? Gave your Duke a chance to skedaddle with his army before getting squashed under the boot of the Royal Guard?' Kaelith maintained his jovial tone. Yet he spoke quietly and kept half an eye on the staff, now upending chairs onto the empty tables.

'From what I've seen, the head is very much alive and recruiting.' She nodded over towards the table at the far end where Volchak had been sat earlier.

Kaelith said nothing. Which said a lot.

'We want to meet him.'

'He's not much to talk to - or look at, for that matter.'

'You will be heading to the prison and then over the bridge?'

'That we are.' No point denying it; the cattle carts only went that way from here and they certainly would not be walking north.

'Once over the bridge, head to the coast. When the capital is visible on your horizon and the cliffs give way to the sandy shore, bring him to the beach and we will talk.'

'Will he survive?' Kaelith asked, feigning to care. He suspected she saw through him. Man had saved his life after all, twice now.

'Perhaps. But for you there will be a chance at life again.'

One of his eyebrows peaked.

'Plainly?'

'We will deliver one of your horses to you. You can take it where you will from there. Back out to the West, I would expect?' She smiled a knowing smile towards him. That was unnerving.

'Just after the bridge. A beach. Got it. What of the others?'

'Bring them, we have something to offer them as well.'

That surprised Kaelith. He had already concocted his reason for dragging Volchak away... Or, more specifically, he expected with enough wine he could deal with Harkner.

Flea couldn't exactly walk and Stirc probably didn't care. Bringing them would be more of a hassle.

He stood.

'A pleasure as always,' he said bowing low, nearly hitting his head on the table.

'Indeed.' She didn't move.

As he stood, Kaelith caught the slightest glimpse of her releasing her left hand from where she had been hiding it. Just like last time, she wasn't exactly holding a rock.

Chapter 16

Cramped, uncomfortable and hot - Stirc had not enjoyed the past few days bouncing in the back of the second wagon. He had insisted he travel in the second of the two with the patient, despite having to share the canvas-covered cart with the larger of the buffoons. But logically, he supposed, it made little difference which one he was in. The journey would be cramped, uncomfortable, and hot regardless. He did not want this one to die. She had done the same for him, in a fashion, so he would ensure she lived.

Despite his many protestations, the carts wouldn't stop, day or night, to allow him to comfortably examine the wound. Progress had appeared to have been slower than he had hoped. Possibly a miscalculation with the mixture, possibly because of the severity of the wound. His compound had worked wonders on stemming blood flow and regrowing skin over in his experiments, but it appeared internally repairing damage and countering the effects of blood loss were beyond his current understanding. He had taken copious notes and, despite his surroundings, had quietly enjoyed the trip for the first few days. The larger man barely spoke to him, other than to ask about the girl's progress, and she had been fading in and out of consciousness for the past three days now.

Several times a day, the Commander, or his new Breachman, the 'farm boy' as Stirc had to keep reminding himself, had left their wagon and walked alongside his to converse with the big man. Or with Stirc himself. The carts were slow and a break would be as easy as hopping out, stretching your legs or doing what business needed doing, and then jogging to catch up. The carts were slow, but they were constant as they rolled on south, day and night. At this rate, the prison would be within sight in a day or two.

They had passed out of the flatlands shortly after leaving the village and the air outside had grown fresher now they were nearer the coast. It was still warm, summer was quickly coming on, but there was a pleasant breeze each time he strolled outside of the cart. Despite this, it was clear that beneath the canvas a steady uncomfortable heat of three bodies stuck in a small space would be the standard. Stirc had theorised that if they opened the front of the wagon alongside the open back, it would actually have made a dramatic improvement, but he had no one to share his thoughts with.

The girl may have been interested if she was awake - she had been inquisitive after all. Of the group of them, she had seemed to harness a sharper mind than the larger man or even than the Commander. Stirc had found her somewhat irksome with her questioning on their march, but upon making some particularly interesting observations about her healing progress, he caught himself wishing she had been alert enough to share in some of them. He had even attempted, on the third day, to share one of his simpler notes with the man Harkner. Stirc had presented how the discolouration around the wound was potential sign of infection. Yet that it too early to determine whether it would take root. The reply he had received, regarding his own mortality should she succumb to it, had not been welcome.

'Commander.' Stirc had taken a rare break and jogged forwards to speak to Volchak.

Kaelith poked his head round the corner, blonde ponytail bouncing and dancing as the cart trundled on. The mercenary's eyes looked Stirc up and down, so he put on his best glare until the man got the message.

'Think I'll have a word with the cart man…' Kaelith hopped out, a little too close to Stirc for his liking, and trotted up towards the head of the carriage.

A rough hand extended from the back of the cart and Stirc took it, using it to steady himself as he navigated the thin steps and sat in the back. Much more room with just the two of them, cooler too.

'How is she?' Volchak clearly expected this to be an update.

'Improving.'

Truth was, Stirc couldn't be sure. She wasn't feverish. But she wasn't awake either. Her wounds had all but closed, but he wondered whether something had gone awry. Stirc's same compound had healed the mercenary far more quickly and he hardly seemed the healthiest of men to begin with.

The two men sat for a moment. Stirc regarded the Commander, whilst he seemed lost in the horizon. Up close like this, he didn't seem that imposing, certainly not a man who gave off an air to be feared. He wasn't a big man. Stirc had spent five days now in the equivalent space with a big man. Volchak wasn't old, wasn't young. He seemed to Stirc to exude melancholy… *Cheerlessness*. Probably what one of the old cattle would look like after too many of these trips. Stirc had seen the way he had split the man's skulls though at the Order temple, had seen his blood-soaked hands when he returned to him from the road. He hadn't seemed cheerless then, more accomplished.

Time for business.

'Commander, when we reach the prison, I assume we will all be leaving the cart and you will undertake your draft?'

'Aye.'

'I notice we were without new recruits from Brieth?'

'Felt it was better to move on after our… evening. Those that had signed weren't likely to be willing when they found out what happened.'

'But they attacked us?'

'Don't think they'd care. Lot of anger in that village. We'd taken that farmer's son; we'd been there in the name of the King and killed those two men and him. When those people found out…'

'Hmm,' Stirc said.

'Did you wonder why the Order Temple was empty?'

Stirc had wondered. Not only why the physicians had left but why they had sent no new ones to replace them, when they returned to the capital.

'There were four graves within the grounds. Kaelith found them. We reckoned the village took them and killed them.' Volchak was grim, as usual.

'But that would be treason! They'd have been burnt as secessionists!'

'Aye. Maybe. But no one seemed to know. Seems news wasn't flowing to the capital much from Brieth, from what I could tell.'

'They had joined the Duke?' Stirc had not considered this before. In the temple he had just thought these were thugs out to rob and kill him.

'I don't know. And I don't know what would have caused them to if they had. Lot of angry people out there, it seems. When we get to the prison, it'll be different. Some of those men will choose to join me. It'll save them, for now. Just need to deal with the jailor.'

'Your ranks will swell with criminals and murderers?'

'Aye. Most Breachmen come that way.'

'What is to prevent them from fleeing? Or turning on you?'

Stirc watched the man. Instead of replying, his eyes glanced down to his feet, where his axe lay wrapped in an oil cloth.

'Some will.'

Stirc felt now was the time to raise what he had come here to say.

'Then I shall take my leave of you before then. I will continue by cattle cart to the capital.'

Volchak shrugged, nodding slightly.

'And I'll take the girl with me.'

The air was still.

'Why?'

That was less confrontational than Stirc had expected.

'Her prognosis is far from certain; I need help from several members of my Order to understand her ailment and seek an effective treatment.'

'Your patients rarely come back.'

That was fair. The Order were firstly an educational organisation, undertaking experimentation and analysis on the human body but caring not for whether their subjects survived. It usually wasn't relevant. *A physician's purpose was not to heal the sick.*

'I recognise this. But our understanding of anatomy can save lives, Commander. From what I see you've been under our knife before yourself.' Stirc nodded to the man's face. He saw the subtle shift as Volchak ran his hand across his scarred cheek.

'The girl saved my life...' Stirc quickly shut his mouth, having surprised himself, but he'd started so he'd finish. 'No thought to her own safety and no way of being found out had she chosen to let me die. That is commendable, and she should be made healthy again. The facilities at the capital will serve this purpose.'

'What of your Order superiors, if they decide she would be a better subject than Breachman?'

'I will give you a signed document that she will be returned to active duty to you. That should suffice.' Stirc felt not entirely convinced this was true, but he would try. The registrars were hardly going to be concerned with a single subject of a physician.

'Will she live, if you don't?'

'Perhaps. But her chances increase dramatically with me.' That was certainly true.

Volchak sat a long while, his grey eyes not leaving Stirc. The melancholy was still there in his face, but Stirc sensed something else as well. Was it menace? Or determination? The air around the Commander seemed a little darker.

'I will take your signed order. But I will have your word as well.' Volchak hadn't perceptibly moved, but the space seemed smaller in the cart now.

Stirc looked at the man and frowned.

'I'll return her to you, Volchak. Alive.'

More moments passed.

'She lives, Stirc. That was the arrangement. That is still the arrangement. She can go with you.'

Volchak leaned back. The air was lighter, and the space returned to the carriage.

Stirc nodded and stood up, holding the bouncing side of the cart as he climbed down the first two steps.

'Stirc?'

The physician paused, listening but not looking back.

'You're taking Harkner with you too.'

Chapter 17

The prison came into view long before the road reached it. Volchak was sore from the bouncing and scraping, and from hitting his knee on the cart as he climbed back in every time. The cut on his leg burned, but he would not trouble Stirc with it; he was still not sure about the man's motives. Volchak had taken to walking alongside the cart in the evening to try to stretch it out, or because he couldn't bear any more time listening to Kaelith's tales of adventures across the world. It was peaceful - walking in the long grass, looking over the brush and rocks to the cliff edge that hid the River Vioene below to his left. He had walked up to the edge several times, although never too close. He'd probably slip, fall in and either smash himself on the rocks, or the fast-flowing water below would sweep him away. He knew this portion of the river had always been the most treacherous; solid rock walls, twice the height of a man made for not a lot to hold on to… but a lot for a barge to crash into if the water was feeling mischievous. Volchak knew very little about boats. He had travelled once down from Yrfrite on a copper barge, but he'd been unconscious or feverish for most of it from the wounds he'd sustained at the battle the week before. He had seen them in the harbour at the capital. Under large cotton sails they had still seemed small and fragile against the raging waves on the beach. Maybe that's why they used the river, he supposed. Long as you didn't crash into the walls, at least you didn't have to worry much about being tossed overboard on a raging whitecap.

The burnt-orange sun dipped into the sea on the horizon as he walked. Looking to the horizon, he saw the fortress perched on the edge up ahead of him. The stone circular towers were resolute against the evening sky. He figured that within a day's cart-ride they would reach it, and he would hand Flea over to Stirc and his Order. Volchak wouldn't trust the physician to look after his own leg but would hand off one of the few people he actually knew who was also still alive. He guessed that it said a lot about him, not much of it good.

The next morning came and he awoke sore from another uncomfortable night's sleep rattling around in the small carriage with a thin oilskin for a mattress. His head ached from only Kaelith and the incessant snoring for company. Volchak paid the cart man for two large supply rolls, and then a further silver for the companions still riding in the second cart. With Harkner with them, it was very unlikely any harm would come... well at least to Flea. But it never hurt to have a little extra assurance. As the road curved away from the cliff edge to the right, Kaelith and Volchak bid the others farewell.

'Keep them safe, Harkner,' Volchak's repeated. He'd already been into this with the man several times. Whilst he was even more reticent than Volchak to entrust Flea to the Order. Harkner had seen first-hand how she hadn't yet come to wake and seemed to be getting desperate. Volchak remembered when Harkner first joined him. He'd marched right into the Breachmen tent as they camped outside the capital before the first march against Yrfrite and thumped his heavy stone hammer down. 'Where's the fight?' He had been all smiles and bravado then. Not a lot had changed in the last year. Not a lot until the last week on the road. He'd been worried, that was obvious, but argumentative, frustrated with the journey and verging on treasonous. He'd swear and shout about volunteering. This wasn't what they were here to do, no glory to be found in the King's army anymore. Volchak would argue back, pointing out that he had volunteered and what had he expected to be doing? Sipping tea with the King after a hearty dust-up? Volchak knew war was sitting around waiting for someone to tell you where to go and who to fight, fighting them, then sitting around waiting to find out where you were going next. All the while trying not to get killed. Harkner had got in his head that the entire war was a farce, as if they meant it to irritate him. Last night had been the worst. He'd shouted at Volchak that the King and the Duke were as bad as each other, a couple of squabbling children. Luckily for him, Stirc hadn't heard and Kaelith didn't care enough either way.

Of course, a volunteer was not unheard of. After all, Volchak had left two more of them back in Brieth. But most volunteers only did it for lack of other choices - just like the prisoners would. Harkner had seemed even happier after they'd passed this way headed north the first time. Volchak had recruited the last of the prisoners, including Flea, and Harkner took an immediate liking to his 'little sister'. He had had made a firm claim of her. Strange though, not as lovers. Women made for fine warriors. But they could be trouble for the infighting they inadvertently caused. Seemed that when you recruited your division from the cut-throats and low-lives of the world and then throw in something to fight over, then a fight is what you get.

But that didn't happen with Flea. Harkner had a genuine will to protect her - a 'big brother' - and none of the others had argued with this bull of a man. Volchak was actually going to miss having him around.

***

The pair walked towards the entrance to the fortress, flanked by the two enormous towers on either side of it.

'No welcoming committee?' Kaelith said as Volchak hammered on the heavy red wooden door.

'They need little in the way of guards.'

A small bookish man's face appeared as he slid back a small section of the door, about wide enough for an arm.

'Papers?'

Volchak handed the leather-bound folder he had carried all the way here from the Commander's tent on the hill and the gap slammed shut after receiving it.

'Hospitable bunch; I will be sure to tell my friends.' Kaelith said.

An hour passed, as the two of them waited before the towering stone walls. They watched the cattle carts disappear down the road and head south. Kaelith seemed relieved to see the back of Stirc. Volchak suspected his newest recruit held on to some less than fond memories from first meeting the physician. Volchak scratched at the scar on his cheek.

The man's face re-emerged through the small opening in the door.

'You may enter. Touch nothing. You will leave your weapons at the gatehouse with the clerk.'

'My orders are that we will retrieve prisoners, and to keep our weapons whilst inside.'

The small man's face scrunched slightly, as if sniffing the air.

'Very well. Enter.'

Volchak knew better than to lose his axe in here. This was the Ropers' fortress. The hands of the Order weren't always that precise about who they deposited here. This wasn't a place he wanted to find himself without an axe to hand.

As they stepped through into the square courtyard, Volchak sighed, his neck throbbing slightly as he looked around. Little had changed from his last visit. Time had a different meaning here. The prisoners all had far too much of it, yet for the prison itself, it meant very little. They crossed the courtyard - seeing only three other figures, two large men and a woman, perched on what appeared to be wooden bleachers set up on one side. Their conversation dried up as the three passed them, staring intently with... craving? Yearning? Hunger? Volchak shuddered and fell in step behind their guide, gripping his axe in his right hand tightly. He had spotted the chain-mail tabards from across the square, and up close it was clear they heavily worn, rusted and torn in places, from what must have been years of hard use. He knew chain-mail wouldn't always stop a sword, of course, luckily for Kaelith. Certainly, it would not stop his axe. A metal axe would both crush bone with its weight and tear through the weaker chains. But against wooden spears, antler blades and clubs? The weapons of the desperate and downtrodden? Well, it'd put the wearer at a distinct advantage. Especially if they meant to take you alive. Volchak met their gaze but they didn't look away. *Ropers.*

The two of them entered a wooden structure built onto the interior wall, a dining hall of sorts, dimly lit and musty. Inside, more robed figures sat eating, or scribbling in manuscripts with their feather quills. An air of must and decay hung heavy in the air, yet the space was decidedly sparse with little furniture and no adornments upon the walls. Kaelith let out a small cough and addressed their guide,

'Forgive my ignorance, my fine fellow. But aren't you supposed to have prisoners in your prison?'

Volchak snorted, not derisively, but ironically. And followed the man through a large heavy door to the rear.

There, he saw them. A lump rose in his throat which Volchak swallowed down. *Just like last time - eyes forward.* He walked on.

Walking through the centre aisle, on each side of him were each of the rows of prisoners. Most of the robed men pacing back and forth between them, attending to the prisoners' basic needs, some carrying buckets of waste, others holding buckets of what might be food - it was hard to tell the difference. These men's robes were all dark grey, undyed fabric, and plain, other than a rope tied around each of their waists - vibrant red ropes.

Many of the blocks had a prisoner secured on them, tied down with thick braided ropes. The ropes wound out from the side of the blocks around each wrist, ankle, neck and leg. Pulling them taught and holding them in place so that the prisoner could not move under the tension. Volchak could see down the length of the long hall. Drains ran down the middle of the slightly angled floor. Two long rows, every few strides another block with another body tied to it. Except - many were empty, many more than when he had last stood here. The ropes were retracted into the holes on the side.

'I....'

With that, Kaelith closed his mouth. Volchak had found something to shut him up.

'Please.' Their guide bade them to follow him, down the centre aisle to the end and through an arch, that evidently opened into the tower which must be overlooking the cliff.

Several of the prisoners were held in a seated position; behind each stood a robed figure fussing over dials on each of the blocks. As they manipulated the dials, so did they manipulate the prisoners. Heads were turning, arms lifting and falling as taught ropes pulled them in various directions. Volchak saw Kaelith trip on the stonework as he walked under the arch, mesmerised by what appeared to be one of the robed men controlling a waving prisoner, dial moving left, then right, then left, then right.

As they climbed the stairs, and left the horror of the King's prisoners behind them, Kaelith whispered.

'You knew?'

'Aye. Been here before. Twice.'

'But how are these men alive?' Kaelith said. motioning back down the spiralling staircase behind him.

'Not just men. All manner of folk are in there. Even a few army officers, if they have stepped out of line. Maybe now you understand why some criminals choose to join the Breachmen?'

Volchak stopped and turned to him.

'You think what we have them do, charge the shield wall, is madness? Why would anyone choose that? Well...' Volchak nodded over Kaelith's shoulder.

'So... Miss Flea?'

'Aye. A month in there. She was lucky, after a fashion. I came through here with Smiele's army on the way to Yrfrite shortly after she arrived. Just long enough to make her choice, but not enough to ruin her. Most aren't so lucky.'

The guide had disappeared from view when Volchak turned and hopped up the stairs at double pace to catch up, chest rising heavily as his leg stung. *Bandage would probably need changing after this.*

Apparently, the man was quite put out when they arrived at the door.

'If you please...' he motioned, feigning politeness, into the opulent room.

The jailor stood at the window, looking out of the arched window above the cliffs to where the sea was visible, possibly in an attempt to appear brooding and thoughtful. Volchak got a flash in his mind of pushing the man out. It was a long way down. He shook it off as he stepped into the room.

'Commander Daveron. You are well?'

'Commander Volchak. You are still alive?' The man was abrupt, yet it was hard to ignore the excitement in his voice. Probably not at Volchak being alive, but at knowing he was not forgotten by the outside world. That he still had a role to play.

Daveron swept a look across them and then sauntered to his chair. He flung back his red cape, attached at the nape of his neck, back as he sat at the heavy oak desk and motioned for the pair. The bookish man handed him the leather-bound folder.

'Thank you, Irvyn.' The man who had been guiding them bowed and scuttled from the room, one last look of disdain at the visitors.

'So, Volchak. Come to avail yourself of some of my guests?' Daveron flipped lazily through the papers in the folder in front of him. 'Smiele needs more meat for his grinder?' The man chuckled. 'Hasn't taken over the entire world yet, still a little more for him.' He fingered the red braided cord that hung over his chain-mail tabard.

'Aye, that's about right.'

'Didn't think to take a few of them off the road? Hear you left quite the mess in Brieth.'

Volchak didn't move or speak. Seemed news moved faster than a cattle cart.

'Who's your man there? Not the famous Harkner – too small. He dead?'

Volchak raised an eyebrow at that. He couldn't place how Daveron would have known Harkner, other than from their last visit, he was hardly famous then. 'Harkner's alive. This is Kaelith, farmer we drafted outside of Brieth.'

'Looks a bit clean for a farmer.' Daveron was no fool, Volchak thought but kept silent. 'Just the two of you, then?'

'Rest gone on to the capital. Mustering there for the next campaign.' It was accurate enough.

'Good. Go after them. I've got very little for you.' Daveron sat back in his chair and tossed the paperwork down in front of him. He stared at Volchak and shrugged.

'Eh?' Kaelith played the part of the ignorant farm boy well, or maybe he wasn't quite sure what was happening.

Volchak sighed and rubbed his eyes.

'How much?'

'Won't cut it this time, I'm low in stock. The Order has been putting in requisitions almost daily and I'm not bringing them in half as fast as they are chopping them up.'

Volchak realised maybe Stirc could have come in useful here after all, but then, what would have happened to Flea? *Too late now anyway.*

'I've spread most of my Ropers across half the countryside. Word came that your battle didn't go very well and Fedal started losing men.' An excuse? Maybe, but more likely, it was true. 'The rest of them are chasing the damned horses. Apparently, several of them were seen headed west after the battle... Something you'd know nothing about, I'm sure?'

'Nothing,' Volchak's head hurt. 'I need men. The King's orders are right there.' He nodded at the desk.

'Then the King can come and look for himself. I've got very little for you and if I give it away, then I've got nothing to keep the men... entertained.' Volchak glared at the man, Kaelith shifted uncomfortably, but Daveron appeared to be sizing the Commander and the man up.

'Two.'

'Two?'

'Yes. You can have two. At a price.' A wicked smile appears across the jailors face.

'How much then, Daveron?' Volchak had danced this dance before.

'One hundred. Each.'

'No.' Volchak didn't have it, nor would he have paid if he had. Volchak paused and realised, he probably would have paid it - better than the alternative. Regardless, the man would either give him the men or he wouldn't now he had nothing to offer. This is the place Volchak didn't want to find himself.

Daveron tutted, looking over the folder in front of him once more, then closed it. He did not hand it back.

'It is not for a Breachman to determine the worth of prisoners of the King. I'll remind you I have complete authority over this facility, by the mandate of the High Registrar of the Hermetic Order. Treatment and disposal.'

'You mean capture and delivery. The Order answers to the King, and the King demands supply of soldiers for the Breachmen.' Volchak stood firm, his chin slightly raised, but palms were slick against his axe. The man clearly had delusions of grandeur, but who was going to disabuse? Certainly not Volchak; certainly not whilst stood in the man's own fortress. If Daveron ignored the orders, nothing would happen immediately, but eventually Smiele would return with the Guard and soon have this resolved. Well, maybe not soon. The army was overstretched, and under strength, at the moment. This could be a problem.

'The Order answers to the King...' Daveron pondered this a moment, '... for now. I'll give you two, then, on your way out.'

Volchak turned on the spot and marched for the door. The room had grown darker and the thick stone walls were clearly those of a prison now. Kaelith followed.

Chapter 18

This was why Kaelith hated the very idea of being in the prison.

Actually no, the idea of being strapped to a wooden block and forcibly fed, cleaned and kept alive but unable to move before being shipped off to be experimented on - that was why Kaelith hated being in the prison. But this meeting was certainly coming in a close runner-up.

As they took a door into the courtyard, the three ropers that had lazed in the afternoon sun on the bleachers were now nearer twenty. An ungainly mob, muscles, scars, black teeth and unpleasant manners. What's more, almost all of them wore a chain-mail tabard, some barely held together, some gleaming in the sunlight. Most had simple wooden weapons, some antler blades, a few spears. But all had thick woven rope wrapped around their bodies, in lassos at their sides or slung over their shoulders. These were certainly the Ropers; clue was in the name, after all. If their commander was being honest that most of them were out scouring the countryside, then he must have commanded quite the force indeed.

Volchak had been adamant they were in and out quickly. That, and keep hold of your weapons. Originally, it'd have been five of them, and one an Order physician. Also, they'd had their orders that Smiele had given Volchak in that folder. It had dawned on Kaelith those orders now sat back up the stairs under the hands of a man who had suggested he would fulfil them, all of two men, after being denied pay.

Seems that Volchak might have been on to something. This wasn't a very safe place to be them right now. The realisation had clearly hit him as well. As they stepped out into the square, the group formed an impenetrable wall around them, each keeping a good ten paces away but clearly giving no ground. Kaelith reached for his sword as he saw Volchak bring his axe to bear in both hands.

Daveron emerged from the door behind them, smiling, his red cloak whipping through the gap, arms outstretched.

'My loyal soldiers!' he addressed the gathered crowd.

'A special treat from his Majesty this fine afternoon. The famed Commander of the Breachmen has agreed to a friendly sparring match between Breachmen and Ropers!' The crowd cheered a muted, yet entirely aggressive cheer.

It was not lost on Kaelith. He had said Breach-*men*. Not Breach-*man*.

'A fair fight, of course. We will arm and offer two of our esteemed guests the choice!'

They brought two men out from the same door, where Kaelith and Volchak had entered before, ropes around their wrists and naked from the waist up. The Ropers handling them seemed quite relaxed. This was obviously not a random occurrence. They looked little like emaciated and tortured prisoners Kaelith had seen in the chambers through that door. Both were bulging with muscle, thick set necks attached to heavy browed bald heads. Clearly not twins, but there was certainly something… uniform… about them.

When Daveron spoke, both their heads dropped; Kaelith knew when a fight was imminent.

'Chiv, Nyten.' The prisoners' heads dropped further. 'Your three-year sentence is up for parole, and you are offered a choice. The Breach or the Rope?' Another cheer from the small crowd, although Kaelith suspected it was more at the thought of the Rope rather than the Breach.

'You will fight these two men. Survive and your ropes will be cut and you will be free to leave. Choose to lose...' *Or not survive,* thought Kaelith, 'You will be committed to eight years at the breach with the Commander here.' This seemed little like a bargain, either way.

Weapons were brought out for the two men. One chose a long wooden spear; they gave the other an antler blade and shield. Simple weapons for sure, but a man fighting for his freedom was much more dangerous than one who wasn't.

The Ropers had shifted onto the bleachers, bringing the prisoners with them. As most shuffled onto the benches, eight of them spread out into a wide square, on the corners and edges. Kaelith had spied the door from which they entered and considered running, but thought better of it. He was quite literally standing in the fortress of men and women trained in tracking down and capturing people.

Volchak spoke quietly to the man behind him.

'Daveron, this is treason.'

Kaelith knew it would be a wasted effort. Within these four walls there was a very different king.

Daveron waved his words away.

'The Order deems it training, Commander. And what is more loyal than a well-trained, armed and drilled Breachman!' A cheer and thudding of boots against the wooden stand.

Chiv, or Nyten - *did it matter?* - squared up opposite Kaelith. The prisoners thick head was still angled down, as he stood still. Kaelith tried to see it from his perspective. Probably spent a long time tied to one of those blocks, manipulated and moved by the ropes which had left clear scars on his neck and wrists. Maybe there were beatings? At some point, they must have chosen him as a fighter for such an occasion; although, looking at him maybe it was quite obvious from the start. He probably just wanted to get away, back home, maybe a family. Did it matter? Not really.

Kaelith held his rusted sword out in front of him, in one hand, and raised his other behind him in the air in a nimble fencing pose. He bounced on the balls of his feet and practiced a few cuts. The sword was too heavy, rusted, with a rather disgraceful looking notch in it. But now was not the time to worry about the aesthetic, although he expected he always looked rather dashing.

Having prepared himself, he glanced at Volchak out of the corner of his eye. The Commander just seemed downtrodden – resigned even. Volchak watched the man opposite him. The prisoner held his long spear vertically. So, that was a military man then, maybe even an ex-Royal Guard? The way he held that spear seemed a bit familiar to Kaelith.

'Begin!'

That caught Kaelith completely off guard - he was watching the other man. Chiv, or Nyten, rushed at him with an alarming speed. Seemed he was right about fighting for freedom; the man was possessed, Kaelith thought. The antler blade's three vicious looking prongs darted at him. Kaelith caught them late on his sword and ducked out of the way of the shield that followed behind. Seems this man was a fighter as well. Kaelith's feet waltzed around the man, who turned and came for a second pass, more calculated and cautious than the first. Probing with the sharpened bone weapon, he occasionally tapped the end of Kaelith's sword before feigning a strike, or striking. Jab, move, stab, move. Being the master swordsman that Kaelith knew he was, he parried and deflected and parried again. This was turning out to be slightly one-sided. His constant defence was making him dance around his half of the square whilst 'Chiten', in his mind he was both men now, kept coming. His opponent tried an overhead swing. Lazy, too slow, Kaelith sidestepped with a slight flourish and stamped on the man's wrist as it connected with the floor... Expecting him to drop the blade and submit. Master sword work. Instead, the man dropped his blade and grabbed Kaelith's leg. *Bugger.* Swiftly lifting it, he pitched Kaelith onto his back and seized the antler blade again, thrusting it at Kaelith's torso as he lay on the ground. Sword up, blocked, caught on the blasted antler blades, twisted, dropped. Ah.

Kaelith scurried to his feet a few steps away, but this time without sword in hand. His opponent stood facing him, head lowered to the ground again. *Maybe it was over?*

***

It hadn't started. Volchak had seen the other man spring towards Kaelith and had to trust the gentlemen mercenary wasn't just good for a tall tale. He faced the prisoner opposite him. He'd lowered his spear towards Volchak but neither had taken a step. Seems neither was too keen to start this business. Volchak took a half step forward, and the man matched him, spear now maybe ten paces away, sharp end held firm. Volchak wondered what eleven more of them would look like next to it, especially in heavy plated armour.

'Don't die,' he murmured, under his breath. The man had seemed to hear him as he tilted his head to the smallest of degrees, as if listening. That's all Volchak needed. He charged.

Four steps to within reach of the spear, the axe head spun, knocking the spear head to the side to give Volchak space to turn his body and miss it entirely. It scraped his leather armour as he slid down the length of it and swung the axe back overhead towards the man. The prisoner tried to bring his weapon up instinctually, but Volchak was inside his reach and the haft just pressed harmlessly against Volchak's body. The axe came down into the man's shoulder, no chain-mail or even leather to deaden the blow. Not clean through, but it crushed the man to the ground in a pile of his own gore.

Turning to the other men, he saw Kaelith on his back, furiously blocking the antler blade the other prisoner wielded as it tried to jab him in the stomach. The last block clearly a bad idea, but what choice did he have? Sword horizontal between the antlers, the prisoner twisted it and disarmed him. Kaelith slinked away onto his feet as the sword skittered away in the other direction, but now he stood now defenceless. Volchak launched towards the man.

Smack! Volchak's face hit the dirt hard, the wind gone from him. As he had launched himself, he had felt his ankle tighten and then jerk back, launching him forward, spinning onto his face, nearly cutting himself on his own axe blade. A tremendous weight appeared to be pulling him back. Peering down at his ankle he saw it had been lassoed by a muscular dark-skinned woman with a deep yellow grin. Something had blurred his vision and he felt the warm wet trickle down his face. He'd split his head against the haft of his own axe. Lucky he hadn't landed differently. He'd be picking up the other half of his head. Looking up, he saw the antler man launch forward at Kaelith and...

* * *

'Nooo yer don't…!' Kaelith turned at the last moment and the antler met air just a fraction to his side. Seizing the man's wrist, he twisted further and then spun round back against the prisoner's back, now holding the antler blade himself. He continued his movement a full turn and moved to jam the blade into the side of the man's head, but he found his shield held up in defence and scratched against the solid wood. As he moved for the second blow, he found his arm wouldn't react, turning his head to give it a piece of his mind, he saw a bright red rope firmly tangled around the antler blade. It snapped back and left his grip entirely back towards the thick-set man who had thrown it. *Guess those were the rules of the fight.*

He stood for the second time without a weapon; however so did Chiten opposite him. Kaelith looked around, down, between them to his left, at what lay on the floor.

'Call it a draw?' He asked with his best 'charm you into not killing me' smile.

In the same instant, both flung themselves to the floor. Kaelith went to his right and the prisoner to his left, as they scrambled in the dirt for the axe that was laying there. Volchak had dropped it when he was ensnared. Kaelith wondered whether he had been skewered by the man with the spear, although given that half of Chiten man appeared to be a bleeding pile of bones and flesh now just past the Commander made it seem unlikely. Kaelith knew his chances of getting out of here were slim if either of them, particularly himself, was dead.

All four hands grabbed the axe haft at the same time. One of Kaelith's on the grip just under the blade but the other on one of the blades, gaining little purchase. Chiten's grip was solid in the middle and his determined face mere inches from Kaelith's. The rotten breath directly in Kaelith's face threatened to bring up his breakfast. They both strained against the other, with Kaelith's hand sliding and splitting against the sharpened blade edge.

He saw the wide circle of rope, at the edge of his view, come sailing through the air.

***

Volchak had freed his leg; it seemed the woman had meant to trip but had no plans to reel him in. As he struggled to his feet, his empty hands searched the ground for the axe but it was not nearby. Either the woman had dragged him quite a way, or it really had bounced hard off his head, with the blood creeping down his face, he suspected the latter. The two bodies dumped on top of it and came up, each gripping the handle tightly. It was Volchak, now unarmed, who searched for a weapon.

He saw one. Volchak jumped forward and seized it straight out of the air. A lasso of rope had been thrown towards both Kaelith and the prisoner. It seemed Volchak's move had been quite unexpected as the rope wasn't jerked back immediately, giving him time to wrap it round the prisoner. His eyes bulged as Volchak pulled the slip knot tight around the man's waist. Volchak pulled it, hard. The man stood a good deal longer than Volchak expected. Maybe his thick legs were even stronger than they looked. Or his will to stay alive was. Whichever it was, it kept him gripping the axe. After what seemed far too long, the prisoner slumped to his knees. Holding the axe, Kaelith took a breath of his own and then split the man's skull with it. His swing was dangerously close to Volchak, who had fallen back on to the ground with the force of dragging the prisoner down.

Volchak stood, staring at Kaelith, then his eyes darted down to the axe in the mercenary's hands. They shared half a breath between them, and he held out the axe with a grin. Kaelith thrust the haft into his chest, as if holding it was burning his hand.

'Not a big fan of this army of yours; awfully rough,' Kaelith chuckled as the pair turned towards Daveron.

Chapter 19

The beach came into view quickly as they crossed the bridge. The river below was no longer a torrent of fast flowing water but a slow, wide, meandering snake through the flat landscape. You could swim it - Volchak had - but with weapons, armour and supplies you'd be taking an awful risk. The sole bridge to the thin sliver of land on the eastern side of had little to offer other than beaches, cliffs, and headland. If the capital hadn't been on that side, the bridge wouldn't have even been built at all.

'You think there'll be Ropers waiting on the other side?' Kaelith asked.

'No. I think Daveron had his sport. If he'd meant to keep us, he would have.'

'Don't the army have rules against such things?'

'Aye. But who would know? Not like anyone else read those orders. Far as anyone would care, we were just lost on the road. Or deserters.'

'Not me.'

Volchak turned and looked at him. Puzzled. Kaelith took a few steps forward onto the bridge and looked back at him with a smile.

'No one knows the great Kaelith joined the Breachmen in the first place.'

Under-foot, the wooden structure seemed as solid as the ground; each of its sections like a great spine laid out underneath, allowing men to walk fourteen abreast across it. Volchak had marched with the army five times over it, so he knew it could hold many hundreds of men at once, but still he felt the slightest unease as he crossed. There was the faintest of movement, creaking of the board underfoot, wind that seemed to whip up fast on it and threatened to pitch him over the side, even if the side was a good ten paces away.

Kaelith seemed ill at ease as well as they reached the middle, maybe a hundred paces in. He kept checking behind them every few minutes, as if still expecting to see the Ropers closing in. Volchak guessed that Kaelith hadn't crossed the bridge too often and the culmination of their last few weeks' travel was breaking his charming veneer. The fight at the prison had ended well, all things considered. No significant wounds, and every fight you walk away from was a victory. But they had recruited no more Breachmen either. Daveron had been quick to point out that he had offered two men, and Volchak had killed both of them. That is the story that the Ropers would likely spread, and what proof did Volchak have otherwise? He knew when he arrived at the capital with fewer men than he started with, he would face repercussions. The officers were all itching at an excuse to be rid of him, but they had been yet to find a willing replacement. Maybe this time? His fate would likely be in Smiele's hand, who would berate him, punish him, try him for treason or just send him up against the next army alone. Volchak surmised he was likely arriving shortly before they would. Smiele would have travelled directly cross-country south west from the battle rather than the longer road most of the army would take. At least Harkner and Flea would be well on their way by now. Volchak hoped they were safe.

'We should get off the road.' Kaelith's voice brought Volchak back to the bridge.

'Aye?'

'I'm sure they followed us. Feels like the road outside Brieth. Let us head off the road and wait a day, see whether we gain any more company.'

'Only three more days walk to the outskirts.' Volchak thought that just the two of them could easily outrun the Ropers, if they had to. Even if it meant having to ditch their supplies.

'I'm near spent. Doubt I'd make it, if we had to dash,' Kaelith said.

Volchak considered for a moment - *a fair point*. His back burned almost constantly now and the wound on his leg was still an angry shade of red, stinging him from time to time.

'Should have kept your horse.'

Kaelith laughed. 'Indeed. The cliffs have given way. I think a bath maybe thoroughly overdue. It's getting too hot to walk for weeks without one and I'd rather enter the capital a gentleman, if given the option.'

'Rather hoped you'd enter a Breachman; least then I'd have gained one on this trip.'

'Yes, well. I suppose I shall stick around a little longer, at least till I have a fresh shirt.' His shirt was almost in tatters, the ruffles had caught and pulled and torn. The sleeves were tied high up now on his arms. Very different from their first meeting.

They turned off the road towards the beach, just past where the last cliff face ended. They clambered over the large dunes and down onto the flat sand. Volchak stood for a moment and stared out from the shore. He liked the sea. No memory. No agenda. Raw power, of course, but a fair one.

'Why did you do it?' Kaelith stood next to him.

'Do what?'

'The other boy at the farm? Freeing me? Letting Harkner go with Stirc? Take your pick. None of it seems to benefit you.'

Volchak looked out again and shrugged.

'Seemed right. Most of what happens just happens. Ain't usually good. So, if you get a chance, maybe you do something right.' He sighed. 'Then again, maybe I'm just not that smart.'

Kaelith stood a moment longer. Clapped one hand onto his shoulder with a nod and then walked back towards the dune - just as the men emerged from above it.

Volchak raised his axe into both hands and turned to face them. Looking left and right on the beach, he saw that there was nowhere to go. Maybe the cliffs? A small cave? Funnel them in? He'd never make the run. There were men climbing down the dunes between him and the cliff face. And even if he had, there must be thirty of them now. And they were uniformed, leather clad armour and flat caps. These were not the King's men. So he stood, axe in hand. Maybe his days of doing what good he could were soon to be over.

The group stood in a rough line, twenty paces away. Seemed strange as he looked down at each man. There was no obvious leader. In his experience, even bandit groups would have someone gussied up fancier than the rest to stand out as the most important, the one to be listened to. Most of the time, it was the one to aim for in a fight.

From behind the line, that one came, although not what he was expecting. She was tall, clad in black leather armour with a black cloak pulled low, obscuring her face. Trailing in the sand a step behind her was a handsome man with a nasty scar across his right cheek. Not any bigger than Volchak, but sharp, with focussed eyes and a purposeful gait. *Bodyguard, and a tough one at that.*

The woman moved with a certain grace, stepping lightly across the sand, as if dancing, or maybe trying to avoid sinkholes only she knew were there. He glimpsed something at her side, no doubt a weapon, but mostly concealed behind her dark cloak. Volchak noted that one of her hands did not stray too far from it. Leader then. He rolled the axe handle in his grip.

'Can I help you, friends?' Volchak spoke to the woman.

'You are Volchak, Commander of the Breachmen?' her voice was soft and smooth. The first woman's voice he had heard since Brieth, and this was no country girl. *Highborn.* Volchak looked to Kaelith, standing off to the side, about half way between the two groups, facing Volchak.

Ah. So that's that then. She hadn't asked who he was.

'Aye. Who asks?' No point denying it. He had a great bronze axe and a scar on his face, he was easy to describe.

'Tamryn Delacey.'

'And friends?' Volchak nodded to the man next to her. Now they were closer, he could see he carried a rather fine steel sword. Interesting. Not really a brutish weapon, and not a cheap one either.

'These are men from my city. Some of them you've met before.'

'Rarely forget a face.' He looked at the man with the scar. 'One of mine?' nodding at it.

'No.' The man's voice was softer than his appearance. Another high-born.

'This is my brother. Olaf Delacey, Duke of Yrfrite.'

Volchak was as a stone for a moment whilst the introduction passed between them. He'd seen this man before, of course, several times, at a distance of half a battlefield. He'd expected the Duke would be grander in person, filled with the fineries of all the high-born, like Smiele himself. Come to think of it, though, he had never seen him wearing plate mail or waving a sword around in battle. Volchak didn't even remember seeing a separate commander's tent at their camps.

'Come to kill me personally?' Volchak raised his axe back up.

'We've come to talk to you,' Olaf said.

'He's not the best conversationalist,' Kaelith sparked up from where he stood off the side. Looking at Volchak.

Volchak turned his head to the man, frowning. Didn't say a word to him, just slightly inclined his head. Kaelith shrugged in response.

'Kaelith, your horse is waiting with my men at the cliffs. There is a small cave there where my men have kept it, those that aren't afraid go near it anyway. You may go.' Tamryn waited for him to turn and walk away before turning back to Volchak and continuing. 'We need to end this war.'

'Been trying; you keep raising more armies.' Volchak replied.

'They aren't soldiers, Commander. The people who fight with me are just people. They keep coming because they don't have a choice. People who have been threatened with drafting, people who have lost families to the Order's kidnappers, or the army has burnt through their villages.' Olaf didn't seem poised, as if making a grand speech. He almost sounded like he was pleading.

146

'They take up arms against the King.' Volchak looked at the thirty men standing by the dune, most of them carried steel swords or axes. These weren't *just* people.

'No.' Olaf replied. 'They take up arms against the Order, against its army. We fight *for* the King.'

Volchak said nothing.

'I sent twelve men down river when the mine finally ran dry in Yrfrite, with word for the King. None returned. Instead, two divisions of infantry arrived three weeks later and arrested half of my town guard.'

Volchak had been there, of course. He'd remembered the divisions arriving. Remembered he'd been in his barrack tent at the time he heard the first shouts, and came out to see the fires burning. The start of the rebellion.

'The people were angry. We sent twelve more, six by road and six by river. Three returned with the heads of the other nine as a warning from Commander Smiele. He wanted more metal; thought we were keeping it to outfit ourselves.'

'Your people drove out the army, I was there and had to escape on a copper barge.' Volchak remembered clambering aboard as it left the dock, catching the current as he watched the warehouses burn behind him, shortly before he passed out from blood loss.

'I couldn't stop them, hadn't enough guards left to stop them. Hadn't a means to equip or arm them. It got out of hand and soon the army had been routed by farmers, clerks and shop keepers. They came to me to lead them.'

'And you started the civil war?'

'No!' Tamryn seemed genuinely angry at the accusation. Her hand twitched under her cloak and she caught Volchak's glance at it. Steadying herself.

'Olaf meant to petition the King directly, assembled a hundred of the citizens from across the city to go with him as a peace delegation, to plead the cases and act as witness to the mine running dry.'

'So, what happened to your delegation?' Volchak asked. He hadn't ever heard of a peace delegation arriving at the capital.

'You did. You engaged us in the foothills south of Yrfrite. Your men charged us and they didn't know how to fight you off, hadn't seen such ferocity before. Panic set in, and then Smiele's Royal Guard arrived. Only four survived, myself included, barely.' Olaf pointed at the scar on his cheek. So Volchak had given it to him, in a manner of speaking. His fourth charge. Where he got his axe. A massacre? That wasn't how he remembered it. But then... there were only a hundred or so, and they had found very few real weapons afterwards...

'I tried sending smaller groups cross-country, even individuals. The Ropers always caught up with them and we wouldn't hear for weeks till rumour reached us. They cut the city off entirely.' Tamryn added.

'And then you started raising armies?' Volchak was still unsure of the angle on all this.

'Yes. We had to get to the capital. I need to speak to the King directly. He needs to understand what the Order has been doing to his people. He needs to know we aren't rebels.' Olaf was pleading now. He hadn't quite fallen to his knees but his shoulders slumped. 'Every time we ventured out of the city, we were engaged by the army. Every time we fell back and tried to stop the fighting. I begged the councillor each time to let just a small group through, escorted by the army, to speak to the King. Each time, he wouldn't listen. He sat on his beast and just smirked at us, telling us we'd be crushed, offering no quarter.'

Volchak sniffed at the sea air, the breeze a pleasant relief from the warmth of the sun. He wasn't sure what to make of this. The pieces in his mind were shifting and reforming, but there was still a nagging feeling like he was being played a fool.

'Why Kaelith?' he nodded over to the cliff where the man had since disappeared.

'I'm surprised he hadn't told you already,' Tamryn said, with a slight exasperation on in her voice at the mention of him. Actually. He had already told Volchak.

'We had to try something new to deal with the Royal Guard. We had spoken to Major Fedal but he could not act against Smiele with the Royal Guard. Even the infantry divisions would have struggled against them.'

That was interesting news, if true. Fedal had been a very reasonable man, never sought a fight for a fight's sake. Maybe they bought him? Or maybe he believed what they said.

'We sought Kaelith out from rumours of a mounted band that had entered the country over the Western Mountains. But the buffoon ambushed you instead of the Guard and then got himself captured. So, we offered him another chance.' Olaf motioned to the beach where they now stood.

'Over the mountains? Can't be done.' Volchak could be sure of this. For hundreds of years explorers, expeditions and even armies had tried to cross the Western mountains. From where they cut out far into the Southern Sea up to where they disappeared into the Northern Wastelands. He had never even thought there was a world on the other side of them.

'Ever see him again, ask him yourself. Might get something near the truth. But have you ever seen so many horses?' Tamryn said with a smirk at Kaelith's expense.

Maybe she hadn't completely believed him either, but she was right.

'What chance? You haven't answered why you want me.'

'To get me in front of the King,' Olaf was direct. 'I will give you these thirty men, as your Breachmen, to report back to the army with. And when you sit on the King's war council with the other commanders in the capital, you make sure I am with you.'

'And what if you just kill him?'

Olaf sighed. 'If I do, you can kill me next. I doubt they'd let either of us in with a weapon.'

That was a fair point.

'What if I just kill you?' Volchak rolled his axe again.

'Will you?'

Olaf stared directly at Volchak, only a step away. His weapon was not drawn. He was not heavily-armoured and despite his scar, he certainly wouldn't have had the fighting experience Volchak did. Maybe this was his chance to end the war in a more direct way. Volchak would be killed, for sure, can't fight thirty men; let alone the sister of a man you just murdered.

'Maybe. What of your sister?'

'*She* can speak for herself.' Tamryn said. 'I will return to our city and try to keep the peace. And if you do kill him, then I'll really start fighting a war.'

'Can't walk thirty well-armed fighters into the capital without people asking questions. Where did they come from and where did they get their metal weapons?'

'You left Brieth in a hurry. Far as I'm concerned, these are all men who came to volunteer for the Breachmen from the village and surrounding homesteads.' Volchak, of course, remembered only the three sign ups, one of which he'd last seen dead and stuffed in a wardrobe.

'Wouldn't stick - look at their uniforms and weapons.'

Tamryn nodded towards the men and they removed their bronze swords, rolling them into thick blankets alongside their leather armour. They piled the bundles off to the side and retrieved a wide variety of wooden pitchforks, self-crafted short spears, stone axes, and clubs from another pile in the cave's entrance. Within a few minutes, the well-armed and armoured division became a rag-tag mob of angry farmers.

Olaf handed his sword to Tamryn. Volchak's nerves frayed slightly as he watched the movement. He thought it could all be an elaborate ruse to get the drop on him. But neither one of them stabbed him with it.

Tamryn nodded to the men, satisfied with their transformation, then turned back to Volchak.

'You will camp along the beach here for four days, then march to the city. They need not enter the inner walls, but will make enough fuss to be known. They are there to get you in, and you are to get him in.'

'Once I've talked to the King, he might have need of them. They'll be yours to command.' Olaf said. He looked at Volchak square on, standing slightly taller, with his thick black hair fluttering across his face in the wind. Volchak stared back through his own matted dark, greying, locks. The same way he had done many dozens of times before, staring into the faces of many men he had recruited. Olaf held his gaze.

'Okay. I'll put you in a room with the King, but if I'm wrong about all this, then remember, I'll not need an axe to kill you. Agreed?'

'Agreed.'

Chapter 20

'Yeah, I know where we can hole up.'

Stirc had found that Harkner had become far more useful since the departure of the Commander and his pet mercenary. They had talked several times over the past two days, in the cattle cart, as Flea came in and out of consciousness. The big man cared for her, that was much was obvious, although Stirc had certainly questioned his motives throughout their journey together. He would find the man looking at her, as she lay there, or holding her hand and whispering. It was certainly unsettling, but he needed the man if he was to make the required arrangements to have her brought to the monastery in the proper manner – and the proper manner was essential if she was to survive.

On the second day the terrain changed - cultivated fields replacing open meadows. More homesteads on either side gave way to small mills and workshops. In the fields, cattle-ploughs worked and there were more people on the road. That was when Stirc had decided he needed to divulge a part of his plan to his travelling companion – just enough of it.

'Excellent. You will need to keep her there for a couple of days, until I can make arrangements to take on an apprentice at the monastery. At that point you will report there, and you will be bringing her as one of my subjects.' He worked his hands nervously in circles. He had been an exemplary physician until now, adhered to every rule… but this was a personal matter.

'I will be the apprentice? No offence to your brilliant plan, but learning ain't exactly my strong suit.'

'Your sole aim will be to say as little as possible. Believe me, Mr. Harkner, I shan't have much trouble in convincing them. The difficult bit will be, when she is healthy again, how we get her out.'

'I should be able to handle that,' Harkner nodded to his hammer.

'Don't be a fool. The monastery is more like a fortress, only the palace is better-guarded and maybe not even so. It will take tact, guile and some effective planning if we are to have the two of you leave. And that -' He nodded to the hammer '- is never going to make it inside.'

Harkner frowned, but he did not argue.

The cart jerked, as it hit hard stone, and then each bounce became more pronounced as the wheels now rattled along on the cobbled street rather than the smoother dirt before.

'Where is this sanctuary of yours? And will it be secret?' Stirc asked.

'In the mining quarter. And I can guarantee no one sees anything there. We learnt the hard way that if you report something, you were just as likely to be picked up by your lot for it.'

Strange. Stirc had of course known the Ropers were for collecting deserters and criminals. Not the City Watch as such, but more a service the Order provided for the city. He had not heard that they took much of an active role in policing or interrogation.

'You were a miner?' He diverted attention from the 'your lot' Harkner had said a moment ago.

'I was a mason. Carved this myself for the woman I loved...' He picked up the stone hammer, his muscular arm making it seem as light as a feather.

'She will shelter us?'

'No. She is dead. Just over two years now.'

'My apologies.' Stirc said, the slightest softness in his voice.

'Aye. A real beauty though she was. Powerful woman.' Harkner sat back in the cart, put his enormous hands behind his enormous head and looked out across the buildings as the rattled past. The cart trundled into the factory quarter and the stone walls reflected the warm summer's heat back onto the road, creating a feeling of heat and industry.

'Three years we had,' he continued, lost in his own thoughts. 'I was a herdsman, raised cattle; I could have been a cartman you know. Good solid beasts we had, fast too when I got them going.'

Stirc sat silently. It all seemed very quaint but largely irrelevant to him, though he supposed it was not wise to interrupt a man who was building a reputation for crushing skulls.

'When the Order came, it was just a single clerk, to inform me the crown had purchased my little farm. I was to be relocated to the mining quarter. Well, that's where I met her. Mining was good work, the best work, the one thing they'd always need more of in the capital.' He smiled. 'I hadn't the heart to argue, I mean, as a mason I got to see her every day!' He laughed to himself.

'Things grew harder for us. She in the mine, me in the masons. Nothing went the way we had hoped it would. And then...'

He trailed off. And they sat in silence a long time.

Until it was time to move.

Stirc climbed out first, holding the two packs as best he could on his bony frame. He had removed his Order robe and wore nought by his undershirt and trousers. Harkner insisted that no one would give him a second glance, but he wondered whether the man was just attempting to prank him.

Harkner carefully held Flea's limp form in his arms and then climbed down the steps, more deftly than Stirc would have expected for a man his size. His hammer had been slung over his shoulder and its head wrapped in an oil cloth as best they could manage. Stirc felt absurd next to the two of them, the undressed man and the giant with an unconscious girl.

But he needed not to have worried. The streets were a cacophony of activity of all kinds and they simply vanished into the mix. Miners, workers, bakers, merchants, industry men, gangs of youths that made for a vast array of people, none of which paying the others much mind.

'Between shifts! This way,' Harkner had to speak loudly over the din. The streets here were narrow and Stirc's thin body, carrying an oversized pack, was bumped and tossed across it as he tried to follow the man through the swell of people. The houses on either side became more run-down and miserable. The streets narrowed and widened as the buildings leaned in, and then would suddenly end and split in two directions. Stirc had spent very little time outside the monastery and had never been to this part of the city before, so he had to trust that Harkner knew this route.

But it soon appeared his fears were unfounded. They stood in front of a rather sad looking house, roof sagging slightly and one of the top floor windows boarded up completely. The place had an air of decay that fit in nicely with the street's. Neglected paving slabs cracked with thick weed growth stood in front of a splintered front door.

'Still here, then.'

Harkner kicked the door hard, and it crashed open. There were far fewer people on the streets now they had escaped the primary thoroughfare. A few heads turned in their direction, then quickly scurried away as if nothing had happened.

'Like I said, no one sees anything here,' Harkner grinned and entered.

The house itself stank of mould and neglect. The furniture had all been smashed or stolen, so they laid Flea down in the room with the boarded windows and allowed her to rest. They made a makeshift camp from the skins and blankets in their travel packs. Harkner propped the door back up with several pieces of wood and set about stashing their supplies upstairs in the other room. Stirc fussed over Flea, making notes on her reactions, on the colour of the wound and consistency of the skin forming over it. He applied several more anti-septic chemicals to try to fight the infection that had taken hold. The angry red skin burned hot to the touch, no matter what he tried, it would not cool. Her brow was beaded with sweat. He knew this was already beyond his knowledge and in a few days, it would be beyond the help of those he could call on.

'You will remain here, then. Keep her watered, feed her what you can, but be mindful she does not choke. As her fever worsens, she may start to seize. If that happens then dab this on her temples.' Stirc handed over the anti-convulsive that he had worked on in his fifth year at the monastery. He had just about perfected it four years later. 'I will return tomorrow and we will need to move quickly.'

'How will you find us?'

An excellent question. Stirc had not thought of that.

'We will wait at the Eastern entrance to the mine at sunrise. Come then. It is the end closest to the monastery.'

'You can provide a map or directions?'

Harkner was grinning again. 'You won't need them. Just be on the streets before sunrise near the monastery and follow the crowd. They will all head down there to work the day shift.'

The man was smarter than Stirc had given him credit for.

'Then I will take my leave of you.'

He looked over to the body on the floor and felt a slight tugging in his chest and a strange sensation welling up in his eyes. She had been the first person to care, enough to put herself in harm's way.

'Don't run. Harkner. The Ropers would find you eventually, yes, but if you want her to live, stay.'

'Just make sure you come back for her.' Harkner looked at him, no cheer in his eyes. He was seeking help.

'Tomorrow.'

Chapter 21

'Ah familiarity, safety, the warm embrace of the known,' Stirc muttered as he stepped under the raised wooden portcullis that was the mouth to his long-time home. He presented his papers to the two halberd-wielding guards as he approached. It was only slightly crumpled and worn from more than three months away. They seemed wary of him, despite his full red robes, but in short order they had bowed and stepped aside.

As he passed through the thick stone walls, calmness overcame him. The world around was quieter here, despite being nestled between the constant thrum of the mine and the bustle of people in the markets. The high walls on either side hid the world around him, the way he liked it. His pace slowed as he took in the ornamental herb gardens. The marble was polished a fine white and the summer bloom was in full flow. Black-robed interns buzzed around the flowers, pruning or trimming to perfection. Across the small lawns at the far end he saw several of his red-robed peers. Deep in discussion over one of the study tables, pointing and gesticulating at the diagrams in front of them with the enthusiasm that only the scholarly can understand.

He followed the wall, keeping it to his right as he walked down the lightly-gravelled path. After so long trudging in the dirt and then bouncing in the back of the cart, it was good to feel its familiar soft crunch. Like walking on frosty grass, not that he would consider stepping on the grass within the monastery. It would not be well-received.

Ahead of him, the main keep jutted out in to the yard with its heavy stone arch. He looked up at the building, raising high into the air and counted the windows as he had always done. Six up, twelve across, simple and perfect symmetry. Organised and arranged as it should be.

Six more guards stood outside, unmoving. An intern stepped from the archway at precisely the right moment to meet him. Sygan, he knew the man - not the most diligent and lacking a certain imagination, but intelligent enough.

'Physician Stirc. Welcome back. I trust your journey was insightful?'

'Certainly.' Stirc saw little need to provide any more, as the man gestured for him to walk alongside into the main hallway of the keep.

'You will report to the Registrars?' It was not so much a question. Sygan reported directly to the four of them on all matters that pertained to the keep. He would revel in the opportunity to report a break in protocol by a returning physician.

'Imminently. I have some articles to deposit in my quarters and then will meet them in the lecture theatre.'

'Then I shall inform their staff.' The slightest nod. Sygan had never managed a full bow - and he disappeared down a side passage and was gone.

Stirc reached the heavy oak double doors but did not enter, instead turning into one of the two large stairways that split from the main hallway. His feet tapped lightly on each stone step, smooth and precisely as he climbed. As he passed doorways to other floors, he saw more red-robed men milling about, or more black robes on errands back and forth between the various chambers.

Upon reaching the fifth floor, he exited towards his room, a further three hundred and twelve steps from the stairwell. Opening the thin wooden door, he smiled. A thick layer of dust lay across his table and bookshelves, and on each of his curios and anatomy models. No one had used his space, and why should they? His wooden bedframe and thin mattress were nestled in the alcove against the far wall, the privacy curtain drawn back as he had left it. He placed his pack down on the bed and surveyed the rest of the room. His block was immaculate, clearly having been kept free of dust and neglect, exactly as it should be. The plain, tiled floor around it had been kept clean. In fact, he noted that the cleaning had been more thorough than one would expect, right up to the edges of the room instead of just around the block as was mandated. No doubt an over enthusiastic intern had been trying to curry favour. Stirc would surely raise it at some point, and the individual would be suitably penalised for their wastefulness.

He removed the glass vials from his satchel within his robe. The large conical white fluid was more than half gone. He placed it inside the drawer, next to his collection of formula's – all encrypted in his own personal cypher. His tools were placed next to them also. He hung the travel cloak in the wardrobe. Stirc stopped for a beat as he opened it, looked at the space inside, space enough to hide in. He glanced around the room quickly, nothing and no one there. He breathed out and shook his head with an almost embarrassed smile.

'Learn anything interesting?' The voice made Stirc jump, hand slipping on the wardrobe so the door banged against its hinges as it swung fully open.

He turned and regarded the red-robed woman who stood in his doorway. The door across the hall from his was now open, revealing an almost identical room, save for some additional apparatus in the corner.

'Torrak. Well met.' Stirc steeled himself, reached for the wardrobe door and closed it, heart thumping in his chest. He glanced at the drawer on the stand, which remained open and casually walked over to it and closed it from view.

'You have kept well these last few months without me?' Stirc turned and faced the woman, the wooden block between them.

'Indeed. Without your incessant need to hog the live subjects for the floor, my research has made steady progress.' She replied.

'I am pleased.' Stirc meant it too - he had need of it after all.

'What of your report on the campaign?'

'Whilst yet to formulate a final draft, it was underwhelming. I witnessed several major engagements. Each very one-sided victories, the Royal Guard left very few wounded for my attention. High Commander Smiele's effectiveness was…' he paused, considering 'self-evident.'

'I had heard differently.' Appeared news travelled faster than cattle carts. 'The last battle, a loss?'

'A stalemate, from what I could assess. The rebels retreated faster than they could be caught and were never fully engaged. I don't doubt they are half way back to Yrfrite by now.' He left out the ambush and the horses, not sure what news had made it out.

Torrak stood smiling, a knowing smile, *a dangerous smile*.

'I wouldn't keep the Registrars waiting for your report. I understand they are keen to speak to you.' She nodded and retreated towards her room.

'Torrak?' she half-turned to listen, her robe giving the slightest hint of a female form as he turned her bald head. 'I may have something for you, actually.' She fully turned; eyebrow raised.

'Aye?'

'I've sent for a new live subject. A specific type of wound I wish to test my compound on, and I believe it will coalesce nicely with your work in infection control.' Stirc's heart started beating harder, but his face remained stoic. 'If you have capacity, of course,' he bowed his head slightly.

Torrak sniffed.

'One more experiment? Aye. Least you have learned to share in your travels. Bring them to me and we shall work on them together.'

Torrak didn't say anymore. Turning on her heel, she walked back into her room and closed the door behind her. Stirc unclasped his aching hands from between his robe sleeves and made towards his door close it.

Chapter 22

Stirc entered the theatre through the door at the end of the hallway and stood respectfully on the inner edge, head bowed so that his red robe blocked out the view of all but the floor. It was a white marble, sheer and stainless. No doubt you could eat off it with no particularly unpleasant side effects; an absurd thought, as there would be no reason to.

He heard the footsteps tapping as they approached.

'Physician Stirc, please do be seated.' The man continued past. Stirc kept his head bowed until the black robe was out of view, then raised his head and padded across the great circular room to the table at the far end.

As he did, he raised his eyes across the four figures sat at the table, each in white robes seated beneath four large imposing marble statues. He counted them off inside his head, calming his nerves for how this next part would go.

One. Bone, a skeletal statue.

Two. Bedlam, bound in ropes, head pitched back, screaming.

Three. Body, man without skin, muscles defined with eerie accuracy, the texture of them cut finely into the marble as it flexed against chains wrapped around it.

Four. Brain, half a skull. The mottled texture of the brain underneath seemed to carry a slight grey hue.

They were flanked by the four other plinths, all standing empty.

'Sit, Stirc, sit.'

'Thank you, Registrar Muldren,' Stirc replied.

'Your journey was a fruitful one?' Registrar Kade was by far the most athletic of the group. His imposing form sat a foot taller and seemed to perch forward, as if ready to pounce from his chair.

'Indeed, Registrar Kade.' Stirc bowed his head. 'I was able to discern several fascinating diagrams about the impact of bronze on the upper larynx.' In reality they had delivered him a several day-old body from the first engagement near Yrfrite where Volchak had cut a man's head clean off. They hadn't provided the head.

'Hah!' Kade threw his arms up and chuckled. 'Brilliant!' Wounds of the body were his passion. 'Then I look forward to your publishing!'

'And what of your compound - adequate field testing?' Yorinth said. She had taken an active interest in his work prior to his first presentation to the group. Her bony fingers wrapped on the large white table.

'Well, yes, actually of perpetual usefulness. Several real-world tests have been conducted and it has proven highly effective against superficial lacerations.' Stirc was getting animated. 'Increased healing factor considerably, with the subject feeling only mild discomfort.' Stirc looked around the group, Yorinth seemed pleased but Kade waved away the comments about feelings, that did not interest him. 'Whilst on the matter, in fact, I am looking to bring in a subject where a more serious internal injury has been experienced so that I might conduct further experimentation.'

'Good, good. The King will be pleased.' Muldren flashed a grin to Yorinth, who nodded her head.

'What of the war?' Caldor asked. The others almost froze in place. Muldren stopped grinning. Until then the man had not acknowledged Stirc's presence in any way. His intense stare focussed now on Stirc – who shuddered under the gaze of the one he knew as Brain.

'High Registrar.' Stirc bowed in his chair, almost appearing to kiss the table.

'I am afraid I am not specialised in military strategy and I would imagine you have received more accurate reports from... The...'

Stirc trailed off – Caldor continued to stare at him with an emotionless face.

'Ahem, that is, I mean to say.' Stirc flustered. 'I witnessed three major engagements. Well, no, two, I suppose. In the hills to the West, the army met with a medium-sized rebel force. Victory was decisive and swift, the Breachmen and infantry pinned them down and the Royal Guard decimated them.'

'What weapons did they use?'

Stirc had expected this would happen. He bowed his head to acknowledge the question, but continued to speak as if uninterrupted.

'The third and final engagement was more of a stalemate. The infantry engaged, but the Breachmen were ambushed by...' he hadn't meant to pause for dramatic effect, but now he had, he forced himself to spit out the words '...mounted warriors. On horses.'

The three Registrars shared a worried look. Caldor just stared forward, unmoved.

'Is that all?'

'No. As ordered.' Stirc knew that Caldor was aware of this already, but went through the motions. Stirc had considered the advice Kaelith had given him, a good lie was as much truth as possible. 'I was escorted to Brieth by the Commander of the Breachmen, who had survived with two of his troops and a prisoner - one of the mounted men. Indeed. We were set upon by Boatmen two days outside the village.'

'Outcome?'

'The Commander and the Breachmen killed seven of them. The sole casualty on our side was the prisoner.'

'A failure, then?' Muldren chipped in with a frown.

The four were all staring at Stirc. He could feel the proverbial rope dangling above his head as he sat there. Each of the statues behind them seemed to lean forward menacingly. Maybe the light from the tall windows behind them shifted, or maybe they weren't lifeless marble after all.

'No. No. Not at all. I have... something. I can deliver a prisoner as instructed. I tricked one of the horsemen from the battle into accompanying me to the city. He believes I will intern him here. He is playacting as one of the Breachmen, as some kind of elaborate ruse. But I can confirm explicitly he was in the ambush.' As much truth as he could, as much lie as he dared.

Kade frowned at Caldor, lowering his brow who nodded slightly.

'When will he you deliver him?' Kade asked, still looking to his right. His voice echoed around the expansive hall.

'Tomorrow. I shall deliver tomorrow.' Stirc sincerely hoped that Harkner wouldn't reconsider and disappear.

A long pause. Inside the hall, all was still. Stirc felt the weight of the place pressing down on his shoulders. Each of the Registrars performed their surgeries here; their presence now bore down on him. Stirc recalled how, as a as a young man, he had stood in this hall and watched Registrar Kade entirely remove the skin from a living subject. He had seen Yorinth remove the teeth from a disgraced Royal Guardsmen – *no, a subject*. When he thought about it, Stirc could recall the clink sound as it landed on the plain white marble table. Muldren had talked one of the interns into biting off their own finger and presenting it to him as a gift, the red blood washing onto the clean marble beneath his feet as he slumped on the ground.

Caldor stood slowly. His face remained blank. Stirc had never seen Caldor perform surgery.

With a bow of his head, he turned and walked past the four statues towards the door nestled in the wall behind them. The others stood, waited for him to be several feet away, and then followed. When they had left Stirc sat a moment, wheezing.

'We shall make arrangements to receive your guest.' Sygan's voice made Stirc's heart jump into his throat and he squirmed in the chair. When he stood and faced the small black robed man, he could feel sweat on his brow and held the back of the chair to steady himself.

'Thank you.'

Sygan grinned, clearly pleased with himself, as they both left the lecture theatre.

Chapter 23

The smell was unbearable. Thick dust, gas and soot hung in the air. Stirc felt choked even through the mask he had fashioned for himself from a bandage. This was his second ever visit to the mine, and it was now two too many. The guards at the monastery had given him some hassle upon leaving, insisting that his orders did not allow a further visit to the city, despite his insistence to the contrary. It was only threatening to go and retrieve the Brain himself that made them surrender the door. Which was good for Stirc, as they were completely right of course. This was an unauthorised trip, but one he expected would be overlooked when he delivered what he had offered.

Harkner had been leaning casually against the corner of the last building, before the street opened up onto the large barren square before the entrance to the main mine. Harkner had been correct it had not been hard to find. Upon reaching the district it was obvious that most people in this part of the city were headed underground that morning. Some were dressed in heavy overalls and carried heavily dented wooden helmets - the miners. Others wore thick leather armour and hoods - smelters. They all walked towards the gaping maw of the mine itself. Huge wooden beams held open the gap that could easily have swallowed the surrounding buildings. The ground was smooth from centuries of people trudging across it; it was impressive and terrifying to behold, that entrance to the underground world beneath the city. And Stirc knew the eastern entrance was the smaller of the two.

'Wasn't convinced you were coming back,' Harkner grinned at Stirc as he approached.

'It had crossed my mind. Where is the girl?' *Subject, Stirc. Subject.* He couldn't seem to control it.

Harkner brought him around the corner where to he had placed her behind a stack of wooden mine carts. Firmly in view from where he stood, but obscured from most of those headed into the entrance. There were an assortment of business types milling past, in more comfortable tabards and trousers but all with a worn and slightly grubby air to them. Stirc supposed no one could come down here without getting covered in the dust.

Stirc felt Flea's head - hotter than it should be even on what was soon becoming a boiling summer's day. She groaned slightly, responsive to a degree. *Good.*

'Bring her. When we arrive, say nothing. With luck we will head straight to my chamber unopposed.'

'Luck? I've always been lucky' Harkner chuckled. Stirc watched him bend to pick up Flea, his confident veneer slipped slightly as she barely moved and he manoeuvred her into his arms.

The walk back to the monastery took another hour as they constantly pushed against the apparently never-ending crowd shuffling towards the mine. They arrived mid-morning, the sun was already beating heavily down on the entrance. One guard had removed his helmet. Stirc took a mental note for later – a breach of protocol. The guard eyed the three of them warily and stepped forward, leaning slightly on his halberd.

'Physician, you have returned.'

'Evidently. I trust no repeat of this morning?'

'No physician. I have had word. You are to report to the Registrars immediately. I shall escort you personally.'

Stirc nodded, straight-faced, the slightest bead of sweat trickling down the back of his bald head. The guard held his gaze and stepped aside. Stirc had already taken another note. A guard was to leave his post to ensure compliance. *This could be a problem.* Stirc glanced up at the metal head of the halberd. Nothing he could do now.

'You are to deliver her to the fifth floor to my chambers, thus marked.' Stirc handed Harkner the orders he had presented the previous day to the guards with his name written on it at the top. He did not know if the man knew his letters or not.

'Forgive me, Physician. Your companions are to accompany you.' The guard was pre-warned then. *Torrak.* Seems Harkner's luck had not rubbed off.

'Very good.' It was not. He had hoped not to have to do this in front of the big man, better to betray a man cleanly at a distance. Maybe not the bravest way to do it, but he had never claimed to be the bravest.

They stepped into the courtyard. Stirc kept a steady and purposeful pace this time. His entourage gathered the looks of several of the black robed attendants as they passed, but he acknowledged none of them. This had to be played perfectly.

As they stepped into the lecture theatre, the sunlight danced around the hall from the large windows on the far side of the circle. Stirc held his chin high with hood moved down onto his shoulders to reveal his bald head, shining in the light. He walked purposefully towards the table.

Half-way he stopped in his tracks. On the table was a subject, bound at each of the key points by thick red ropes which protruded from the ground beneath it. Each rope was

171

furnished with a metal manacle, denoting its importance and significance.

The four Registrars were no longer seats in the shadows of their plinths, but stood at points around the table examining the subject. It seems they had already started operating, to a small degree. There was a faint trickle of blood running down the length of the table and dripping onto the floor. It appeared to be coming from under the subject's left arm.

'Ah Stirc, excellent. Come in, come in.' Yorinth beckoned him forward. 'We are extremely pleased to see you. Your companions may wait outside.' She motioned to the guard, her dark hand emerging from her white robe and then disappearing as quickly as the wave took.

Stirc didn't argue. There went his plan to deliver Harkner as his prisoner. But events had overtaken him already.

He approached the table and Kade stood in front of him, half a step away.

'You have been dishonest with us, Physician.' His imposing form casting a shadow across Stirc, holding what seemed a tiny scalpel in his large hand. It was, of course, regulation size.

Stirc swallowed.

'I…'

'Remarkable!' Muldren could not contain himself. All but shoving the far larger man out of the way to get to Stirc, seizing him round his bony shoulders and walking him to the table whilst chattering away.

'Your reports made it seem like the progress was slow, but we have re-opened and examined the wound and your work is exceptional. A significant puncture almost completely healed in a manner of weeks; the man should have bled to death within a matter of hours.'

Stirc was completely flummoxed.

'Errr…'

Caldor stood alone at the head of the table. Stirc saw what he was holding and panic set in. His first instinct to dash across the table and seize it from him, hide it, protect it. But he still had enough sense to know that would not have ended well.

'Impressive.'

Yorinth stepped back in front of them. 'You have certainly delivered. Well done. Maybe not quite as we expected… We thought you were bringing him yourself. But the Ropers pulled him in on the bridge several days ago and arrived here this morning.'

Stirc looked at her confused, then tried to appear as if he knew exactly what she meant.

'Good.' *Who?*

Kade spoke. 'When they arrived, they brought him to us. We interrogated him. He told us the full story.'

Stirc looked beyond him. He saw the torn shirt, the ponytail and the terrified look in the man's eyes.

'Yes, yes… very sharp of you, very sharp. Arrived and told us of your plan.' Yorinth said.

Stirc's heart was thumping. How had he known about Flea, and Harkner? And where did they get the vial?

'The prisoner said you'd promised him sanctuary here. Brilliant!' Muldren spoke quickly. 'Very sharp… You'd told him to wait on the bridge and you would send for him.

And, of course, a horse as well! What a find! We shall make adaptations for autopsy for that, in time.'

'And when we heard he was one of your subjects after the battle and that you'd applied your compound to a wound? Well, we just had to see for ourselves. You were holding out on us!' Kade boomed with laughter. He smacked Stirc on the shoulder jovially, hard enough to make him step to the side.

'It wasn't... complete.' Stirc's voice shook, he was still unsure what to make of all this.

Caldor spoke, suppressing the energy immediately.

'Physician Stirc. Your actions in service of the Order were exemplary. Your application of our craft, has yielded a tremendous discovery, capable of life extension and recovery, which will significantly improve our ability to operate and examine.'

Stirc had even never heard of Caldor saying more than a single sentence at once. Yet he continued in a flat tone, no different than as if reading the most basic of instructional tome. 'And you have delivered directly to us a prisoner of significant strategic value above and beyond the expectation. The mercenary holds information critical to the superiority of the Order.' Stirc's eyes held firm but his mind reeled, not understanding what the High Registrar meant. 'By unanimous vote this morning, we have elevated you to the rank of Registrar of the Hermetic Order. You shall hereon fulfil the duties of Registrar of the Blood. You may provide representation to this council and choose such help and field of continued study as you should choose.'

Stirc's eyes widened at each word until his gaunt face stretched and he felt it ache.

'Thank you. Honoured... peers.' He bowed low, neck cracking slightly as he lowered his head.

'Please, a demonstration from Blood!' Muldren almost cheered.

Kade handed Stirc a scalpel, Caldor placed the vial down on the table beside the subject, the white liquid sloshed heavily against the glass.

'Yes... quite... well.' He reached into his robe and took out his tools, those he hadn't left in the drawer in his room. He placed the bloodied scalpel down on the table and took his clamp and applicator.

'The application of the compound is relatively simple. Please rotate ninety degrees to the right.' Yorinth manipulated the dials on the far end of the table and the ropes shifted Kaelith onto his side. Blood was steadily seeping from the wound under his arm, as it had when he first met Stirc.

'The difficulty actually comes from preparing and handling the compound itself. It will stem blood loss incredibly quickly, and then will form a thick crust which will dissipate after one to two days.' Whilst speaking he clamped the wound and built a circular layer around the hole that Kade had apparently cut in the man's underarm. Precisely where the spear had stuck him several weeks ago.

In under a minute Stirc had finished. The bleeding had stopped entirely, and the wound was encased and sterile. Muldren squealed with joy and Yorinth clapped her thin hands slowly, gazing at the table.

'Intriguing.' Praise from Caldor was another first, although he did not share the excitement of the others.

'My thanks, High Registrar. If I may? I have a subject outside with a more severe internal wound. I wish to further study the application of the compound. I would humbly request Physician Torrak's assistance.

'You do not need to request. Registrar.' Kade replied. 'Continue your work. You shall have access to whatever resources you need. We shall provide the requisite attire. And we shall erect the statue of the Blood for your seat.' He nodded to one of the empty plinths. Stirc mused slightly how this would create a pleasant symmetry - with Brain in the middle.

'We will see you for council tomorrow. It will intrigue you to hear of some of our most recent... developments. Someone retrieve this subject and monitor his recovery over the coming days. Quite remarkable.' Yorinth nodded and turned away, headed for the door far to their left. Kade followed.

'Yes, indeed, entirely spectacular work.' Muldren swept off to the door on the right.

Stirc stood alone with Caldor.

'We will discuss plans for production.' Caldor nodded to the compound sitting nearly empty on the marble table. 'Timing is….' A pause as he looked over Kaelith, still pinned on his side, '…excellent.' He turned without a further word and walked past the statues to the back of the room as before.

Stirc looked at Kaelith, whose eyes were bulging as he strained against the ropes.

Stirc just shrugged slightly, and walked back the way he came.

Chapter 24

Volchak poked at the small fire, sending sparks into the warm evening sky, as he had done the past three nights. He sat alone, as usual, about twenty paces from the other larger fire where the Duke and his men roasted meat, chatted, laughed and drank. He nudged the bottle next to his foot; it slipped in the sand until the dark liquid inside balanced it out. Maybe he shouldn't be feeling glum? He had a full belly and was warm. No one had tried to kill him today, and he had an entire division of Breachmen under his command. Probably the best armed and well-drilled he'd led in years. They'd look fine when he reported back to the capital, of course. Even Smiele might be impressed. But they were hardly likely to charge a shield wall made up from their own army.

'What am I doing here…?' He slurred; head foggy.

'Trying to poke holes in your fire from the look of things.' Duke Olaf stood a few feet away, on the edge of his firelight. 'May I join you?'

Volchak nodded.

He regarded the man; full thick brown hair, the same plain leather his men wore, a small stone axe hung loosely at his side. His face was slightly soot-smudged from taking his turn watching their fire over the past few days. The scar on his face danced in the firelight, offsetting his rugged features and purposeful manner. His scar was smaller, neater, less craggy than Volchak's. Seems this was every man's idea of a gallant hero, straight from legend. Volchak smiled.

'That's more like it, friend. Why do you not join us?' Olaf said.

'Laughing, drinking, sleeping next to the rebel forces? Not for me. I draw the line at sneaking their commander in to see the King'

Olaf chuckled and offered out another of the plain green bottles they apparently had stored in the cave, expressly for this prolonged stay.

'No, thank you.' Volchak nudged the one by his foot. 'I'm set.'

'You know, you're not quite what I expected.' Olaf said as he took a seat on the shingle next to where Volchak lounged.

'Shorter, I suppose. Most people say that about me.' Volchak was looking at the fire.

'Ha, try being mistaken for your sister's butler half your life.'

Volchak thought about that for a moment. Probably wouldn't mind being her butler; she didn't seem too bad to spend time around in the short time they'd spoken.

'No, I mean your reputation.' Olaf continued. 'Executioner. Slayer of men. Fearless Commander of the Breachmen. Wasn't sure you wouldn't try to fight the lot of us single-handed on the beach. Or just cut my head off and be done with it.'

'Thought crossed my mind.' Volchak reached for his own bottle. 'But, I guess, comes a time when no matter how many heads you chop off, there always seems to be two more. Maybe I thought I'd try listening to one of them for once.'

Volchak paused. 'Before I chopped it off?' He smiled and Olaf chuckled. There was a longer pause as they both stared into the small yet fierce fire. 'Fearless? Truth is, I've been pretty much afraid the whole time. It's why I fight.'

'They drafted you?' Olaf seemed genuinely interested.

'Aye. Near fifteen years ago. The Boatman invasion.'

'I remember it. My father was Duke then, rallied the city to build a fleet to fight them off. Turned out they'd landed on the coast and never even got past Brieth.'

'Aye, I was in the South then. Three charges, two pitched battles before they retreated to the ships. What a mess...' Volchak sighed.

'What were you before the draft?' Olaf asked.

Volchak sat a moment. Thinking. Genuinely trying to remember a life before marching, rain, cold tents and colder food. Before drills, the wars, before Smiele and the Breach. It was a long time ago.

'A clerk. Worked for an ore merchant. Used to catalogue the shipments out of Yrfrite, as it happens. Worked in the warm. In the quiet.'

'Quite a way to come since then.'

'Aye. Quite a way.' Volchak wasn't sure why he seemed so willing to talk to the man; he doubted even Harkner knew of his life before the Breachmen. Maybe because he asked? No one else really lived long enough to ask.

'I remember the fleet, seeing it finished in the harbour at Yrfrite. My father said it would save us... then when news arrived that the Boatman had landed. I remember seeing how worried he was.' Olaf said.

'Worried? What for, wasn't he safe?'

'Worried for the King. Or the King's father, as you'd know him. They were close.'

The fire crackled as Olaf stoked it.

'He gathered the Yrfrite Guard, few more than this, and what common folk he could and marched south with them. I wanted to go, but he wouldn't take me - too young. Took my sister though; only seventeen, but she could handle herself better than most.'

Volchak thought of Flea. She was seventeen.

'I don't remember the Yrfrite joining the battle.' And Volchak didn't. He remembered his third charge. It was by far his bloodiest and longest. He scratched the scar on his face. Two full minutes pressed into the Boatmen and their large rectangular shields. Trying to get his stone hammer over the wall to drag one down, clawing at their eyes with his other hand, trying to get a purchase on anything. The Royal Guard had arrived, their spiked-halberds pushing, skewering the shield wall with Volchak still in amongst it. He thought of the light reflecting off the blade as it passed his face, the pain in his ribs as they marched over him. Crawling…

'They never did. As I recall, you and the Royal Guard pulled off a glorious victory, celebrated for months to come.'

Volchak rubbed at his ribs, remembering how he spent the months after the battle.

'What would your father make of all this then?' He waved his hand over men on the beach, over the beach itself, over the entire country.

'It was him that wanted it, before he died.'

Volchak looked at Olaf, puzzled.

'We never rebelled, Volchak. Don't forget each man there is loyal to the King. Just ask one of them.' Olaf paused, jabbed the fire with the poking stick. 'Have you ever met Caleb?'

'Who, the King?' Volchak said. 'No. Not really. Seen him once. At a war council.'

'And tell me, did he speak?'

Volchak thought. He had remembered Smiele and that balding, emotionless man in white. They presented the rebellious actions of Yrfrite and it's leader, the same man Volchak was now sharing a fire with on the beach. The abandonment of the copper mine. The trade blockade. Declared the Duke a traitor.

The King had… just sat back on his throne.

'No.'

'I knew Caleb. We grew up with him. You couldn't pay to shut him up, even before he became King.' His look held Volchak's eye. 'This entire war. Not a word, not even an attempt. Known him for thirty-two years. Every time I had to talk to that idiot councillor, I pleaded for an audience with the King. The dolt wouldn't even consider it as part of our surrender.' Olaf poked angrily again at the fire, then tossed his stick onto the top of it.

'Then why fight? Why not run?' Volchak had asked himself that enough times.

'They sent the army, they were going to take the city. That monster Caldor wanted it for himself. "*A source of unending subjects*" our prisoner had said.'

'Who?'

'There was a Physician in Yrfrite. We captured him, well more saved him before the crowd got to him. He told us of the plan to install Caldor as the authority in the city. Didn't even try and hide it.'

Volchak remembered that march up north. 'You came out to meet us on the field. And lost, if I'm not mistaken.'

'We didn't lose.' But there was no wounded pride in Olaf's voice. 'You fought, and then chased us all round the country, for months. We kept the army there whilst my sister made safe the city.'

Volchak pondered this for a few moments, sipping now at the bottle but barely noticing it was empty. The Duke's lines had collapsed, but every time the bulk of the force had slipped away.

'Hmmm. Maybe Smiele wasn't as clever as he thought.'

'Oh, he's clever. Almost caught up in the West, back against the mountains. We came away with less than half of what we had hoped. Had to make back for the city.'

The sixth charge, Flea and Harkner's first. Volchak felt the scar in his side twinge at the memory.

'I wouldn't leave them - the city I mean. And I can't leave Caleb. He needs our help, I'm sure of it.' Olaf said.

Volchak was quickly sobering at this, head swimming with memories of the battles, of what had happened. Or what he had seen happen. He wasn't really in the position to understand. Smiele pointed him at the enemy and he charged. It was a brutal but simple existence. Olaf watched him for a few minutes as the fire died down.

Olaf stood. 'I don't think Caleb knows, or he knows and can't do anything about it. That's what you're here for.'

'Thought I was just there to get you in the room?'

'You'll be there when I speak to him. Then I expect you'll decide whether you're loyal to your King or your Commander.'

Volchak put his hand on his axe. Thinking. Maybe a chance to do something right.

'You know, I'm glad it might get to do some good after all this time.' Olaf said, nodding his head to the axe. 'Ever since you took it from my younger brother, it has caused my people nothing but hurt.'

Olaf stepped out of the light, and back to his men gathered around the larger fire. Volchak just sat, stared out onto the cold black glass that was the sea before him.

'Damn.' He muttered to himself.

III

Chapter 25

The room looked to Flea exactly how she would have expected it to look, save for one or two insignificant details that didn't seem right to her. As her bleary eyes came to focus, she had flashes of the cart journey, being stretchered, awake, asleep, stone corridors, this room. She tried her hand on her chest, it wouldn't move. She wasn't in her supple leather armour but a scratchy white gown. She tried to turn her head, but couldn't. Her eyes swivelled left and right, gazed round the room. Large bookcases, a mixture of papers and tomes. Amongst them, models of what seemed to be parts of a person. The far corner held a contraption that resembled a wooden helmet but to cover the full face and shoulders. Flexible hoses protruding from it and then ending in all manner of vials and cylinders on tables. Standing above her, a stern-looking woman staring down from a deep orange background. She smiled – no, she sneered. Her red robe bleeding into the orange behind her. The eyes seemed deep, intent, blue, no red, grey. Edge was black. The robe was white now. No, it was shining. No, it was white. It was Stirc. The room was spinning. She tasted metal, copper, or blood. It was wet. Water. She drank. It spilled. A stark tiled floor.

When she opened her eyes again, something out of place, a large armchair with a large man draped across it, one leg over the arm and head tilted back with mouth open. Most likely snoring. Harkner. He was here. She rested her head back from straining against the ropes on to the hard wooden table she appeared to be lying on. Seemed he was far more comfortable than she was. She tried to turn on to her side, a stabbing pain as she rubbed against more ropes. The pain shot through her both front and back and she quickly thought better of it, remaining on her back. Staring up at the chipped alabaster ceiling, she tried to piece together the fragments which kept coming back. Stirc on the ground, then a man in the wardrobe, Volchak. The pain. She shuddered with it, making her back stab at her again. Had he stabbed her? She couldn't believe it, but his face, then pain. She was starving; her throat parched. Someone had been giving her water. Where were they? She tried to raise her head to call for Harkner but found it wouldn't move. Held in place. Her wrists ached. Her eyes were getting heavier again. Fading.

Something else was out of place here, but what? She slept.

***

The rancid water bubbled up around Kaelith's open mouth. He'd had worse mornings, but this was definitely in the list of his top three. He forced himself to roll over onto his back, the pain stabbing through his side as he did so. Staring up at the moss-covered stone ceiling, he felt the water draining down his neck and onto his rags that had once been his dashing white shirt.

The cell looked exactly how he expected it to look. As it had always looked. He pushed himself, still lying face up on the floor, back with his legs, till he was completely out of the puddle that permanently sat in the centre of his cell. His nose and lungs full of the scent of it, or was it the slop bucket, or maybe fear.

'I must remember to make a complaint to the management...' he rasped, throat raw from screaming and skin chaffed from the ropes. 'I'll not be recommending this place, my friend.'

His friend didn't answer. No surprise, it was just a bundle of rags in the far corner, not moving.

He lay for a few more minutes, the pain subsiding where his puncture wound, wounds were. They had kept re-opening him and then healing him, then re-opening, then digging around, then healing. Time and time and time again. Even in his own head, he had grown... bored with it, or he would have had it not hurt so much each time.

He propped himself up onto one elbow painful on the hard stone floor. He rubbed at his eyes with the other hand. They stung as the putrid water got into them.

'Nice to see someone else getting all the attention I 'spose?'

The rags didn't answer.

He flopped back down.

'Must be nice. Bit of company too. I once spent a week in a hold of a small trade vessel, rode it right across to Yrfrite. Didn't talk to a soul. Been chattier ever since...' he trailed off. The bundle was not engaging.

'I've given them all of it, you know. Answered all their little questions, such as they are. Would be mad not to. It's only the main one that asks them, the others just poke and prod. The main one asks...' Kaelith felt his lip quiver. Strange, he thought he had passed the weeping stage a few days ago.

'He wasn't a friend in the end, my friend I told you about. Thought might get me out of this.' He waved his arm across the interior of the foetid cell. 'Shouldn't have brought him up. Thought they might believe that he brought me there. That probably killed him. Shame. Don't get many friends in my line of work.' Kaelith shrugged, pausing mid- way through to wince and lower his shoulders. The woman had seen fit to remove the skin higher on his back this time, before they applied the white paste. He wasn't sure they'd got everything back in the right place.

He pushed himself further back, against the rough stone wall and attempted to sit up against it. The pain stung at him and he thought better of it, instead shuffling down to lie with his back gingerly touching it.

'Bit of a mess, this one. Can't kill me, need me to get to the other side of the mountains. Didn't tell them all, didn't answer all their questions. Would be mad to. Not mad though. Not yet. Might be though. Can't say I enjoy my time out of our room.' He looked over at the friend. No reply. The bundle was piled up in the corner, edges trailing into the puddle on the floor, wicking the stale water up into the fabric.

'A month, I think, maybe less. The first time, they left it four days before they came back. Think it's been six since, maybe five. It's been five. Or maybe six.' He closed his eyes. This certainly hadn't turned out the way he had hoped it would. *Damn Ropers*. He knew the bridge was a bad idea. But it was his best chance to get across the river and back out west. If only they hadn't stirred up that damn prison so much. The dark-skinned woman caught him with a rope round the ankle and his jaw still hurt from where it hit the wooden floor of the bridge.

'I hope they haven't hurt the horse. Hopefully, they feed it.' He sat up straight and alert. Turned to the bundle of rags. 'They'll know it needs feeding won't they?'

No answer. He slumped back down with a pang of sadness. Closed his eyes.

'It's not my favourite. He got my favourite with that axe of his. Head clean off. Wonder what they did with him.

Tricky, that woman, very tricky. Might have just killed him right on the beach. Not sure why? They were talking. Plan. Might be she wins and I get out of here, you know. Got to keep hoping. Could get out. Might be they run out of the paste. That'd be nice. A bit of a break.'

He had opened his eyes whilst talking, and peered across the uneven floor towards the bars, thick, hewn straight from the rock itself. This must have been some kind of underground cavern connected to the big white room. The incessant dripping though - were they near the harbour?

The room with the table. He shuddered, another stab. 'Wouldn't recommend it to my friends.' His golden hair lay brown and stained over his neck now, matted in places, missing in others. Not quite the gentleman mercenary image he was going for. 'Trouble with friends. You don't get many in this line of work. They won't win if they get through them, though. Mountains. I know the path. But someone else can find it. If the Order get to the other side, not sure what they'd do. Maybe another city? What if they name it after me?' He chuckled. He was, after all, the kingdom's greatest explorer, even if no one knew it.

He heard a shift of something heavy, muffled, as if far away.

'They can't be coming back,' he whispered to his friend. 'I've only been in here a day, or two, or more.' How long was it since he was last dragged down?

'No, the answer's no.' No one had spoken. 'I'm not telling them. I saw it, why it was there. It took me years to find it, but I made it through. Made it back. Brought them back. They were mine to take. I was famous. Or I would be. They can't take them.' Kaelith was weeping now. He wiped his face with his hand. More pain.

'I won't tell them the way through.' He sniffed hard, whimpering to himself.

He dragged himself further across the cell, right up to the pile of rags in the corner. He placed his head onto it, tears dropping onto the torn, damp, stinking material.

'I might tell them.' He choked out a sob.

A hand reached out from under the ragged bundle of rags piled in the corner, and gently patted Kaelith's shoulder.

Chapter 26

Stirc fussed over the chemicals, muttering to himself cheerfully as he mixed and measured. The familiar yet sharp smells filled the air. The compounds congealed and the soot gathered on the base of the vases as he heated, cooled, mixed and spun them. His measurements were, of course, precise. He was a Registrar of the Order after all. His brilliance was mandated. Finally, as the fifth vase rapidly cooled in the cold water to his right, he was finished. After only two - *or was it three?* - weeks of diligent work. His only breaks taken to check upon his subject's slow but ultimately positive progress. He had concocted five times the amount as before, hence the additional challenge. Several small improvements as well. Five thick glass bottles were each filled with the viscous white liquid and lined up carefully. He caressed one, as a mother would a small child, adjusting it slightly to form perfect symmetry with its siblings on the white marble table. A slight iridescence was visible in the right light – a pleasant by-product of his improvements.

Stirc looked proudly at them, then looked around the room at the wondrous faces of the many physicians who had gathered to see him finish his demonstration. They wouldn't be permitted to see the entire process, of course. He was not ignorant of their ambition, but the final flourish was theirs to behold. When he stood on this side of the table; he had a slight penchant for the dramatic, snatching away cylinders at the very point of boiling or tipping powders at the very moment they would catalyse.

As the applause faded from the observers, and the room emptied, only his most recent intern remained. Harkner stood a solid two feet above all the others, and even with the largest of the black robes they produced, it hung short at the ankle on him. He didn't glide like the others, he still marched. Certainly couldn't hide him in a crowd, despite the same bald head.

'You enjoyed that.' It wasn't a question.

'Why yes, Intern Harkner, I believe I did.' Stirc was still admiring his cylinders as other assistants, in plain brown garb, cleared away the apparatus.

'She's up and about. Or rather, she is up and wants to be about.'

'Excellent, excellent. It seems Torrak's work is of some merit.'

'Saved her, didn't it?' Harkner's voice was gruff, grating against the serenity of the surroundings.

'In a manner, yes. It breached the wall on what was killing her, although I think I still had rather a part to play in it all myself.' He was grinning as he motioned to the flasks on the table. Harkner shrugged and picked them up in his arms, none too delicately. They made a sharp clink, threatened to smash. Stirc released his breath, and grinned again when he saw they did not.

'She needs all this?'

'No. This is for Caldor. For the war effort.'

'Hmph. What I gather there ain't much war being fought. The Commander got back with his new Breachmen from the prison and they've sat around the taverns and brothels and ain't done a lot since.' The word Stirc would use to describe his tone was… jealous.

'And how, may I ask, have you gathered this? Given that they permit only Registrars to visit the capital beyond the gates?'

'I'm big. Can see over the walls.'

Nonsense, of course. The walls were twenty feet high. Stirc rather suspected an arrangement with some guards at the doors may have been struck. Harkner seemed to thrive amongst the lesser folk here. But Stirc did not need to report the man. Who would he report him to, anyway? Only the High Registrar bore more power, and he would hardly be interested. Caldor spent his time below, with the prisoner in that workshop of his, on the lower levels.

'Registrar Stirc.'

Had he summoned the man by thinking about him? Seems the Brain was aptly named.

'High Registrar.' Stirc bowed his head and turned. 'Yes. Thank you, Harkner, you may deposit those in my chamber as per my instructions. I will revisit our subject presently.'

Stirc turned to Caldor and saw that he watched Harkner, face neutral as it always was, head past the five statues to the back of the lecture theatre and disappear beyond the door.

'How was your demonstration?' Cold. Emotionless.

'Quite exemplary, I am pleased to report.'

'They will soon be able to replicate the compound?'

'Not yet. This took me many years to perfect, and it is as much an art form as a scientific one. Some show promise, and I shall work with them.' Stirc bowed his head. But he wouldn't work too hard, he would be less irreplaceable if he trained others to replace him.

'Join me.'

Even as a Registrar, he knew an order when he heard one.

He followed Caldor past the newest statue, the swirling liquid frozen in marble form emanating from the heart placed at its zenith. It was an intricate as the body, as strong as the bone and as complex as... maybe Stirc was getting ahead of himself. It was as impressive as the other four, that was for certain. They exited the theatre through the same door as Harkner, although Stirc knew he would have taken a right and headed up to the fifth floor rather than continue down the corridor as they had. Harkner was gone by the time they reached the end of the long corridor and started down the wide wooden staircase. Stirc had not been permitted into the workshop, none but the staff of the High Registrar were. He had not sought to challenge this. Now it appeared he was to be brought into the centre of things.

Through the heavy doors were two guardsmen, stood with their gleaming halberds ready. *Unusual.*

Stirc paused in the doorway as the guards opened it for Caldor, aghast at what he saw. Rather than a workshop, a single room, there was an enormous cavern that opened up, rough-hewn into the very ground itself. He double-stepped to catch up to Caldor, as they made their way down one of the many wooden walkways that snaked around the walls, connecting different levels and passages between chambers. From the top of the walkway, he could see down into chambers like an owl in flight, head swivelling as he turned it left and right into each room.

'I wasn't aware....' He said, evidently to the back of Caldor's head. Which did not respond.

'Few are.' Sygan had appeared behind him. Had he followed them in - or had he been waiting inside? Either way, he caused a jump in Stirc's heart that threatened to send him off the edge of the walkway. It seemed quite impractical not to have a handrail to grab.

'I did not see you there.'

'Indeed. The High Registrar's workshop is in the site that once housed the Order's mining operations' His high-pitched voice cut through the thrum of activity below.

'Mining operations?'

'Yes, inactive for several hundred years. The Order built the monastery after the palace, of course, and there was a reason this site was chosen.' Stirc did not know this. Which surprised him, as he had been here thirty years.

'Follow.' Caldor's voice was getting fainter. Stirc had stopped completely to talk to Sygan, and now had to rush again to catch up. It seemed most of the work here was what Stirc was used to. He saw blocks, ropes, the usual medical apparatus. But then, in the next cavern he saw a smelter, a kiln - equipment that seemed more at home in the palace armoury than here. Most were decommissioned, cracked, dust covered or simply dumping grounds for unused equipment. But, as he continued to keep pace with the High Registrar, it was obvious that there were a number that appeared lit. Stirc had seen an anvil, an actual, fully metal anvil - in one of the workshops. Black-robed apprentices milling around it silhouetted against the firelight of what may have been an active forge.

'High Registrar?' Stirc called at the back of the thick bald head, as it ploughed on through the corridors. Stirc was quite confident now he could not find his way back. Maybe that was the plan. He would pay more attention on the walk back.

They came to a small chamber, with what appeared to be a single way in or out. Caldor spun on his heel and faced

Stirc, who almost didn't quite stop in time so that he remained uncomfortably close, not that Caldor seemed to notice.

'Your compound has had unintended side-effects. The subject has become incoherent, and unreliable during questioning. You are to review the subject, and adjust your formula accordingly.'

Stirc stood dumbly for a moment. Why couldn't this be conducted in the sterile environment of the lecture theatre above?

'Side-effects? Who is the subject?'

'The prisoner you retrieved,' Caldor said.

Stirc thought Kaelith was long dead at this point.

'I was not aware of its use on the man… subject. Had he not recovered from my last application?' Stirc asked.

'He did. Seven further applications since.'

Stirc tilted his head slightly. He had delivered a vial of his compound at the High Registrar's request but he was confident that they were trying to deconstruct it and determine how to reproduce it. Seems he had, in fact, been using it. Seven times, though… that meant seven wounds opened then healed. He swallowed; a cough threatened to escape from his throat. He looked into the cell for the man.

Kaelith lay sprawled against one of the damp stone walls, his clothes in tatters and the colour of deep brown ichor that seemed to surround him. He lay half in the dirty pool on the floor. His hair was a single matted clump plastered down one side of his face, obscuring most of it. Had it not been for his chest rising and falling, Stirc would have thought him dead. Filth and grime caked his bare legs and feet, leather boots gone and trousers tattered to well above the knee. His shirt was little more than a shredded sash, and on his body even at this distance, Stirc could see the angry red flesh of several large scars. No doubt the result of the use of his compound.

'What side effects?' Stirc asked. *Beyond transforming him into what seemed little better than a breathing corpse?* he refrained from adding.

'His information has become erratic.'

'Well that maybe a result of the interrogation rather than...'

Caldor's face was still, no smile or sneer. But the way he glared at Stirc seemed to exude a fury that Stirc had not witnessed before. It seemed Caldor considered this Stirc's problem to fix.

'His information is of paramount importance to the Order.'

Sygan had taken a step back, he faded into the half shadow of the doorway. The room became very close, Stirc was suddenly aware of the weight of the ground above him.

'I... shall do as instructed. I shall examine him. Bring him to..-'

'Here.'

Silence for a moment. Stirc stepped back and then nodded slightly, bowing as if falling to his knees in slow motion but stopping before he reached the ground.

'I shall remain with the Registrar to ensure he does not lose his way.' Sygan bowed even lower as Caldor strode back through the door past them both, acknowledging neither.

'Well then.' Stirc stepped up to the wooden door to the cell and pulled back the mechanism that held it shut. He stepped inside and closed it, Sygan had not moved from the doorway to the cavern.

When Stirc knelt beside the man and inspected, he had to actively try not to think of the acrid smell that filled his nostrils or the disgusting grunge that was gathered around his knees. At first Kaelith did not move, the man just stared upwards with no hint of recognition or even awareness. Stirc watched the man blink, once, twice, shuddering slightly, which sent little ripples through the brown pool that lie around his filthy legs. For a moment Stirc saw the two blue eyes focus on him.

'Stirc…' the slightest rasp.

A hand shot up and grabbed Stirc's shoulder and pulled him close. Stirc squawked in surprise and prepared himself for the headbutt, remembering the sting in his nose and the blood down his robe. This one would be less easy to disguise.

Instead - Kaelith pulled him close to his mouth, and whispered. As he did, Stirc's eyes flashed to the bundle of rags in the corner, and widened.

***

'What happened to you?' Harkner was lazing over the chair in Torrak's room, one leg resting up over the arm of it. Torrak, it appeared, was not there. That was lucky. Stirc did not speak. He strode into the room towards the wooden block, leaving a brown stain across the white tiled floor as he did so, and knocked one rope that hung unused on its side.

'How are you, my dear?'

Flea stirred, blinking up at him.

'Better, Mr. Stirc.' There was more strength in her voice than the previous day. It seemed Torrak's vapour therapy was proving more effective than Stirc had expected, although progress had still taken time. He glanced across at the wooden helmet in the corner, its tubes sticking out at odd angles into the various cylinders on the floor. Crude but effective way to get the gases into the lungs.

'Good, good.' Stirc pried open the gap in the cotton tabard he had provided her, with one of his probes. He inspected the site where the spear end had emerged. Noticeably improved. Only a faint redness and barely any swelling. She didn't move.

'And you have been walking, Harkner tells me?'

'Aye. Just a little bit, just around.' Her eyes circled the room.

'Excellent.'

'What will happen to us?' *Us,* that stung Stirc. His eyes glanced up to Harkner, who had his eyes closed, but couldn't have been asleep, not at the angle he was sitting.

'I will deliver you back to the Commander, healed. That was the arrangement.'

She smiled, nodding, but her face sunk slightly.

'Unless you would rather remain?' It was not meant to sound condescending. Stirc had meant it. She could stay and take an apprenticeship here. Learn the wonders of anatomy, devise her own experiments. Become a renowned and respected Physician, maybe even a Registrar, one day, with her own statue next to his.

But he had said none of that, and so Harkner answered for her.

'We will go back. Not staying here to be poked and prodded to death.'

Stirc looked at Flea. She nodded thoughtfully, the slightest shrug in her shoulders.

'Then, a few more days and you will be well enough, my dear. But there is something I need you to take with you to the Commander. A message.'

Harkner opened his eyes and sat up in his chair.

'Aye?'

Stirc looked at him, then to Flea. He hesitated – this was an awful risk he was about to take.

Chapter 27

'Drag it down!'

Volchak's shout was angry, frustrated and loud. Loud enough to be heard over the clash of the Breachmen against the solid shield wall. The men crashed again into the shield wall, jabbing with their antler blades, thrusting with their spears and swinging with their hammers. They prodded and probed the wall, seeking a weakness in the enemy to embed their weapons in. The shields splintered, and the line flexed back, but the enemy was mostly unmoved.

'Disengage!'

The men had fallen back about ten paces, then stood in a solid line, brandishing their wide variety of weapons.

Not a single enemy casualty – after all, the enemy were large logs dug deep into the ground with shields mounted to the front of them. Very hard to kill. They were spaced just under a shield-width apart, so their large wooden shields overlapped to form a solid wall. Volchak looked at it, unbroken, and sighed, rubbing his eyes.

'You aren't there to kill them! Stop fighting them and try to breach them!' He paced back and forth in front of them, gesticulating at the line of logs behind him, poised as if at any moment he'd charge them himself.

'You. Step forward.'

A short man with thick arms and a closely shaved round head stood forward, brandishing a plain stone axe.

'Sir.'

Volchak spat to his side and walked right up to the man's face. He was about the same height and met his eyes, close enough to embrace him. Instead, he seized the man's stone axe and pushed it against his chest, hard, thumping against the leather breastplate.

'Get to the other side of that wall,' Volchak was quieter now. Most could still hear him, but his voice was vicious and sharp.

The man moved to turn to the side towards the log wall but was held fast, as Volchak gripped the axe and didn't move.

'Sir... I?'

'Get to the other side now!' Volchak kicked out. The man's leg buckled from under the him and he dropped to one knee as Volchak snatched the axe from his hands. Volchak flung it with both hands in an overhead throw, which sent it flying across the training ground well above the log wall. It bounced along in the dirt before coming to a stop.

The man kneeled for a moment, as if ready to rise and tackle Volchak. He then seemed to check himself and sprinted across the gap between the line and the shield wall. He barrelled into it at full pelt, leaning into the charge with one of his thick shoulders. He caught the spot between two shields, and one broke under his weight as he careened through in between two of the logs. As he landed face first onto the floor behind it was clear that he had achieved his goal. Volchak could see the man laying down on the ground through the newly created gap in the row of shields. There was a now a breach.

Volchak strode over towards the edge of the wide shield wall, walking around it and past the man who was now sitting upright in the dirt. Volchak walked to where the axe had landed and picked it up. It was heavier than his. He knelt and seized it up, back aching slightly as he did. When he returned to the man, he held out a hand. With a nod, the man took it and stood. Volchak handed him back his axe.

'Well done. Breachman. Return to the line.'

The Breachman hesitated just a moment as he took the axe in his hand, looking from it to Volchak. He then turned and walked back towards the line.

Volchak sighed in relief. His other hand loosened on his own axe handle. It wouldn't be needed on this one.

**

'See, that's ... the problem ...' Volchak slurred ever so slightly as he spoke over the top of his ale, motioning with the half-filled flagon towards Olaf across from him. The man had drunk about the same, but apparently it didn't have half the effect. The Duke didn't drink to forget.

'What problem?'

'Your man. Should have swung. Should have pushed back...' He belched, breathing in as if to stifle it and simply making it worse. 'Should have tried to kill me, even. They always try. It's all too clean, they'll notice.' Volchak waved his arm in the general direction of the door, signalling somewhere as to whom "they" were.

'So, your point is they are too disciplined?' Olaf was unsure.

'Aye. Exactly. They are going to notice, eventually. Not one. Not one has tried it yet, in here…' Same arm, waving around the well-lit tavern. Spilling some contents of his flagon onto the clean table and spilling onto the carpeted floor beneath it. '… or out there.'

Olaf sat back in his chair, staring at his own flagon whilst tilting it in one hand.

'You may have a point. Tamryn has equipped them well, so to speak, but these are our best men.'

'Don't usually get the best. Supposed to be the worst.' Volchak finished his drink.

'And you, then?'

'Ha! Best of the worst!' He laughed as he slammed the flagon down. The barman quickly came and retrieved it. Volchak ignored the man's slight huff as he wiped the table and stormed back to the bar. Most of the cliental seemed to ignore the pair of them. Save for a few sideways glances, and the occasional eye-roll when they thought they wouldn't be seen.

'Indeed. I see your point though. We have had several spectators recently at our most recent training sessions, several physician's assistants if I am not mistaken.'

'Damned Order. And they say I am a violent man. I don't kill them what aren't trying to kill me, you know. Certainly don't butcher them. Don't torture them…' Volchak trailed off. A moment passed, and he waved his hand. Apparently, this was signalling for another drink.

'Before we met, I heard a tale… that you were attacked by twelve men on the road to Brieth?'

'Seven. And wasn't just me. Harkner and Flea stood with me. They killed three, more or less.'

'And the other four?'

'Never killed someone what didn't try to kill me first.' Volchak repeated, as another jug was put in front of him. The rotund barman backed away quickly.

'I heard a farmer died?'

'A boy. How did you hear?'

'Tammy has had eyes on you for months. Ever since Fedal wouldn't help.'

'Tammy, eh?'

'I wouldn't tell her I told you. Used to be a sweet child.' Olaf grinned.

Volchak was staring ahead. He hadn't heard.

'A boy. Maybe sixteen. Drafted him the day before. Tried to put him out of the way, said I'd keep him safe. Lied. Probably bought me a few moments though. Buried him. All I could do.'

'Why do you do it?' Olaf asked. 'The draft? Army just shows up in villages, in the districts of the capital, in my city. Demands twenty-five years. They might as well just kill them there, that's their whole life.' Olaf was no longer grinning. 'Any surprise - the people are angry? You've taken their sons and daughters.'

Volchak sighed.

'Always been a draft. My first draft was the one they picked me at. Straight from my parent's house right here, in the mining district. I was smart. Good boy. Good with numbers, good with planning. I was too afraid to do anything else and went with them. Smiele was a captain then, small patrol, chose me himself.' He took a long draw on the flagon. Olaf had not asked for another. 'Cried for a few days. They beat that out of me soon enough. But I saw people resist. Saw Smiele cut down a father in a shop doorway. Man had only one arm, kept saying he'd paid the price. He was lucky in the end. I remember Smiele taking the boy and tossing him out into the street. He tried to run. Ropers got him. The screams as they dragged him towards the monastery.' Volchak had grown quieter. Over the activity in the tavern, he noticed Olaf had leaned forward.

'You know what the physicians do?' Olaf asked.

'Aye. Every campaign they sent some with us, one or two. They hauled that wooden rope contraption up and down the country. When we fought on the Boatmen on the coast… When we were chasing you around. I saw them do wondrous things to wounded men; patch them up, stop them dying. Even saw one heal your man Kaelith. He had no business surviving that.'

'He's far less my man than you think. Tamryn has him employed, but I don't think loyally. Too afraid to give away the secret of his horses and where he gets them.'

'For someone who talks so much, he rarely says a lot.' Volchak took another gulp of his ale. 'But I saw the other side, too. The experimenting. Saw men go in whole and come out in pieces. Heard the screams. That was the choice. Bring men for the draft, or send them to the monastery. Or join them myself?' Volchak frowned.

'Did you ever think of running?' Olaf looked at him, his eyes piercing through the haze of ale. Volchak just stared back, sullen.

'Every time. But where? Two cities. Seven villages. It's a small world. Maybe I could hide in the mountains. Maybe, but doubt I'd survive long. And in the flatlands? Ropers would find me eventually. Breachman was my way to run. Ten years back, and all I had to do was not die.'

'Gone well so far for you.' Olaf sat back and smiled. 'Best of the worst.' He motioned for another drink.

Volchak leaned back in his chair, the tension lifted from the table, the sound seemed to penetrate their bubble again and the light of the tavern seemed brighter.

Several minutes passed, Volchak finished his next drink and Olaf started his.

'What happened to Harkner and …?' Olaf asked

'Flea.' Volchak smiled at the thought of them. 'Still alive … I hope. Sent them with … a friend. They've been with me for a year now. He's tough. Volunteer, don't get many of those. You'd like him. She deserves better, I'll be happy if I can keep her alive and out of all this.' He waved around with his hand again. 'If I can.'

Olaf nodded.

'They ever try then? Take a swing? To kill you?'

'Ha. No. Think they are both a little scared of me. Seen too many scraps. Or maybe they are just too clever to start a fight they weren't forced to?'

Olaf looked around. Two physicians' assistants sat near the door. Neither one had touched the flagons in front of them.

'Volchak?'

'Aye?'

'This place is delightful. Spotless.'

Volchak looked at him, puzzled, tilting his head and looking around at the surroundings. This was certainly one of the nicer taverns in the merchant quarter. The floors had thick carpets and the windows were clean glass with heavy curtains. The ale was crisp and clean, and expensive. Maybe he came here to make them feel uncomfortable. They couldn't argue with a grizzled old warrior even if they didn't want him breaking the veneer of their very fine establishment. And besides, who would they call on to remove the Commander of the Breachmen anyway? A member of the High Commanders' personal staff surely belonged in a place like this. Just a shame he was a low-born brawler. But he didn't think that's what Olaf meant.

'Ey?' Volchak said, looking up at his companion.

Olaf sprang to his feet and up-ended the table in one fluid motion. The two flagons went flying across the room, erupting in a cloud of ale as they spun. A great roar emitting from him as he side swiped Volchak hard from his chair with the back of his gloved hand. Volchak's limp body rolled across the carpet, gathering it up into large folds as he skidded to a stop against it. He lay on the ground, stunned.

'That'll teach yah to shout at me, yah scum!' Olaf shouted as he turned and stormed out of the tavern, knocking against the table where the two black-robed men sat as he did so, spilling ale from both their full flagons.

Volchak shook the stars from his head as he lay in the folds of the carpet, and grinned slightly, face already stinging.

'Smart man,' he said and raised his arm, signalling for another drink.

Chapter 28

Flea was a ghost. Gliding from corridor to corridor, fading into dark corners or peering through dusty windows, gone before anyone saw the shape of her. Since her first treatment in the strange contraption that woman Torrak had built, she was far clearer of mind, the pain had sapped away from her closed wounds and she was steadier on her feet. By the second week of daily treatments, she had completely recovered, but still feigned weakness. She learned in the mine that if folk think you can't do a thing, they rarely look too hard at whether you do it. Now, she was doing a thing.

She had quickly started to understand the rules of her new prison. By simply listening to the men and women as they went about their days, or chatted to each other when they thought no one would hear, she'd learnt far more than they would have wanted known. The white robes had complete control. They could seize any research or take over a chamber, if they determined in was in their interest to do so. There were five of them, Stirc was one now. She hadn't seen the leader yet, the man they called Brain. His workshop was hidden and off limits. The red ones did their own thing but tried not to get caught doing it. Stirc was the only physician she'd known and it was obvious most did not share his caring attitude towards their subjects. Torrak was okay. But she was being told what to do, so Flea figured she didn't have a choice. The black robes did what they were told, and they were the key to this place functioning. They buzzed around this hive of activity, carrying, recording or passing messages.

They had quarters on the sixth floor but no blocks of their own, rooms filled with scrolls and books and notes. She'd found a black robe for herself in the wardrobe in Torrak's room in the first few days, old and slightly tatty, but the overall effect was enough. She left it there, but retrieved it whenever she wanted to go a place. Harkner had a black robe too, too short for him, but he didn't do much, mostly lazed about the room she slept in. She had to wait for him to leave with Stirc, or sometimes he went off alone, before she would be up and about. He was always caring, making sure he let her know he'd be back and even roughly when. He'd been gone a lot more lately. That's why she didn't tell him about the little reconnaissance missions - he'd worry, or worse, tell Stirc. Then, she'd be back on the ropes. She'd seen plenty of subjects tied to a wooden block like the one she slept on. She assumed that's why the security was so lax about movement within the place. In fact, everyone she had seen - who wasn't in the Order - was tied to a block, which was both reassuring and unsettling. Being caught was not a pleasant prospect – but she wanted to learn more.

The fifth floor was all wounds and healing. The subjects here were in various states of near death, or some just on the wrong side of it. Punctures, cuts, slices, amputations. Most of the physicians here worked with chemicals like Stirc had. She had seen them mixing, boiling, stirring, or applying them to their subjects. Sometimes when she snuck into unoccupied rooms, the bottles were all neatly lined up ready for the next 'subject'. *Person.* Flea had heard one physician belittling Stirc, insulting his 'compound', and recounting the failures of the Head Registrar for appointing him. She was sad, Stirc's bottles of white stuff were very important to him. He was her friend, and she didn't like this other man's evil yellowing teeth and bony arms. She'd waited for the nasty man to leave and she had snuck into his unlocked room. Upon seeing the five chemicals neatly arranged on the side table, she had quickly taken a glass pipette from his shelf and mixed several of them with one another. On the shelf behind was a clear liquid that smelt acrid when she removed the lid. She took that too and dripped some more into each of the five. Satisfied her mischief was done, she stole back out of the room, winking at the man that was roped down onto the table. He had watched the whole thing and never made a squeak. Being dead tends to keep folk quiet.

Not all of her wandering had been so jovial. The third floor had the word BEDLAM carved the length of the corridor in dark burgundy letters. There were distinctly fewer black-robed people flitting around here. However, the screaming from several of the rooms had piqued her curiosity, and she had peered inside one. A woman, roped to a block on her back, appeared to have a large glass dome over the lower half of her body that was filled with dozens of wriggling spiders. They fell over each other and scuttling over her body as they tried to escape up the sides of the glass. The woman's head was thrashing against the rope and blood seeped down the side of the block where she had torn her skin against it. Flea had retreated in horror and hadn't been back to the third floor since.

She found the Registrar's room on the second floor on her third visit there, and upon peering inside the glass window she saw his white robe hung on the wall. The man himself, topless, muscular and at least as big as Harkner, was straining against a victim who seemed, to Flea's eyes, completely healthy. The big Registrar was forcing his prisoner back onto a strange wooden block. It stood upright with a large L cut out of it, making it more of a large seat. At first glance, it didn't appear to have any means by which to hold the prisoner, until Flea moved and saw thin metal wires instead of ropes across key places. As the weight of the Registrar's bulk held down the healthy one, his large hands seized one of the metal ropes and wrapped it around the man's head, tight against his jaw. He wound a second wire around the neck and a third the torso. Flea wanted to continue to watch, but a neighbouring door opened noisily and she quickly feigned an important errand, She strode purposefully towards the opposite end of the corridor before marching down the steps there. Strangely these stairs were far longer than she expected and the door at the bottom spat her out in front of two armed Guardsmen, not Royal Guard as they both had red cord hanging from their metal plate mail like the Ropers wore, but still with halberds. One turned towards her as she made her way through the unguarded door to her right in one fluid motion, as if this were her route all along.

The large circular room she stood in was a stark bright-white, against the relatively dim interior of the rooms above it. There were large windows above her - *must have been above the shallow staircase she had walked down* - and five gigantic statues stood between here and the other side of the room. She had seen the symbols on the back of four of them before, in the Order temple in Brieth. The large round room, however, was not empty. She froze in step as she looked ahead and saw a large gathering of both physicians and interns gathered on the far side of the large marble table. But most worryingly, on her size of the stable was a white-robed figure she knew, Stirc.

Within a moment, she went to turn to head back through the door behind her. She was confident the guards wouldn't recognise her, might not even realise it was the same black-robed figure going back in. At that moment, the door she had come from opened again and a warm breeze hit her face. She saw a white robed man stride past her with no acknowledgement at all of her presence. He was stocky, muscular, a thick bald head on a thick bald neck and an emotionless look on his face as he walked forward towards the group. For a moment she looked at the man and could only think how much he reminded her of the Commander, but then she quickly fell into step behind him. She figured those men of high-rank who were used to being followed by their subordinates wouldn't notice or care when one did. She was right. When he reached the table, Flea disengaged and melted into the larger crowd. One black robe stood almost two feet above the rest, and she was wary to stay both out of sight of it, and of Stirc who was presenting.

The glee on Stirc's face was self-evident. He moved with a certain grace and poise, as if dancing with his chemicals. A slight bit of smoke rising here, a flask dashed away from overflowing there. It was clear he was putting a bit of flourish into his display but the audience was completely enthralled, except that single tall head which occasionally seemed to look around the room - Harkner. And the man in white, he just stared blankly as if nothing was happening. Flea caught herself smiling at Stirc and his enthusiasm. He had saved her life, of that she was fully aware, but the more she had learnt about this place, it seemed he had more compassion in him than anyone here. In her weeks of stealing around the physicians and their subjects, she had heard none of the others ever ask if their subject was okay, nor refer to them as a person at all.

The presentation did not have a final crescendo, no large puff of smoke for a grand finish or elaborate spin of a flask. *Shame.* But as the white compound she had seen locked in his drawer formed in the fifth of the cylinders, the audience collectively started to applaud and then filter away. Flea was at the front of the charge, knowing she had to beat both Torrak and Harkner back to the room. She was quick though, known for it, as she darted up the stairs.

Chapter 29

Volchak scratched his face, then tugged at his neck, pulling at the tight collar of the uniform he had been given to wear. The high-necked wool irritated and threatened to choke him, as he walked down the marble corridor. His clean leather boots squeaked against the polished floor. He was flanked by Olaf, who appeared far more comfortable in his borrowed uniform than Volchak did. *Damn him.*

The two walked down the opulent corridor with several Royal Guards behind them, their halberds tilted back so as not to knock against the chandeliers that lined the ceiling. Each of the portraits of the kings on either side, dour on their thrones, resplendent in their military outfits or glorious atop their castle walls, judged the pair as they did so. Being unarmed always left Volchak with a sense of unease. He had the small antler blade he had tied under his belt but that was hardly much use against a halberd. Even in the supposed safest place in the kingdom he missed the familiar weight of his axe. They had been summoned by a Royal Guard whilst training two days prior and were to attend a war council to be held in the presence of the King, in the royal throne room. Volchak had attended a war council twice before, so he knew more or less what to expect. A lot of ceremony, a lot of talking from those far more important than himself, then eventually a lot of walking, a lot of waiting and then a lot of bloodshed – mostly his.

They had been met at the curtain wall by one of the royal attendants. The man's blue doublet was impeccably clean and impeccably fitted. He had taken them into the side entrance of the castle to deposit their weapons and change. Volchak scoffed at the outfit they provided him, but knew it was hardly his choice to make. The heavy wool was too hot for the summer and it restricted his movement without providing any of the protection he was used to. *Impractical.*

The throne room was on one of the upper floors, with a large balcony overlooking the courtyard they had crossed. As they entered through the heavy doors, which had actual ironwork re-enforcing them on both sides, he was still taken back at the sheer wealth of it all. A vast hall, a long dark wooden table in the centre, on what seemed to be the most luscious carpet he had ever walked on. The red velvet seemed to burn in the light as it sank under his feet. The walls were draped with hangings, banners and heraldry symbols, vibrant and shining. Around the room, at strategic spots, were pairs of halberd-wielding Royal Guards, in their full plate mail armour. Reflections from the large windows bounced off them as Volchak walked past. He wasn't sure at first whether there were men even inside them with how still they were, but then the two escorts had taken up their own positions in the room, and he suspected there were.

The throne sat at the far end of the long table, maybe twenty-five paces away. It was set back on a high dais, away from the floor. Wouldn't be able to reach the table from there, although Volchak supposed there wasn't any food or wine on it. Volchak and Olaf bowed low upon arrival in the room, Volchak's back aching and neck stabbing on the left side, causing a slight wobble in his bow. The King sat sternly, unmoving, almost shrouded in shadow on the high throne at the far end and didn't acknowledge them. The light from the windows behind the throne was largely blocked by the crimson Order standard on one side and the blue royal banner on the other. Volchak glanced sideways at Olaf as his companion looked up at the King, as if he was expecting him to recognise him instantly and come down from his high throne. He didn't. *More's the better,* thought Volchak. If the rest of the crowd realised the rebel Duke Olaf was in their midst, and that he'd brought the man here, then likely he'd get to see how good an antler blade would be against a full metal halberd, or eight.

They were seated near one corner of the table. Maybe it wasn't deliberate, but they certainly felt like the least important seats, far from the King and far from the map spread out across the other half. No matter, he had planned on saying as little as possible anyway.

Volchak looked around at the other men, most of whom he knew, and most with far larger entourages either seated or standing in the cavernous space behind.

Smiele sat far to Volchak's left, at the other end of the table nearest the dais, two of his lieutenants joining him. He remained in his lavish steel chest plate and his sword was rested on the table next to him - seemed he was too important to disarm. His two lieutenants, sat farther down the table were equally adorned, though with a little less grand inlay on their armour. Opposite sat three of the registrars from the Order. The thick-set one opposite Smiele with a blank look on his face, eyes fixed forward. The skittish man that Volchak remembered having been appointed onto their council at the start of the war was glancing around and smiling, teeth chattering despite the heat of the room. Volchak had been introduced to the man, but couldn't remember his name. He knew he took the position of Bedlam, so he just thought of the man as that. Seemed to suit him. The third made Volchak raise an eyebrow though. He recognised the gaunt face and bald head as soon as Stirc sat down. He caught his eye, and Stirc nodded ever so slightly, before resuming staring at the edge of the table in front of him with intent. He obviously meant to share Volchak's tactic of letting this all happen without his participation.

There were two empty seats before Major Fedal sat, a single captain alongside him, both their battle dress uniform, neatly washed and pressed. More practical than the blue garb that Volchak wore and clearly less restrictive. Like Volchak however, neither of the men carried any weapons. Fedal had acknowledged Volchak as he sat down, and he had bowed his head back. Opposite him, and closest to Volchak and Olaf, was Commander Daveron. He lazed in his chair, head on its high back chatting as if to the ceiling rather than to the two women on either side of him. Both of them were fierce-looking. Volchak recognised them from the prison. The sisters, or maybe twins. Both were adorned with thick ropes, black and red, wrapped around their bodies and hanging from their belts. Their toned, sharply-featured bodies still wore their armour, and their boots had distinct mud stains on them. Daveron himself had donned full chain-mail, including a coif. It clung heavy to him and made him sweat, but caught the light and sparkled as he moved his arms. He looked almost as radiant as Smiele.

'Commanders, esteemed colleagues of the Hermetic Order,' said the small, black-robed man, as he stood in front of the dais at the head of the table. 'His Illustrious Majesty King Caleb Domenici II, Protector and Ruler of Tydrian, has bid me to welcome you to his war council. I shall act as chair for this gathering of his army and advisors.'

Volchak stole a glance to his right at Olaf, who seemed strained, trying to catch the eye of the King, high above them. As if showing his face would spark the monarch into action. Volchak hadn't promised him he would be able to get them an audience with the King, just that he could get them in this room. The rest was up to Olaf. Volchak glanced over Fedal who looked back. Neither man gestured but the look spoke enough between them, Fedal's eyes had gone wide when he spotted Olaf.

'Following his successful campaign on the flatlands, High Commander Smiele has returned to replenish his forces and update us on his battle plan.' The small man bowed and stepped back, inviting Smiele to stand.

'Four successful engagements saw us drive the majority of the rebel forces back into the West.' He was confident, commanding and spoke with unchallenged authority. Volchak didn't feel it was the right moment to ask just how successful that last engagement was. He remembered it differently, it seemed.

'Ha! Send off the blighters!' Daveron chipped in with a thump on the table. No one appeared to notice.

'We are confident that the Duke has been recruiting,' Smiele continued, 'but that his numbers have now stagnated at around a thousand men. The majority are poorly-equipped militia, farmers and citizens of Yrfrite. We have waited whilst we studied their movements and readied our forces, and we are confident that we now have the opportunity to end both their hold on the city, and decimate his army itself. Forcing a rout and the surrender of the treacherous leadership.'

Volchak saw Olaf looked away from the King to Smiele. Apparently, this was news to him also. Unwelcome news. Volchak turned back and saw the woman next to him had her hand on her belt. He tensed up slightly, feeling the trail of sweat pass over the scar on his face.

'We shall send our force north, along the river road. There has been a small uprising in the village of Brieth. An Order temple has been desecrated and several people were murdered there. No sign of the physicians who manned it, no doubt murdered by the rebels.'

'That village is awfully close to the capital to be rebelling,' Daveron remarked, to no one in particular. *It was awfully close to his prison, more like*, Volchak thought.

'They shall be crushed and the conspirators will be surrendered to the custody of your care, Commander Daveron.' Smiele nodded to the man, respectfully. 'They will learn that rebelling against his Majesty and his Order will only result in one thing.'

Stirc looked up then to Volchak. He shook his head ever so slightly.

'I'm sure I can find somewhere to accommodate them.' Daveron smiled back menacingly.

The room was unbearably hot now.

'This will also serve as bait for the rebel army, who will soon hear we are mobilised against them and will have to come to intercept us, lest we reach their city first. We shall aim to engage them here.' One of the lieutenants revealed a long wooden rod and he indicated the hills to the South of Yrfrite in a single, clearly well-rehearsed, movement. 'Meanwhile, our second force will dispatch and move cross-country to the Western Road to shadow their movements and attack from the rear.' The rod pointed to a longer path. 'Thus - cutting off any escape and ensuring their destruction. We shall prevent them from ever reaching their own walls.'

'No such second force exists?' Fedal protested. 'And if it did, how would we stop the Yrfrite spies from discovering it and warning the rebels?'

'Ah, both excellent questions, Commander Fedal.' The small black-robed man stepped forward again. Apparently, he was part of this presentation as well. Smiele remained standing silently, a slight smirk on his face.

'To answer your first question. I would invite my compatriots to step on to the balcony to my left and look to the courtyard.' He motioned with his black robed arm.

Volchak and Olaf stood, warily, and walked to the side of the room, along with Fedal, Stirc, and Daveron. They had all heard, yet ignored, the steady thumping coming from the city outside. They all stood in the portal to the wide balcony and looked over the side. Volchak felt Olaf tense up as they both saw it.

Below, stood at least two hundred and fifty men, heavily armoured with chain-mail hauberks, plate mail gauntlets, and helmets. They each carried a large square shield and long steel sword hoisted over their shoulders. The light shone and bounced and danced from the sheer volume and variety of metal in the palace grounds. These were clearly not Royal Guard, clearly not an infantry division either. This was something else entirely.

The group on the balcony stared for what seemed like several minutes. Then, collectively, they turned as the white-robed, stocky man stood and spoke.

'The Order Guard.' His deep voice boomed around the throne room. Flat, but loud.

Volchak looked back. When he focussed, he could see their chain-mail was tied with red cord, a large red rope hung from the two banners on either end of the formation and the Order standard was visible on each. This unit would be more mobile, more defensively viable, and more manoeuvrable than the Royal Guard. This would make them hard to contend with once a shield wall had fallen, and a melee ensued. And there were just so damned many of them. If Smiele had half the metal in the kingdom before, this was clearly the other half.

Volchak walked back to the table, leant a hand as if to steady himself on it, and spoke directly to Smiele.

'That force far outweighs anything the Duke could muster. Why not march the entire army to meet him and demand surrender?'

'Commander Volchak,' Smiele spoke as if he had just seen him and not even known he was there. 'We have no intention of sending these traitors back to their homes, to fulminate over their loss and cause trouble. We expect to crush every single last one of them.'

Before Volchak had time to reply, Fedal was standing next to him.

'How did you get this much metal to equip them? Why haven't we used this for the infantry before now? My men fought with wood and stone.' He thumped the table, hard. Behind them, Daveron, the two Ropers and Olaf re-entered the room. Only Stirc stayed on the balcony. Seemed he was reluctant to return at all, gripping the edge of the parapet.

'The Order provided,' the small black robed man said. 'And in return the King has agreed to grant them autonomy over the city of Yrfrite. They are to be our glorious allies to the North, who will provide us with protection in any and all our hours of need.'

Olaf froze, half way back to his seat.

Volchak played that back in his head. The King had agreed to surrender the second city of the Kingdom of Tydrian to the Hermetic Order.

'Sir, are you-?' Fedal was cut off.

'What's more, Commander.' The black-robed man spoke directly to him. 'In answer to your second question, regarding how we stop the rebels from uncovering this plan?

Well Commander, Daveron can provide us some assistance in that area.'

'So I can! I was made aware of a series of unfortunate information leaks and have recently concluded my investigation.' Daveron said.

Two hands clamped down on Fedal's shoulders. He tried to turn to face them, but they held firm and pushed him down onto the table in front of him. Red rope wound round his wrists. His aide made a dash for the door only to be stopped by the guardsman who struck him with one gloved hand, knocking the man onto the floor as one of the Ropers moved to tie him up as well.

'Commander Fedal. You have been found guilty of conspiring with our enemies to undermine the King's rule. We have sworn testimony of you meeting with their leader and his commanders with a view to share our plans. I hereby release you to the custody of the Order, there to serve your punishment.' Smiele seemed first immensely proud of himself, then immensely annoyed as he watched the man turn and shout towards the King frantically.

'Your Majesty, they don't want a war, they only want to..-' Daveron cut Fedal off with a punch to his stomach.

The King remained seated; his head turned toward Fedal with one slow movement.

'Deliver him to my workshop.' The Head Registrar said, coldly.

'Well, err...' Stirc had emerged from the balcony to an altogether different scene from when he left. They muscled Fedal out the door past him, the aide behind.

'He does not get the choice of the Breachmen?' Volchak probed, gently as he could.

'Ah, the Breachmen. That brings me to our next order of business, Commander Volchak.' As Smiele spoke, Volchak could almost feel the rope slipping around his own wrists. He moved one hand discreetly behind him to where the handle of the small antler blade was hidden.

'We find the barbaric and uncivilised form of warfare that the Breachmen undertake to be wholly unnecessary with the advent of the Order Guard. You will remain in the capital, in a ceremonial role, and we will no longer require criminals and murderers to fill your ranks.'

And with that, Volchak was free. Smiele had saved him. No more fighting, no more blood, no more breaching. He was wholly obsolete and would live the remainder of his short term in peace here in the capital. His legs wobbled and he placed both hands on the table to steady himself. He felt his stomach lurch and wondered for a moment if he might pitch forward onto the table, not unlike Fedal just had.

'Naturally,' The black-robed man added, 'the reduction in draft terms will be removed forthwith.' The man smiled, and Volchak understood.

The world broke.

Volchak launched himself across the table towards the man – bare-handed. He meant to rip out the throat that just condemned him to ten more years slavery with a passing comment. Even as he did, he knew a halberd would skewer him. Or maybe Smiele himself would finish it with that sword of his. He'd go down how he had always expected - violently. Maybe he'd even get to throttle Olaf's precious King at the same time.

The bald, white-robed man stopped Volchak dead, mid-air. With one arm he had completely arrested Volchak's attack, and slammed him down onto the table.

'Enough,' was all the Head Registrar said. Volchak's face was bleeding from the impact against the hard wooden table. His vision was blurry as the man swept him off the table as he would a troublesome cat, with what seemed like no effort at all. Volchak landed on his face on the floor.

'Escort him out! He needs no more part in this!' The black-robed man shouted to the guards.

Olaf appeared at his side and propped him up onto his knees, then to his feet. Volchak looked up, neck wrenched and back burning, as he coughed up some of the blood. He was ashen faced, with tears forming in his grey eyes.

By the time they emerged from the palace back into the city, both men still in their military dress uniform and weapon-less, Volchak was walking unaided again, having regained his breath and senses.

'Spoiled your chances I think,' he wheezed.

'No, I got my moment. Whilst you were having yours.' He nodded to Volchak's clearly broken nose.

'Aye?'

'It is far worse than I thought. The King... well, it isn't Caleb anymore. He's a ghost of what he was, thin, battered. I don't think he has any wits left. But... they've bound him with metal thread to that throne.' There were tears in Olaf's eyes. 'Like a physician's subject. I got up close behind to whisper to him and I saw it. It's so thin, subtle... but every part of him. He's being tortured in front of them all.'

'But they must know...'

'Who's left? Smiele, Caldor, Daveron? I think it is them Volchak. Give away my city? The Order Guard? I don't think we just lost this war. I think we might only just have realised we already lost it.'

'You need to get out. Take as many of your men as you can and get out of the city.'

'Come with me?' Olaf had a hand on each of his shoulders. Volchak looked over the bridge of his bloody nose.

'I've got my own fight. I'm going to stay, and go after Smiele myself.' Olaf looked solemnly at Volchak, who glared back and continued, 'He chose me on the draft, saw something in me. Trained me. Moulded *me*. Kept me alive all this time. I need to know why he'd cast me out now, what it was all for. He made a killer, my whole life. Why?'

Olaf frowned, then nodded.

'Tonight, then. I don't doubt we are watched, so we will leave it till the darkest hours and my men and I will leave. We have a boat ready to sail us north.'

'Smart man.' Volchak coughed, then smiled – the blood was thick red between his teeth.

'You can still come?'

Volchak shook his head. As they continued to walk back towards the Breachmen training ground. Neither of them noticed the flash of white robe, nor the noise of feet pounding on the road back towards the monastery.

Chapter 30

Volchak ached as he ascended the rickety wooden stairs at the far side of the Breachmen training ground, as he had done a hundred times before. Just like each of those times, it held his weight, creaking and shifting slightly but refraining from casting him down onto the bare ground below. He stepped onto the wall and looked over the parapet. His face stung, even with the pleasant warm breeze, where he had first hit the table then the floor. Just another pain to carry, he supposed.

He looked over the district before him. There were several wide dirt streets reaching towards the training ground, at the edge of the walls to the city, but no buildings were within thirty strides of it. He shrugged. He was used to standing alone. But as he looked beyond the gap, to the squat orderly houses that stood on either side of the road, he frowned. Wondered how many of them were empty this evening, or where children stayed with grandfathers and mothers, or those too young or sick to fight. When he counted off the Royal Guard, the Order Guard, the Infantry... a lot of empty houses. At the far side of the district stood the curtain wall, tall and thin solid stone, with the ramparts set to protect against thrown projectiles. Impressive, clean, solid. He nudged the outer city wall on which he now stood, moss covered and cracking, and a small piece chipped away under his foot. He supposed the palace would have been the target of an invasion, not the training grounds. Still, it summed things up nicely. As he turned, he looked over to the mining quarter, the hum of activity and torchlight casting its permanent orange glow as the evening shift began. Hundreds of people were marching towards the Eastern gate. He glanced over the fields on the other side of the wall, proud crops stood tall in the last of the light, interspersed with the many cattle fields. He sighed; guess he'd be haunting this wall for the next ten years. He couldn't get to Smiele anyway, not past that curtain wall, or that army, and not without his axe. His arms felt light without its familiar weight. He doubted whether he would ever see it again; all his wealth and power in a heavy bronze weapon, and he didn't even know where it was.

The Breachmen grounds were empty; most likely they would stay that way. The open dirt arena with the row of logs splitting it down the middle. He rubbed his shoulder, thinking of the many times he had force his way through that line. It really was a barbarous way to fight. Throw the worst people you can find against a shield wall. Maybe it was better it ended.

He heard the staircase creaking again, as the figure's head emerged above the precipice.

'Still alive then?' Harkner pushed back the hood on the black robe he wore, revealing his messy locks and familiar grin. He shrugged the pack on his back onto the floor to his side.

'Aye. Flea?'

Harkner nodded.

'Safe. For now. Will keep her that way.' He replied.

'The Order?' Volchak motioned towards the robe.

'Stirc's idea. Not a bad one either. Have you spoken to him?'

'Was at the war council, didn't say much.'

'Lively debate was it?' Harkner motioned towards the cut across Volchak's nose.

'My talent for finding fights seems to extend to politics as well. If you've come to re-join, I hate to disappoint. The Breachmen are finished.' Volchak sighed and looked back towards the palace, leaning on the crumbling stone wall in front of him.

'Not quite. Seems like there is one still standing.'

'Ha. Not the first time.'

'Why?' Harkner's tone was unusually reticent for the man. Volchak had seen him crack jokes standing opposite enemy armies, or in the face of odds neither of them had a hope of winning, or for no reason at all.

'What?'

'Why did you do it, all this time?' Harkner asked.

'Do what?'

'Keep living. Even before my time you'd been through some fights, I'd heard. You always wanted a bloody reputation? Or glory?'

'I...' Volchak rubbed his eyes; they ached, his neck ached, his arms were two dead weights, dragging on his shoulders which also ached. He leant back against the wall. 'I don't even know. I just wanted it to stop. Do my time and never raise a weapon again. Looks like only one of those will happen now.' Volchak paused and breathed out a sigh. 'Why did you? The only volunteer to live this long.'

'Had to.' Harkner's face was grim.

'How so?'

'For her.' Harkner nodded his head back towards the city, towards the monastery and its shadowy walls.

Volchak looked at him, the giant of a man, his black robe hanging a good foot above the ground from where it should be. Muscular shoulders and a wide face, a soft face by most accounts, always smiling. It wasn't smiling now.

'I don't understand... You met her after you joined. What made you join?'

Harkner shook his head and reached down and picked up the package he had placed at his feet, whatever was inside was heavy. His arms bulged as he held it in front of him. It was well wrapped in heavy skins, two straps hung from it.

'Knew her before. When she was little. Knew her mother. She... never made it out of the mine.'

Volchak stood silent and still, the warm breeze ran across his bloody face. A bead of sweat was forming on his brow from the thick woollen tabard he still wore.

'Accident, they said. Happens. Entire section collapsed. She left behind a young one, but she didn't know me. I just kept my distance, looked after her. Had to, for her mother.'

'Your little sister...' Volchak whispered, almost to himself.

Harkner didn't notice, or didn't care to stop. He stared into the evening across the fields. 'They kept her in the mine; I paid them to. She was safe, fed, warm. Couldn't have her with me - they'd have taken her away. Wasn't my blood. What if the Order got her? The army? She was safe in the mine. Then, that foreman. Should have seen it, stopped it sooner. Didn't know, till she had killed him and she was at the prison. I tried to buy her out; Ropers took it all and got her out alright. Sent her to you.'

'And you volunteered?' Volchak said.

'And I volunteered.'

Volchak thought back, Harkner had joined him over a year ago, here in the capital. At the time, Volchak figured he'd just lost his family in the mining accident like so many others and had nothing left to lose. Turns out he was half right. He'd lost half his family but had just one thing left to lose.

'You never told her.'

'She didn't know. Her mother... Her and I... it was new... but I loved her.' He shrugged. *More to it then,* Volchak thought. Harkner had slowly shed the oilskin, the enormous bronze axe glinted in the evening light. In Harkner's hands it wasn't oversized, it was big enough to be practical. It had clearly been cleaned and sharpened, looked five years younger.

'Harkner, you're a genius. How on earth did you get it from the palace?'

Volchak stepped forward and put a hand onto the haft, just as he looked up into the man's face.

That face. No smile, no joke to crack, no comradeship. Just deep lines around his eyes and a heavy frown, maybe a glint of wet in his eye. Volchak tightened his fist around the haft and made to take it, the axe didn't move.

'They've got her still. At the monastery.'

Volchak applied more pressure as he tried to pull it, slowly, as if teasing it from the man's grip. He failed. A shadow fell across Harkner's face.

'Harkner...' Volchak's tone was guarded. This was going in a direction he hadn't expected, but most things in his life went in this same direction eventually.

The big man's eyes came to focus on Volchak's, a good head's height shorter than the other man. Harkner's other hand, a giant paw, rested onto Volchak's woollen shoulder and shoved him away, hard. Volchak had the wind knocked out of him as he bounced off the castle wall, nearly pitched over it with the force.

'They'll let her go, let us both go, if I take care of you. That was the deal.'

'Look, they won't need you once they've gotten rid of me... Why would Smiele have you walking around...? The Order will-'

'I've seen that place!' Harkner interrupted. 'She can't stay there! Not my girl! Smiele has offered me a command, she'll be safe and I'll have a seat at the table! You'd do the same! You've done the same!'

'I don't care about their table!' Volchak shouted back, knowing no one would hear this though. The gap between the grounds and the buildings, the empty area below - there was no one left to hear. 'This isn't about your freedom!' *It never is.*

'Oh please! Commander of the Breachmen. Fearsome reputation. You're a killer, Volchak! You've built a life out of it! Hundreds? More? Everywhere you go death follows you like an old friend. You're a monster!' Harkner spat out.

'That's... not how it is...' Volchak could only cough out, it caught in his throat as he tried. He wheezed for breath, holding himself up by the wall. *Damn, but he ached.*

'Brieth? The Boatmen? Kaelith's horsemen? The Rebels? I've seen you kill and kill your way out of everything you come across. You'll kill us too eventually, I know it. I'm going to save us. Save her, from you.' Harkner turned slightly towards the monastery at the mention of Flea, as he shouted.

That was Volchak's chance. He launched at the man. Went straight for the axe handle but was met by the solid wall that was Harkner's body as it was wrenched away. Harkner reached out and kicked Volchak in the unprotected chest. It may as well have been his enormous stone hammer, as it hit it knocked him back against the wall.

Bouncing back from the wall, having banged his head hard against the stonework, chipping even more from it, Volchak regained his footing. With his right hand he seized the small antler blade from his belt – it had already dug a nasty bruise onto his lower back from the encounter earlier, so it was hard to forget. He waved it in front of him, swishing it back and forth.

'Can still walk away from this friend…' Volchak could taste the blood in his mouth again as he tried to move to the side, needed to get more space behind him. Harkner matched his step. For a long time, they had fought together, got to know each other well, and it started to show now.

'This is the only way for us to be free of the Breachmen. Of *you*.'

Harkner feinted forward, then swung the axe high; Volchak saw it and ducked under, felt the air move past his head as he seized the man's ankle and raised it to tip him backward. Harkner squawked as he pitched onto his backside and Volchak was on him with the antler blade. He stabbed through the robe once, twice, three times. Quickly, viciously. Stab. Stab. Tears of blood and sweat were gathering in his eyes as the final thrust snapped the blade off and his hand punched the big chest under the robe. Solid. Metal.

Damn.

Harkner threw Volchak backward and sprang to his feet. He groaned slightly as he did, bruised, but not pierced. The cuts in his robe parted and caught the light. Chain-mail ringlets gleamed back at Volchak as he held his ground.

'Smiele and Caldor are the future of Tydrian now. You're the past. About time you accepted that.' Harkner backhanded Volchak with his gloved hand, knocking him to the ground. Volchak made to roll away against the parapet and pushed himself to his feet.

He felt the axe connect. He was crushed against the wall, driven to the ground with his back to it. He looked up at the massive shape towering above him, and sighed. His throat croaked into a bloody cough. The man just stood there.

Volchak knew this was how he died.

Chapter 31

Stirc rushed through the corridors. The air here was cooler than outside, but he had still worked up a considerable sweat. A lifetime of limited exertion had left him frail. Up the ten flights of stairs, three hundred steps exactly (he noted to himself, fewer when running - as would be expected) and he entered his room. Flea was standing by the wardrobe, peering inside. Why not in Torrak's room? No matter. No time.

'What's wrong?' She looked at him with concern.

'We need to get you out. This evening.'

'Where's Harkner?'

'I don't know.' Actually, he had seen little of him in the past few days. 'I've come from the war council; the Order is taking over.'

'What do you mean, taking over?'

'From the King.'

'But the King is in the prison, you told me... Kaelith said so?'

'Yes, well, he was very much at the council. I don't know. Caldor was controlling him somehow.'

'I know how.' Flea smiled, as if merely commenting on the passing of the weather. Stirc peered at her.

'You do?'

'Yup. Seen the big white robe one practising. It's one of those-' She nodded to the wooden block, '-but with special metal wires, not ropes.'

Stirc looked at her, steely eyed. Then smiled.

'And where, exactly, did you see this?' Flea didn't answer. She sheepishly looked back into the wardrobe. 'We shall have to discuss the rate of your recovery and how accurately your results have been reported another time my dear. For now, I think it best we get you out of here. And you won't be going alone.'

'Harkner?'

'If we find him, yes. But he is safer here as my intern. Seems several of the other Registrar's have rather taken to him. You however, are not. Especially if you are not quite as ill as I had expected. People will ask questions, if they haven't already, about my lack of public demonstration on a subject I've been keeping here. No, you will be safer in a much more dangerous company, royal company.'

'Huh. Never met a King before.' *She understood.* 'Should I get Torrak's gas?'

'What for?'

'Well, truth be told. From the white liquid thing-y, I only got a little better. But first time I had the gas-stuff... Well, I've been alright ever since.' She sheepishly smiled again at him and shrugged her shoulders. A picture of innocence.

'Indeed? Remarkable.' And it was. Had he known, he would have likely reported these results to Caldor long before. He had thought the gas had merely halted the infection, but it seemed to have cured it. Inadvertently, her dishonesty had served a purpose. Or perhaps he was just too fond of her to mind.

'Fine, we shall grab some...?' She fished the cylinder out of his wardrobe, alongside a black robe.

'Oh, goodness!' He laughed at the girl as he rolled his eyes. Seemed she was far better suited to saving someone than he was.

'Right well, despite your resourcefulness, you need to keep with me and keep quiet. You are an intern of the Order until we are past the gates, then we need to find your Commander and get you both out of the city.'

'Mr. Volchak is alive?'

Stirc seemed puzzled. 'Yes, quite so I saw him a few hours ago. Although he did not see me.'

'Harkner said yesterday...'

'Well, Harkner is wrong. Now put the robe on and let's go!'

They navigated the corridors, a Registrar and his subordinate. Down three floors, then they took the back staircase towards Caldor's workshop. As they passed between the guards, they were unchallenged. That was convenient, seemed he had free pass now. Getting back out may prove more difficult.

They hurried, without obviously hurrying, through the enormous caverns below. The activity was far greater than that of a few days earlier. Many of the forges were lit and many more people buzzed around. This was useful, as two more were not noticed even though they were moving quickly. Twice they took a wrong turn - but Stirc had a reasonable idea from his previous bird's eye view - where the farthest chambers were. Within fifteen minutes they were standing opposite the cell door. A thin, grimy body lay on the floor with its calloused feet a few inches deep in a pool of filth. Stirc worked the mechanism to open the door whilst Flea stood watch.

'Kaelith?' Stirc voice at the body on the floor.

'What?' Seems he wasn't asleep or unconscious.

'Where's the King?'

'Dunno. Palace?'

'Dolt of a man. This is your exit if you want it. Have they returned with him?'

Kaelith sat up when he realised Stirc was alone in the cell entrance. Stirc saw his gaunt face dart around and then settle on his.

'They took him several days ago; he isn't here.' The bundle of rags in the corner was gone, only the most rotted and fetid of blankets remained crumpled on the floor.

'Right, well then. You had better come with us even so.' Stirc thought it might indeed be simpler sneaking out of the monastery without the King of Tydrian in tow, although it made this trip somewhat pointless. Stirc fought the urge to admit that he had perhaps put some value in bringing Kaelith out as well.

'Put this on, and keep your mouth shut if you can.' Tossing him another black robe.

'A picture of silence.' Stirc rolled his eyes at the man's response.

'You know it's damp in here. It wouldn't surprise me if there was an old sluice to the river if this used to be a mine...' Flea's ability to find intrigue in the most inopportune moment wasn't lost on Stirc.

'Quiet! Come, both of you.' He snapped back.

'My lady Flea. A pleasure and a privilege to see you again. May I apologise for my current poor state? I have been somewhat indisposed as of late,' Kaelith said. Stirc stopped mid-stride and turned, glared daggers at the man. He grinned and bowed slightly in apology, then snapped his mouth shut.

'Madness' Stirc whispered, wondering if maybe Caldor was right, and Kaelith wasn't just play-acting insanity, maybe his constant torture was having an effect. No time to decide, though.

They quickly exited the cell and were about to start heading for the entrance when a voice rang out.

'Registrar Stirc!'

Damn. Stirc turned on his heel and split the two blacked robed figures.

'Administrator Sygan, a pleasure, as always. What may I help you with?'

'You are needed…' Sygan looked to the two black-robed figures. 'You have taken new assistants? What of the tall one?'

'On assignment. What am I needed for?'

Stirc stood next to the man. He saw Kaelith manoeuvre around behind him out of his sight line.

'You are to accompany me to the lecture theatre where we will meet with the council.'

'I am afraid I am on urgent business and cannot delay. If I may join you later...?' Stirc tried one last time, not for Sygan's sake, but, he supposed, for his own.

'You most certainly may not!'

Just as Sygan finished speaking, the heavy metal ingot slammed down on the back of his skull with a dull clink.

Kaelith must have grabbed it along the way. Insufferable, Stirc thought, but useful.

Stirc looked around for what to do with the body. Kaelith didn't wait for instruction though, and dragged the man back towards the cell. He dumped the body in the corner and covered him the blanket. No choice, Stirc supposed. They needed to leave immediately.

Back past the guards and up the staircase unchallenged. They proceeded along the second floor, then doubled back along the first. Stirc did not stop to look but glanced sideways as they passed. He saw the subjects contorted and broken on the wooden blocks. Some had entire bones removed and others stuck out at curious angles, broken by the ropes. He had never been a fond of the crudeness of Bone's work.

'Registrar.' The guards, at the gate to the monastery, nodded to him as he passed. He was glad of his rank. It afforded him no need of papers nor explanation to the gatemen.

They maintained their disguises until they reached the Breachmen training ground, standing alone at the far side of the army district. It was quiet, the army was amassing elsewhere. Stirc believed that most of these houses would be empty. The group reached the wooden area and entered inside. It was eerily quiet.

'It might be he has taken to the ship already,' Stirc said. The three of them walked around the edge of the large dirt arena.

'Let's check the walls then head to the harbour district,' Flea suggested. Stirc saw no better plan. He wasn't sure what boat the other Breachman had referred to, or why he thought Yrfrite would accept the two of them, but he had hoped they would find it there. Or at least a boat that could get Flea and Kaelith out of the city where Caldor couldn't get to them.

As he walked up the staircase behind Flea, he heard her cry out. Not a scream, but a shout of panic. He rushed up the last steps until he saw the cause.

Volchak's body was propped up against the wall. His own axe protruding him his left shoulder, with a thick pool of crimson blood gathering on the surrounding walkway. Stirc looked left and right but no one else was present.

'Do... something...' Flea was on her knees in the man's blood next to him. Stirc stood frozen at the top of the stairs.

'Now's your moment - save him!' Kaelith turned back to face Stirc, his signature confidence drained from his face.

Right. A challenge.

He knelt next to him and felt the subject's – no, Volchak's, neck. The vein throbbed, alive. He rolled out his equipment next to him, always on hand. From his small satchel he took a small cylinder of his compound, kept just for emergencies. It glowed almost imperceptibly against the darkening sky. Flea produced Torrak's gas cylinder from her bag under her robe - he would get to that shortly.

Stirc took a breath and then examined the wound. Significant penetration, shoulder separated, muscle crushed. Likely extreme blood loss upon removal of the blade. Complicated.

'Kaelith, when I say now, I want this axe out and out of my way. Flea, I need you on the other side with your cylinder pressed to his lips. There will be a sharp intake of breath and that is likely to be our best opportunity. Do you both understand?'

'Aye.'

'Yes.'

'Okay.' He breathed out, steeling himself. 'And... Now.'

Stirc moved his hands with the skill and precision of a practiced swordsman. He even surprised himself as he moved the probe underneath the blade when it was shifted the slightest amount and applied his compound. With the clamp in his right hand, he seized the major artery in the shoulder and forced it shut. Pressure built behind it quickly, threatened to rupture. Stirc released his hand and took a second clamp and twisted it into place. His left hand followed in perfect harmony, as he applied compound to the edge of the wound. Flea held her canister to his mouth as Volchak took a sharp intake of breath, despite being unconscious. *Excellent.* Stirc pressured the two parts of the subject's shoulder together and the compound bound. He brandished his remaining clamp to the rear of the wound, everything faded as he was lost in his demonstration of skill and precision as he worked. All else forgotten.

Within minutes, he sat back. The white Registrar robes were soddened with blood and gore from the operation. But as he felt the Commander's vein, there remained a steady throbbing. There was no fresh blood leaking from the wound. If only for now, he would live.

'Stirc ...' Flea's voice seemed far away as he sat back and admired his work. Before his eyes, he had seen the flesh bind, not regrow, but attach back from where it was torn. The improvements to his formula were self-evident. He would be revered in the Order for this achievement, true mastery over flesh.

Except not. He landed back in the moment with a harsh thud. Only the three of them, well, the four of them, would witness this.

'He will live.'

Flea threw her arms around him. He sat bolt upright, unsure and completely paralysed by her embrace.

'Thank you. Thank you. Thank you.' She whispered as she squeezed him.

'It's ... alright my dear.' This was all he could manage to say. She let him go. Kaelith entered his view.

'We can move him?'

'In two hours, carry him to the harbour district. Look for a Breachman, scarred in the face. Olaf. That's his new number two. He said he can get him onto a boat and out of here.'

'Olaf?' Kaelith seemed surprised.

'Yes?' Stirc replied.

'With a scar on his cheek?'

'Yes?'

'Olaf ... is the Duke of Yrfrite.'

Stirc's head swam.

'Come with me.' Flea cut through the fog in Stirc's head. *Me*.

'No. I will remain. Someone has to see what happens here, find out what Caldor is planning. You are safe. I will seek out Harkner and make sure he is too.'

Flea hugged him again.

'Thank you.'

'Aye, thank you.' Kaelith had no irony in his voice.

Stirc nodded, dumbly. That was more praise than he had received in a lifetime. And all it took was saving the life of a disgraced military commander, apparently in conspiracy with the greatest enemy of the land, a land whose King was being controlled by the head of the Order of Hermetics.

He shrugged. Quite the day.

Chapter 32

'My lady, please excuse my disgraceful attire.'

Kaelith bowed low, as he reached the top of the gangplank and met Tamryn's disapproving stare. His tattered white shirt - or sash as he now thought of it - did little to hide his starved body. His rib cage protruded and his flat stomach threatening to pitch his torn trousers onto the floor at any minute. But despite this, his grimy face beamed. Not just because she was the best-looking thing he had seen in a long while, but also at the fact he saw several large crates of food being moved onto the ship via the hand crane on the dock, and being unloaded behind her.

'And where do you suppose you are going?'

'A daring escape. I shall be fighting off a dozen Royal Guardsmen with nothing but my wit and skill with a fencing blade!' He coughed slightly as he slipped on the deck, nearly losing his footing. It was difficult to appear debonair when half-carrying, half-dragging, an unconscious Breachman around. And he didn't actually have a sword.

'Please, you have to help us!' Flea pleaded from behind, her sweet voice no doubt trying to appeal to the Tamryn's softer side. Good luck with that.

'I *have* to do nothing girl. How are you at this dock, mercenary?'

'Why, the Duke has offered us safe passage back to your city.' It was sort of true, as much truth as he could think of anyway before the lie. That was the trick.

'Where is my brother?'

Stirc had said he would be here by now, collecting his men and then headed to the ship he had said. This might make things more difficult; he was hardly owed much allegiance here.

'Ah well, he will be along. But there is this too.'

He raised lifted the heavy steel ingot, a valuable commodity. More than enough to purchase a ship, let alone barter passage. *But beggars can't be... well, in this case, they can be beggars but with something to offer in exchange.*

'Should buy three spaces I'd hope?'

Tamryn glared at him. Volchak groaned as Kaelith shifted the unconscious man's weight around his shoulders. She regarded the three of them with her stony face.

'Two.'

'Well, the thing -'

'Two. And you can come as well, but you will owe me after this.'

'Deal.' Kaelith beamed and took a step onto the boat. *Never turn down an opportunity to live – can pay for it later.*

Kaelith and Flea navigated around the crew on the small trade boat to the lower deck, where they found a small bunk to lay Volchak's unconscious body on. Had Kaelith not just spent a month being opened, closed, cut and healed by the same miracle compound Stirc seemed to carry around, he wouldn't have believed how the man was still alive. Flea was fussing over his wound. She applied more of Stirc's miracle compound. Kaelith thought he really ought to come up with a name for it. Periodically she opened another cylinder in front of his face. She seemed rather capable and in control, so Kaelith wandered off in search of food. It had been maybe two days since he had eaten anything, and he rather hoped for better fare than what was sent into the Order's cell.

He stepped back out into the warm, dark night and heard the commotion up the street from the harbour. Shouts and loud crashes were chased by firelight as they spilled into view. A small gang of armed men, leather armour and stone weapons, appeared to be retreating from a unit of the King's infantry. Although this infantry was armed with actual swords and appeared to be wearing full chain-mail. They weren't Ropers. They moved as one, at a steady march whilst the others fell back. Occasionally, a brave soul from the pursued would surge towards the pursuers. Swinging a stone axe or antler blade, or stabbing with a spear. He saw these attempts ricochet harmlessly off shield and chainmail. When the retreating group had reduced from twenty to fifteen, they seemed to abandon the fight altogether and run. Straight for the ship.

'My lady Tamryn? I believe your brother has arrived!' Kaelith shouted as he stood at the side of the ship. The group was only fifty strides away now and running for the gangplank.

The crew were shouting loudly and sprinting across the deck as they coaxed the ship into life. Ropes were being pulled and rigging climbed, it was all very dramatic. Kaelith knew as much about sailing as he did about the finer points of baking - which admittedly was not nothing - but was not much help here. So, he ran to the end of the gangplank and helped drag the men up and onto the boat as they arrived. He thought maybe he could kick the plank away dramatically just as the pursuing forces arrived, thus saving the day as he sailed off into the night.

The pursuers had broken out into a steady jog maybe a hundred paces behind the last of the men who were running up the gangplank.

'Tally ho gents!' Kaelith shouted, to no one in particular and no one particularly noticed.

As the last of them ran up the ramp and the boat lurched as if it was about to move. His moment came, just as he was about to kick away the plank - he heard a loud shout from behind.

'The mooring line is still tied! The mooring line!'

Kaelith had no actual idea what a mooring line was. But he could tell a thick rope tied to the stone block on the dock and then to the ship probably wasn't supposed to be there if you planned on sailing away into the night. He turned; Tamryn had come up behind him to the rail holding what looked like a rather magnificent short sword, full steel with gold inlay in the handle. *Exquisite*. She wasn't brandishing it, it seemed like she was about to give it to someone, clearly a sign.

He snatched it from her hands and tore down the gang plank at full pelt, bare feet thumping on the wood. He heard her angry shout as he did but cared little, a daring charge if ever there was one straight towards the pursuing forces. No head bashed in with a rock for him.

The moment his foot hit the dock he spun sideways and sprinted for the mooring line, confident he had just improved his sailing knowledge. In eight strides he was there and he swung the sword in all almighty arc with a shout.

It cut about a third of the way through the line before bouncing back.

Dammit. Thicker than he thought. Well, he guessed, if it was to hold a boat in place, that made sense after all... he shook his head slightly as if forcing the sense back into himself and swung twice more. Once, nearly. Twice... Through.

The line sprang back towards the boat and landed in the water as he turned back, glancing at the oncoming horde a stone's throw away now as he saw the gangplank tumble off the dock into the harbour water below as the boat moved.

'Oh, come on!' He looked around desperately. The nearest man was only about a spear length away. Not much room on the dock, though, maybe two abreast in all that armour.

'Well... why not?'

He struck his finest fencing pose, one thin, muddy arm in the air behind his matted, thick blonde mess of hair. Bare feet poised, his sword out in front. Too damned heavy to do this for long, he thought as he felt the weight of it threatening to pitch him forward.

The first infantryman swung his sword, pathetically slow. Kaelith knocked it up into the air in a single motion and then thrust the other end directly into the man's face. He seemed surprised and shocked as the blade slipped into the skin of his cheek before being whipped out again, and the man collapsed to the floor. *Only place to stab him*, thought Kaelith; *made sense*.

The second man was already swinging wide around Kaelith's guard and Kaelith had to jump backward. The blade passed uncomfortably close and thudded into the shield of the third man who was stepping over the first. Their advance had slowed to a crawl as they bunched up on the dock, but they weren't exactly short of men and Kaelith was getting alarmingly short of dock. He darted forward and swept out the leg of the second man with his own, spinning fluidly through the motion back to standing with a slight flourish of the gleaming sword in his right hand. May as well look good for the audience. The man pitched backward onto another man behind, but righted himself quickly on the press of men behind him.

'Well, there's just an army of your fellows, isn't there...?' Kaelith said as he slowly and deliberately stepped back. They matched him now, no longer sprinting forward as they stepped over their dead comrade, but equally knowing this as only ending one way.

Thud. Kaelith backed directly into the upright wooden post. He glanced upward, saw the loading mechanism and the horizontal arm, and the rope hanging from it.

Kaelith turned to face the second man, who had seen this too. The soldier lurched forwards swinging his blade - just as the hand bow bolt hit him squarely in the face. The man went down, dead, onto the dock. This tripped the third man, who slipped in the blood and tangled with the body and fell over the side into the water. *No doubt he'll regret his choice of wardrobe now,* Kaelith thought as he turned and leapt for the rope hanging from the hand crane. Now, *this* was a daring escape.

He completely missed it. Water rushed up and hit him hard in the chest as he dropped the sword and floundered. It was ice cold compared to the warm air above, and he lost all his bearings. No idea what was up or down, he thrashed and stared until he saw light above him. He saw the faces looking over the side of the ship as it kept moving away and felt a harsh dragging against his side, painful, burning. *Mooring line.*

Kaelith seized the heavy rope with his now empty hands, wrapping it as best he could round his arm as he felt it being yanked through the water. Spluttering, he emerged at the side of the ship and then was dragged up the side by the crew, moving as one. He spluttered and coughed as his face hit the wet deck, hard.

'You're…' he coughed up more water and rolled over onto his back, considerably cleaner than he had been a moment ago, although shivering. 'Welcome.'

'Blundering fool - I was going to cut it from this side.' Tamryn scowled at him, but with the slightest hint of a smile hidden behind. She was reloading her hand bow. Even in the dim lantern light on the deck it was clearly as masterwork of craftsmanship, metal pieces caught the light, including the tip of the bolt. Each shot a small fortune then. Nice to know he was worth it.

'Ah.' was all he replied. He closed his eyes, felt the hard deck against the back of his head and smiled up towards where she was still standing, looking down at him.

'That would have made more sense.'

Chapter 33

Flea opened the small wooden door in to the plain-looking chamber and stepped inside. The stonework here was simple. Heavy wooden columns held aloft a high, but unpainted, wooden ceiling. The windows were small, squat, and frosted with dirt. The floor was smoothed stone and there was a thin wooden table standing in the centre of the room. Around it was a series of basic, low-backed wooden chairs and ordinary looking, stern-faced people.

'Hi!' She smiled as she walked in and sat down at the nearest chair. It was at the head of the table. She looked at the map in front of them. It showed the outline of Yrfrite's large thick stone walls at the edge nearest her, then stretched off down the table towards the South, with Brieth at the other end. Several hills had been shaded in where the Northern Road swept round. On top were several large wooden markers with red and blue markers, and fewer brown wooden ones.

'Miss Flea, thank you for joining us' The scarred Duke sat amongst the men on one side of the table, acknowledged her arrival

'Just Flea.'

'Flea, my apologies.' He bowed his head. Polite for a Duke. She had always found those with titles to be more uptight. Especially in the army. Captains were alright - majors, though, were the worst, she'd never met a Duke.

Maybe they were more polite? She was supposed to meet the King, but that hadn't happened as Stirc had expected.

'… and the terrain could work to our favour if we are on one bank of a hill with the cliff to our left…'

Flea shook her head, emerged from her daydream and started listening again.

'No, that won't work. The second force is going to be arriving from the West shortly after we engage. We will be trapped against the cliff face.' The Duke seemed to have the best grasp on the situation. Guess he'd been in a fair few fights. Flea would know, she had been in some of them herself.

'Then what? We run again? They'll take the city and hand it over the Order. What of the people? We aren't stocked for a siege - we can't hide behind the walls!' A short-haired woman was frowning as she pointed at the pieces on the table with a small antler blade.

'I know, Klyssa. We don't have the men to fight on two fronts. The shield wall can hold against the Royal Guard. We have enough men we may even bring them down. But we don't have the time to try.'

'What about their Commander? You've got him prisoner, don't you? Can't we barter him?' Another man sparked up from the other side of the table.

'He's not their commander anymore. You saw the state he was in when we arrived. He isn't our prisoner either. They've disbanded the Breachmen.'

'Good thing too. Savages.' Klyssa leant back in her chair. 'Shouldn't have him here, Olaf. He's a monster. Killed fourteen men on the road a few weeks ago, along with the men in Brieth. He's probably the reason the army burned the village.'

'Um… It was only seven men on the road…' Flea's voice seemed quite small in the high-ceilinged chamber. Klyssa waved her comment away and pointed back to the map. Flea clasped her fists below the table and sat still in her chair.

'It can't work. We are beaten already. We just don't know it. One hundred and fifty Royal Guard we might be able to fight, but there's near double that in this 'Order Guard'. We can hold one at bay, surround them, bring them down. It'll be bloody but we can overpower them in place. But we can't fight on both fronts. Not without armour and proper weapons. At least, behind the walls, we have time. They'll be here in two days.' Klyssa's voice was raised in frustration.

'Time for what? The Boatman wouldn't come to our aid. Not enough of them left. All our emissaries returned to the docks before Tamryn even left to get us at the Capital. The North? None returned. The tribes there aren't interested in our little kingdom.' The Duke said.

There was a general thrum of agreement and discontent around the table. The men all sat back and scowled as if the map would tell them what the answer was. Olaf stood over it intently.

'Um… I might know what to do…'

Flea saw all the heads turn to her. *Had she said that?* They were looking at her like she said that. She realised she had better do something.

She stood up and reached over the table, although given her size the centre of the table was out of bounds, but that didn't matter hugely for what she had to show them.

'If you can't stand and fight on two sides, then don't.' It seemed so simple. 'You put the shield wall here like the scary lady said.' She nodded at Klyssa, who sat back in her chair, clearly unimpressed. Flea moved the little plain wooden marker to the edge of the hill, with the cliff on one side. 'Then we get our own Breachmen.' There were no spare markers on the table. She reached into her pockets and pulled out a small piece of dried meat she had left over from breakfast. Seemed about the right size. 'Break through the Royal Guard when they are... here.' She moved the blue marker to where the bottom of the valley was marked and put the piece of meat on top of them.

'When they get them all tangled up, then make the army charge down the hill *here*. They will have to spread out thinner and try to fight back, or it'll be twelve men against a thousand at once. They won't be able to use their halberds neither. Would have to use their swords, and they are too big and slow for that really.' Flea shrugged.

'Charge the Royal Guard? Madness. A shield wall is the only thing that can stand up to them, draw them in close and go for the weak spots.' A deep voice from the other side of Klyssa chipped in.

'No, it is not. I've seen it. They are good when they are in a nice row, walking forward. You always just stood in the way and let them. Breachmen can mess that all up. That's what they do. If the Royal Guard can't fight up close with their halberds. they'd have to use their swords. But they are too heavy, too slow, they can't see good out of their helmets. You'd have a chance.' She looked around again and fished in her pockets, but no more breakfast. She pointed to the top of the hill, behind where the Royal Guard and the Breachmen-meat was placed. 'That's where Smiele will be. If someone can get up there, they can stop the fight before it gets too bloody. The Breachmen can try to get there once the army charges.' She took the piece of meat and moved it up onto the hill. 'If you can kill Commander Smiele, and his officers. There will be no one to tell the Guard what to do. Up close you can jab 'em in the soft spots. There's enough of you.'

Olaf looked thoughtful. Klyssa looked impatient.

'Are we forgetting that we don't have any Breachmen?'

'Um... yeah we do.' Flea couldn't really believe herself. She was arguing with a Duke in front of the room of veteran officers. 'I talked to them on the boat. Mr. Volchak trained them himself. In the capital? There's at least fifteen of them?'

Olaf nodded. Clapped his hands together once as he stood.

'Yes, of course. These are excellent fighters Klyssa, and Volchak's tactics are … effective. Even against Royal Guard, they should be able to enact suitable amount of mayhem.' He was studying the stable, head moving from piece to piece.

The deep-voiced man from earlier sat forward. He was an older man, with long grey wisps of hair and a thick beard that hid a leathery face.

'What about the Order Guard? Won't they just catch us beaten and bloodied from the tussle with the Royal Guard even if your men stop it? And in a valley nonetheless? They are arriving at the worst time for this plan.'

A voice from the far side of the table, one that had been uncharacteristically quiet until that moment, suddenly chimed in.

'I am sure I could take care of that.'

Heads turned towards the voice, Kaelith was tilting his chair back against the wall with a plate of food in his left hand. At first glance, he was asleep, or drunk, or both, but apparently - neither.

The lady who was sat next to the Duke spoke – *Tamryn*; Flea knew her name. She had been sitting next to Olaf, contemplating the plan. Flea had heard she was the one in charge when the Duke wasn't. Heard that, and seen it on the boat a few times. Never spoken to her since they first met, though.

'Oh, indeed, and how would you do that?' Tamryn said.

'Well, your most gracious…' a slight pause as Kaelith sought the right word '…nesses. I've had word that eleven of my most loyal and most hardy of compatriots are soon to be arriving in the city. Survived the last little soiree we threw and heard that there might be a small fortune here to collect.'

'And how did they hear that?' Tamryn asked.

Kaelith shrugged. 'I may have been a little presumptuous that their services may be rendered necessary. Plus, I told them you'd pay them what they are owed though from our first arrangement before I left.' He grinned. 'Do that and we will call it evens.'

'Twelve, against two hundred and fifty?' Tamryn scoffed.

'Twelve, *on horses,* against two hundred and fifty. And you underestimate my ability to harass and frustrate an enemy. I only need slow them down.'

'Ha!' Tamryn's laugh was genuine, breaking her serious demeanour. 'Your ability to frustrate is definitely not in question.'

Flea looked at the woman. She was smart and she spoke with authority. Flea liked her.

'I'd never seen a horse till our last battle. Didn't know what to do, even less how I would fight it. I think Kaelith could slow them down a good long while.' Flea earnestly nodded towards the Duke.

'Yes, thank you, Tamryn.' Duke Olaf also nodded in agreement. 'If Kaelith can hold up the Order Guard for long enough, we may retreat and reform on to the hill here.' He pointed down at the hill where they had started. 'And have a fighting chance. Especially if our twelve horsemen are still alive and none of their officers are.' He nodded respectfully to Kaelith, who grinned and carried on eating.

'Miss Flea - apologies again...' Olaf bowed his head and corrected himself, 'Flea... we are in need of someone to command them, and you are our most experienced Breachman.'

Oh, no. She hadn't thought this part through.

'Uh...'

The door thudded open. Everyone turned suddenly to look at the doorway. Flea spun on her feet nimbly and took a step to the side just in case someone was going to try to poke her with a spear again. Light flooded in behind the man, stood there leaning against the doorframe. It was not a large man, hunched over slightly and with his left arm bound tightly across his body in a sling. Wild hair casting a shadow across his face. A hint of stained blue uniform from beneath the bloody bindings.

'No... she isn't...' A voice croaked.

Klyssa and the man next to her shot to their feet and brandished their weapons, her an antler blade and him a mean-looking stone axe. Before they could move, Flea sprang forward and threw her arms around the man's neck and embraced him tightly.

He patted her back with his one good arm and set her down, slightly unstable on his feet.

Olaf was the first to speak.

'I saw you on the boat. You should not still be with us, let alone walking around.'

'Not my choice, this time. I'll lead the Breachmen.' Volchak said.

'Will you be able to keep up?' Tamryn looked at him with a raised eyebrow. She, too, had seen the state of him when Flea and Kaelith first brought him on board.

'For everything the Order has become,' he nodded to his arm and flexed his fingers, 'they have certainly mastered their craft.'

Klyssa and the armed man didn't sit down.

'Aye.' Duke Olaf didn't argue. 'Then the last little problem. Assuming we can breach the Royal Guard -' he indicated to Volchak. '- and then that the army can charge and break them -' he nodded to Klyssa, '- whilst the Order Guard are held up by twelve men on horses -' then at Kaelith, '- we need someone to go after Caldor. Someone to rescue the King from the Order monastery.' Olaf look around the room.

'We don't have any assets in the monastery.' Tamryn shook her head as she spoke. 'I've tried for months to determine a way in, let alone any information about what we would find. The guards are all Order members and can't be turned. And even then, with the sheer number of people they've got in there, we would never make it in unnoticed. Even if we did, it'd be impossible to fight through the halls whilst we look for where the cells are, and a way out afterward. Not with two thousand men could I do it.'

'Err, I know how.'

Dammit, Flea thought, her mouth was at it again.

Chapter 34

Stirc sat quietly at the large marble table, his eyes peering round the previously stark white marbled circular chamber. He settled on the statues as he counted them off. One. Two. Three. Four.... He looked at the fifth one. The frozen liquid seeming impossibly fragile as it stood in a tall amorphous shape. Was it flowing or was it dropping from the heart? Why had they brought him into the council now? He glanced around the room and saw other recent additions, several armoured men stood at intervals, not unlike in the throne room. But these men were armed with steel swords and shields and the garb of the Order Guard. Two large red banners with the crest of the Order now hung from the ceiling, flanking the door to the rear of the theatre, the door to Caldor's workshop.

Caldor stood, having completed whatever reading he was doing at the far end of the table. Yorinth and Muldren both turned to face him from their opposite sides of the enormous table. Kade simply leant against the high back of the large, heavy chair and grinned, arms crossed in front of him.

'Progress. Discovery. The Order. That is the commanding force in the kingdom now.' Caldor's tone was flat, but with the slightest gesticulation of his hands as he spoke, he seemed... excited.

'Stirc, it is time to inform you of our intentions and our capabilities. I expect you have already devised a series of questions?' Kade said.

Stirc might not have been meant to speak, but he couldn't help blurt out, 'What was that, at the war council?'

Caldor didn't frown, his face moved little if at all, but his annoyance seemed to emanate from his stare.

Muldren chirped in, as skittish as always.

'Culmination of over a year's preparations, perfectly executed. Oh, the look on their faces!'

Stirc opened his mouth. Muldren wasn't at the council, was he? So, what did he mean about the look on their faces?

'Nearly perfectly,' Yorinth added. 'There is still the matter of the Breachman who escaped on the boat. We believe that Commander Volchak was with them.'

'Your intern failed in his duty, Stirc. He was instructed to kill the Commander, yet it seems he only wounded.' Kade's voice was brimming with disdain for Stirc. That was clear.

'I was not aware...' Stirc began.

'We had not informed you.' Caldor cut across him, monotone. Yorinth continued for him. 'He was a deserter from the Breachmen, and provided a suitable avenue to remove their leadership. He was offered a role in the army as payment, and your current subject was to be released.'

'I expect that is why she is no longer in my chambers then?' Carefully, Stirc navigated the issue. As much truth as he could, that was the key.

'Indeed.' Kade made a sideways glance to Caldor, who did not react.

'It matters not. The Order Guard will decimate the rebels and secure the city of Yrfrite for the Order as per the King's command.' Yorinth placed her dark hands on the table in front of them. 'The King's command is our command,' she continued, peering deep into Stirc's eyes, as if daring a challenge.

'Aye.' Kade looked very pleased with himself. 'But complete control has required more extreme means, which risked the death of the monarch, which would have caused us significant difficulty. That is why your compound was so timely, it has allowed us to be more... direct with our... supervision.'

Stirc had already reached this conclusion when Kaelith had told him about the other prisoner in the cell, King Caleb Domenici, Monarch of Tydrian. So he sat, stony-faced, as if making calculations in his own mind.

'So, your physical restraints, you plan to reach a point where they are no longer needed?'

'Yes. Yes. Exactly! The mind can be bent and shaped, but you need control of the body. Now we have the ability to do both without damaging it - well, not irreparably so.' Muldren clapped his hands together, clearly thrilled at the prospect.

Stirc looked at Caldor.

'And how did we establish The Order Guard?' He asked.

'One year ago, a collapse in the Eastern Mine sealed the capital's mining tunnels. You know this.' Kade replied. 'What you do not know is that it opened a new vein from our mine of exceptional quality iron. We have been using a portion of our subjects to extract and forge since it's discovery.'

'Our best estimates are that we have nearly tripled the amount of metal in the kingdom, and the Order controls over two thirds of that supply.' Yorinth continued.

'And the men to wield it?' Stirc turned to her.

'Subjects will always choose subservience, and - with persuasion - will fight hard.' Kade grinned menacingly. 'There was, however, one variable we had not accounted for.'

'Horses.' Caldor spoke again.

Yorinth continued for him. 'There was only one breeding pair in the entire Kingdom. A tight control on their import through the docks was kept, because of the potential shift in power they could cause away from the traditional warfare stratagems. This mercenary had nearly two dozen in his charge. Where did he get them from? There must be a source. How did he bring them here? Where did they train? That is why your prisoner was so important.'

'The prisoner who died.' Kade said, shaking his head.

Was this an interrogation? Did they know? Stirc thought.

'Luckily for you.' Kade continued. 'You tricked the other one into walking right into the Roper's on the bridge and then to be delivered to our door, not the army's. Another triumph of your achievements, Stirc.' He seemed, as Stirc searched his face, to be genuine.

'And the perfect test subject for your compound!' Muldren chimed in. 'High value information was extracted; we believe we know the route through the Western mountains.'

'There is no route through the mountains; they have all been attempted over the millennia.' Stirc would not accept this, and he knew Kaelith to be an accomplished liar.

'Incorrect. The mining disaster may have opened a fissure previously covered over, or simply no one had found it before. Our route is *under* the mountains. Yrfrite is perfectly placed. That city will be the staging point for the Order to explore and exploit the land on the other side of the mountains. In time, it will overtake the capital in terms of power and influence, and the Order will control the Kingdom here and beyond the West.' Yorinth beamed at him.

'That is the strategy I have devised.' Caldor said. Again, despite sitting still and giving no outward signs, he seemed ready to burst with excitement from within.

Stirc sat. All eyes were on him. It was clear this was the moment, the test. His responses would be analysed and weighed. He felt the weight of the Order guards around him bearing down on him, the rope dangling above his head.

'I will assist as required.' It was true, therefore they believed it. He just had not decided what that requirement would be.

'Splendid!' Muldren burst out loudly, making Stirc jump in his chair. 'Once these pesky rebels have been dealt with, a world of discovery will open up to us.'

Stirc sat back in his chair and thought of the coming battle. He couldn't see a way this could end, other than what Caldor had planned. Stirc knew that's why the strange man was in charge in the first place.

Chapter 35

Volchak looked over the cliff edge to the choppy sea. Yesterday he had watched a single boat head south, now it was empty again, turning under the wrathful clouds - dark greys and streaking whites above. He listened for thunder and heard it from behind him. Turning, he looked down the hill to see the steady march of the Royal Guard, as they crested the opposite hill and descended. Their armour shone in the mid-day sun, their tall halberds glinting as they caught the light and then bounced it across the hillside where he waited.

He looked to his left and right, expecting to see the familiar gap between him and the next man. A gap that came from a long and bloody life. Next to him Olaf stepped up and smiled, the scar on his cheek breaking up the clean-shaven face that sat over his strong-cut jaw, a hero's face if ever there was one.

'Doesn't she mind you coming up here to die with me?'

'She doesn't know. If she did, she'd just kill me herself to get it done with.'

Volchak chuckled and looked back towards the Guard, steadily progressing towards the valley floor below.

'Aren't you supposed to be on another hill somewhere waving your sword around, giving orders or some such?' Volchak had to raise his voice slightly now over the sound of the men on the opposite hill. The sides were steep, not too steep to walk down but enough to slow them down. What few of Fedal's infantry – well, he supposed they weren't Fedal's anymore - had caught up with the rear of the Royal Guard and added to the noise. They were getting caught up in each other's formation. *Sloppy.*

'Guess that's the benefit of being in charge. Who's going to tell me what I should be doing?' Olaf smiled, wide and joyful. His long steel sword, shone in the morning light, although he held it low at his side until it was needed. 'Besides. We need every trained Breachman we have, and I spent a month under their most famed commander!' He smacked Volchak on the shoulder enthusiastically. Volchak swallowed back the immense stab of pain that wracked through his side and up his neck. The bindings were tight. He had all but finished that gas that Flea had left him, and it looked healed on the outside. But damn, did it still hurt.

Volchak looked to his other side. The man from the Breachmen arena stood beside him, gripping his stone axe. The man's short, thick arms bulged as he gripped the haft, tightly.

'Just get to the other side of that wall.' Volchak nodded at him as the man glanced over to the left, a worried smile appearing on his face.

'Don't die.' Volchak said. A simple statement of fact. A choice the man had to make. A prayer? He didn't even know anymore. Been saying it so long now it was just what he said. Seemed to help others though. The man nodded back to him and turned to the enemy, smile gone from his face and a fire in his eyes.

***

Volchak's chest heaved, and his shoulder burned, as he stamped down the hill. From all down the line he knew the sixteen other men were doing the same. Suddenly emerging from the shield wall - which closed up behind them - to sprint the thirty or so paces to where the Royal Guard were reaching the bottom of the valley. Volchak had timed it well, or was lucky. The small fence on their side had awkwardly fallen under the Guard's boots. Coupled with the hill sharply meeting the valley floor the front few rows had lost some of their composure. There were gaps in the wall of halberds from the first twelve men and those behind had raised theirs to allow for movement.

The Breachmen crashed into the front line. Volchak forced a stray halberd blade high into the air with the head of his axe, before spinning into a heavy swing which crunched against a plated helmet. It didn't penetrate, but it caved in the helmet itself and the man underneath went limp. Olaf's long blade stabbed under the arm of the man behind the first and pushed him backward onto the third man in the rank. Rather than recover his footing from his swing, Volchak used the momentum to barrel into two more guardsmen with his newly-rebuilt shoulder. Their halberds entwined, as they tried to swing them sideways and they were both knocked to the floor. He looked up to see the familiar Breachman crush one of their chests with his stone axe, then swing it in a wide arc, catching another in the side and knocking another down. As it exposed his side a flash of metal came down and cracked his skull open. Volchak saw how his hair had just grown back in as the two halves of his head were forced down onto his crumpled body. Volchak stepped once towards where it landed and stamped on the wooden haft of the halberd, breaking off the heavy head. The plate covered hand landed like a hammer on his shoulder, searing pain forcing him down onto one knee and pounding the wind out of him. The Guardsman had dropped his weapon and tried to wrestle Volchak to the ground. Volchak spun his axe in his hand as he drove the pommel into the man's neck once, twice. The hand let go. With a turn of his body, he brought the axe blade in a heavy swing and carved the man's arm clean off, hitting right at the joint of the armour where it provided least protection. Volchak looked around for the next threat. It stabbed at him from a rear rank but with little force at that distance, cutting a deep groove across his leather chest piece but failing to catch or penetrate. Volchak dropped the axe, grabbed the haft with both hands and pulled, dragging the man who wielded it forward, -knocking down two of his fellow Guardsmen at the same time in a flurry of plated arms and legs. As Volchak ducked to pick up the axe, a sword rushed over his lowered head, straight into the haft of another halberd that was plunging down from above. The severed head of it fell hard against Volchak's back and cut the back of his neck slightly, but a damn sight less hard than it would have had it still been attached. Volchak caught a glimpse of Olaf - moving into a follow up swing towards the wielder and catching him at the base of the neck, cutting the man deep despite the armour and then circling away to another fight. Axe in hand and already low, Volchak swung at the legs of a guardsman facing the other way and swept him clean off his feet and into the ground, familiar crunch of bone, or maybe it was the armour, as it connected.

Facing rearward, he saw the moment the Yrfrite army finished its own charge and crashed into the lines of the Guard. They had spread into a wider line, that was well formed at either side. Many men were skewered onto the halberd tips from the rebel's downhill charge. Despite the semblance of shape at the edges, the middle ranks of the Royal Guard were a tattered mess of fighters and bodies and clashing weapons. As the Duke's army collided with it, an enormous bulge was forced through the middle of the Royal Guard unit right up to where Volchak had breached, and carried him with it as it carved the unit in two. At any moment, he expected to feel a familiar sting of a wooden spear from his own side, someone too confused or too angry to know or care what side he was on. Maybe even just trying to settle a score. But as he re-joined the charge, they completely enveloped what was now a thin rank of the infantry behind the Guard. Volchak swung his axe wide, catching one lightly armoured man in the face and carrying the swing through to the chest of the next one. As the man fell, Volchak saw it – space. The green slope of the hill right up to its crest, the glint from the plate mail armour on that hill seemed to hit him directly in the face.

'Breach!' Volchak shouted as he tore into the hole and started pounding up the hill. He could feel at least one body next to him as he sprinted as hard as he could, away from the melee below.

Chapter 36

Kaelith's men smelt unpleasant. He had expected this, after a day's ride under the hot summer sun and then an uncomfortable night camping in the hills with no water to bathe in. Thankfully they were a good ten strides behind him, riding in a close-knit line, each holding high a spear with a white cotton flag tied to it.

The large unit of men had been visible from the night before and Kaelith had concocted another of his brilliant, albeit somewhat simple, schemes. Kaelith's company had ridden down the road directly at them, no doubt spotted by a few scouts beforehand, but faster than they could relay the message back. The marching column of men had first come to a stop, no doubt when they saw the dust cloud being kicked up as the company increased its pace. Then they had completely fallen out of formation into a wide semi-circle as men abandoned their positions to watch twelve horses riding toward them in a glorious formation across the horizon. Kaelith stood tall in his saddle with his new chest plate gleaming, and his fencing steel at his side. Shame they hadn't got a long-curved blade like he preferred to use. They looked so much more dramatic when waved around for all to see.

'Halt! In the Order's name!' The heavily-armoured man had shouted as they pulled their horses to a stop twenty strides away.

'What?' Kaelith had shouted back.

This clearly completely flummoxed the man, who was probably already off balance at the sight of the horses.

'Stop!' He shouted.

'We have stopped!' Kaelith shouted back, grinning.

'Then. Err... leave your horses!' He had clearly tried to think of what to say at a time like this.

'No!'

There was a long pause, a slight shifting in the heavily armoured gaggle of men who faced them now. Kaelith chuckled to himself. It was the little things he enjoyed.

'I will speak to your commander!' Kaelith shouted over.

'I will fetch him; wait here.'

'No!'

Again, the man stopped, as if unsure what to do. He was mid-stride, one foot raised, and seemed to malfunction completely. It took almost a full minute before here responded.

'What?' He eventually shouted.

'We will wait over there.' Kaelith pointed in no particular direction off the side of the road to the right of the man, who just seemed to shake his head and march away.

Kaelith gently coaxed his horse with his legs whilst leading it with the reins, to the right of the large group of infantry and a hundred strides further away. They reformed their original pattern, facing what was now the side of the group, which slowly rotated even further out of order so that the men could get the best look at the horses.

After five minutes, a group of about twenty of them jogged across the gap towards the horsemen. A small bookish man, with thick black robes and a hood pulled up over his head, was in the centre.

'What is the meaning of this?! Where did you find so many of these animals? Why have you stopped us on the road?'

Kaelith swore he had left this man's limp body in the cell at monastery.

'Caldor sent us.'

That hung in the summer air. Kaelith had kept his ears open even whilst his mind went a bit walkabout in the prison, and people will use many names around you when they think you're stark raving mad.

'For what purpose?'

'We are to be the vanguard force, here to crush the rebels when they engage the army.' Kaelith knew it was the truth and therefore made for the best lie. The truth, from a perspective at least, which was the army and which rebels, was just semantics.

'I...' The man seemed overwhelmed. The ridiculousness of standing one hundred strides off the road conversing with a man on horseback about which of you was going to the be the surprise attack probably was a bit much. 'You have orders?' It seemed the man would fall back on protocol then. Not ideal, but not the end of this little adventure, either.

'Yes.'

Kaelith whipped out a leather-bound folder from his saddlebag. Volchak had helped him with this one. Spending a lifetime around the bureaucracy of the King's army had clearly taught that man a few useful lessons. And Kaelith was a dab hand with a bit of forgery. He handed it to the man.

'This is most irregular.' As the man read through the orders, peered at the signatures.

'Understandable sir. But you don't think you are the Order's only secret weapon, do you? And let's be honest, you are hardly inconspicuous.' He looked over the throng of men, clashing and clinking together as they moved around disorganised.

The small bookish man huffed and handed the orders to one of the armoured men behind him. He took another minute to inspect it.

'This says we are to return to Brieth?'

'Aye good sir, that it does. We will handle the rebels.'

'Well, I…' The man said. *So close*, Kaelith thought. 'Wait, who are you?'

The lie was too big – not enough truth.

The flash of recognition in the man's face was instant. His head cocked, eyes went wide and then he scrambled to shout, as the fencing steel pierced his unarmoured throat. He dropped to the ground.

The silence was thick. Kaelith felt the fight was about to begin. He knew that at any moment someone would move, something would drop, some noise or disruption and it would all break loose. He waited, a moment passed, he waited, another moment. Just as he felt he might be able to explain himself out of this one, his horse let out an almighty snort. And the horsemen shot forward from behind him and passed him on either side.

The Order Guard was wholly unprepared and unable to cope with what had just happened. The man holding the leather binder was trampled beneath the hooves of one of the eleven horsemen who had shot past Kaelith. Most of the twenty that had joined them were either crushed, sliced or scattered within moments.

Kaelith heeled his horse hard in its ribs. It reared up impressively and nearly dumped him from the saddle, damn thing, before shooting forward after the others towards the main bulk of the force. They didn't ride straight through the mob. Eventually, they would have slowed and stopped and then brought down most unceremoniously. Instead, the group carved at the edges, where the disorganised crowd was thin or groups had become separated. They made two more passes before the most organised of them formed solid ranks. Each pass crushed even the armoured men under hoof or allowed the riders to stab uncovered faces whilst shields remained lowered. Kaelith knew fighting on horseback was damned effective, but hadn't expected it to be quite so useful against such armoured opponents. They were thoroughly ill-equipped to deal with the threat and soon were forming a tight circle of shields, with the occasional sword poking out from it.

Kaelith and his men backed off. Two had been killed. One by a rogue sword at an unfortunate angle and the other had been too close to too thick a group and his momentum had stalled. He was stabbed and pulled off the horse and stabbed some more. Shame the horses had died in both cases as well. *Only nine left.*

After ten minutes, gaps started emerging in the ring of shields, as the force shifted slightly back towards the road. Every time they did so, the horseman started up again and rode in circles around them, feigning a charge at anyone who stepped too far from the line. Nearly an hour passed without a single weapon clash, the tight group of infantry moved again down the road, but at an incredibly slow pace. The horsemen were a constant reminder they could no longer march openly. It certainly wasn't a glorious charge to be remembered throughout the ages, a valiant band of mounted warriors standing up to a horde of armoured Order soldiers. But rather a well calculated plan, eating up the hours and sowing chaos and confusion.

The slow-moving stand-off began, and Kaelith had nothing but time.

Chapter 37

Flea stripped off her soaking wet clothes in the darkness and tried to stop her teeth from chattering so loudly. The noise seemed to echo around the damp chamber she found herself in. From the rope tied around her ankle, she dragged up the oilskin she had tightly wrapped in a bundle and wished with all her heart it had stayed dry. She had been rather more focussed on using it as a float to help keep her out of the water than whether she kept the water out of it, as she had clumsily swum up the sluice gate. This area was clearly rarely used, as she had expected. The sluice gate at the mine in the capital was used only when the tunnels were cleaned. This was rarely ever, usually only after a collapse. Being dirty underground didn't stop you digging. She wrapped herself back up in the thick black robe, slightly tatty, but familiar to her after her time here in the monastery.

She took the small flint and striker from her bundle as well. She knelt, facing the gap in the rocks out to the bay and struck three small sparks. She had no idea whether it would be seen at the distance that Tamryn had placed the small rowboat. Flea liked Tammy, even if she hated being called Tammy. Tammy was sweeter than she acted and had made sure Flea had a comfortable bed on their boat and lots of warm food. She'd thought Flea was asleep when she covered her with the blanket. Flea wasn't asleep, of course; she was a very light sleeper and boats were actually quite noisy. Constant footsteps and creaking and the ropes would drag on the...

She stopped herself. *Focus.*

She pocketed the flint and striker; it was probably one of the most valuable things she had ever held and she wasn't about to lose it, and made her way to the door. Unlocked. In fact, no lock at all. That would have cut short a very wasteful trip, or she would have had to wait in the darkness and the damp for a very long time.

As she made her way into the cavern beyond, it seemed a bustle of activity - far busier than when she had last been there, and far brighter as well. She lowered her head and wove amongst the smiths, the assistants, the other black-robed interns who rushed this way and that. The plan was simple. Find the cells, hole up down here until she found an opportunity to stab Caldor with the little steel knife Tammy had given her. Save the King. Get back to the sluice gate. Float out to the bay. Get picked up. Mr. Volchak wins the battle. She gets a royal pardon for saving the King, and she and Harkner can be let free. Kaelith had called it a 'solid plan'.

Flea had no intention of sticking to the plan. She needed to find Harkner and Stirc and get them out, that was what mattered. Luckily for her, once she was out of the cavern, she knew exactly where they would be. Maybe she would stab Caldor on the way out, maybe not. She would try to save the King because that royal pardon sounded like a good thing. But if she got away without stabbing anybody and only saving the important people, then that would not be the end of the world.

After generally staying out of the way as she moved around, she eventually caught sight of the staircase up to the familiar door at the top. She made for the stairs and climbed up. Glancing back, she took in the sight of the glowing ants' nest of activity below her. Definitely busier than when she was last here. Most of the forges were lit, and the number of people had clearly doubled. The staircase creaked and brought her back to the moment as she continued up and opened the door. The two guards did not have time to challenge her. She immediately turned right, as if through habit, and ascended the stairs. They did not care. Seemed to her that maybe they were told to keep people out, not in. Her boots tapped up the stairs as she went. Perhaps barefoot would have been quieter, but then if someone noticed, it would be harder to explain. People don't pay much attention to what's on your feet, till nothing was. She shook her head to bring her out of the daydream.

Focus.

She reached the second floor; it looked precisely as it had before. Quiet. She saw one red-robed physician enter a room about half way down. They ignored her completely as she walked past, head bowed. She passed the room where the large topless man and his throne were. She glanced in through the small slot in the door, and stopped in her tracks.

The Duke had told her several times what the King looked like. Kaelith had then explained, afterwards, that he saw the man as he wanted to see him. But that the reality was very different. Kaelith was right on this one. The thin, bony body had a stark ribcage and almost skeletal arms as it slumped on the wooden replica throne. The blonde hair was long and matted, plastered down the front of the face with a thick and curly peppered grey beard covering most of the face. But the eyes were a stark bright blue, of that there was no denying.

Royal pardon it is then. One minor detail was the large topless man asleep on the cot next to the captive King, his massive shoulders facing away from the door.

Flea removed her boots. If he had time to ask her about them, then it didn't really matter anyway, as it would be too late. Her bare feet were cold on the stone floor as she slipped open the door. Unlocked. What was it with this place and their lack of locked doors? Anyone could come in and take whatever they wanted, even a king?

Focus.

The door opened with the slightest creak, but otherwise she entered silently. It was late into the evening, or early into morning. She hadn't checked beforehand... but guessing it was late in the evening she hoped no one was awake. The eyes of the prisoner locked on her as she opened the door and she held her small hand to her mouth with one finger covering it. She wasn't sure if he could make a noise, but she would prefer it if he didn't. She glided over the tiled floor to the sleeping man. His bald head bulged with veins, just like his muscular arms. At least the size of Harkner, and probably in far better condition. More of a fighter than a Physician, but she shrugged; didn't matter. She didn't see the need to feel bad about this. She had seen the pleasure this man had taken in binding the body last time and she now knew what they had done to the King. After all, they had tied him to a wooden throne about two strides from her. Stirc had told her these white-robed Registrars were evil, and Stirc was very smart.

The man shifted on the cot, rolling onto his back. That was handy. She drove the blade into his neck once, twice, three times, four times, quick and sharp jabs as the steel slipped in and out, and in and out. The gush of blood onto her wrist and the floor made it easier with each stab. The man's face contorted into a silent scream. For a moment, she thought of the foreman and his loud scream as he fell from the walkway. How it alerted everyone and sent her to the prison. No such scream here. One arm raised slightly towards the wound as the eyes swelled from his face, but he was dead before it reached there. Flea stepped back as the blood trickled down into the drains at the centre of the room. That was convenient, much less work to clean up, she supposed. Looking at her hand, covered in thick crimson blood, it did not show against her robe. She wiped it on the man's white robe hung to the side of the cot. That would be quite a lot of work to clean, would be better to get a new one.

She shook her head, fighting off the urge to follow the train of thought, and turned back to the prisoner. She looked at the dials on the back of the throne, all unlabelled.

Tricky. She followed the wires with her eyes. Several of them were tied around the man's neck. Probably want to be careful with this then. She twisted one slightly and the man's head twisted. She quickly put it back, and it moved back the other way. Another of them seemed to raise one of his arms, no not useful. She walked round the front.

'Any ideas?' she whispered.

One wire was bound in thick leather directly across the man's mouth. He could only gurgle a response, which Flea didn't understand. She looked back at the dials. At the bottom, towards the right there was a lever, pushed all the way up. She shrugged, grabbed it, and dragged it down.

There was a click and then a scraping of what sounded like metal.

All the wires dropped loose as the man slumped down in the chair, no longer held in place.

Ah. That worked then.

'Your Royal... ness...' Flea hadn't ever spoken to a King before. 'I think you had better put this on and come with me.' Her voice was soft, but commanding. The man seemed to fight back the urge to cry for a moment, his eyes glistening with tears as he strained against the throne to push himself up. He didn't respond, but his bony hand reached out for the other black robe and took it. His other hand came up and held her elbow. The slightest of nods. She smiled at him, and a few tears leaked from his piercing blue eyes.

Stirc was leant on the edge of his own block with his back to the door. She saw the back of his gaunt bald head lowered as he appeared to be staring at the tiled floor. Both his hands spread behind him on the empty block behind. Flea thought she'd have to wake him up, but apparently not.

'Not now…' he said, not turning as she entered the room with the King behind her.

'Hi Mr. Stirc!' Her voice was quiet but cheerful. She was happy to see him.

He spun, looked from her, looked to the King, looked back at her. His eyes widened and mouth opened, forming a 'what' with no sound.

She smiled, tilting her head slightly, face full of mischief.

'Think it's time we got you out.' She mimicked his voice from a few weeks ago and chuckled to herself. Then back to normal. 'Where's Harkner?' The chair he normally lazed in was empty.

'I… err…' He was still lost for words as his legs buckled and he sat back on to the cot.

There was a noise outside, a door opening and the closing as someone walked down the hall. It seemed to snap him out of it.

'Flea, there's something you need to know.'

⁎⁎

Tears still stung her eyes as they marched down the wooden staircase back into the workshop below. Flea kept them fixed on the back of Stirc, in his crisp white robe, and resisted the urge to wipe them away until she was certain they were out of sight of the guards. Caleb - he had said to call him Caleb - followed, unsteadily, behind. His bare feet occasionally poking out from under the robe. Luckily it was large enough to cover his whole body - too big, in fact. Meant for someone far larger than he was. More tears swelled up.

As they headed for the sluice gate, she suddenly froze in place. Stirc realised, several paces later and returned to her. Until he, too, glared into the cavern mouth where she was standing. She must have passed on her way here, but hadn't even thought to look as she hurried past. At its rear was a small wooden door which stood open, and inside, with his back to them, was a man in a white robe kneeling before an enormous set of shelves. Stacked high, beyond where the doorway revealed, were dozens of glass jars, some stained and dirty, but others transparent. Flea nearly vomited in her mouth, despite all she'd seen, when she realised what they were holding.

In a daze, she headed for the door... focussed on one thing.

She slammed the door behind her. The man didn't jump or react in any way. He simply rose from kneeling and turned to face her. His blank face staring at hers. No anger, no pity, no arrogance. He seemed to see into her and weigh her up, and react to neither.

He had no weapons; she made her move against him.

Flea feigned left and skipped forward, ducking low to the right, as if dodging and weaving round blows that Caldor was not delivering. She thrust the knife upward towards his heart. The blow came to meet her face before the blade met its mark. The back of the man's hand struck and lifted her off her feet. She reeled in the air before landing on the floor several strides to the right. As she tumbled and recovered, rolled onto her feet in a crouch. Flea looked at where he had stood when he hit her. Empty space. A hand gripped the back of her leather armour, the slight constriction of the collar round her neck as it plucked her from the ground and flung her forward. She collided with a large wooden block, an immovable weight that crunched against her face and shoulder as she skidded into it with a painful jolt.

Her world upended as powerful hands lifted and crashed her modest form into the air and onto the block. He cracked her skull against the wood as her eyes searched desperately for something, anything, to help. The block was stained a deep crimson at this end, with the indentation about the right size for a head in the solid block. Flea panicked as she saw the man's blank expression. He stood next to the block, holding her against it. His deep blue eyes were empty, staring through her. With one hand, he pressed her body, squashed it against the block. His other hand reached down and pulled up a rusty, but substantial, metal chain from the side of the block. He reached towards her wrist.

The crash of glass. Fetid green liquid sprayed from behind the man's thick bald head and into Flea's eyes and mouth. She gagged and coughed, spluttered and shook until she regained her vision. Shards of glass covered he legs. The man had his back to her and walked slowly towards Stirc, who backed away with his arms up in the air, cowering. He was covered in the same rancid liquid that was in her hair and face.

No.

She leapt from the block - an impressive jump even by her standards - and landed on the floor behind the man. Her hand swept the ground before her as she rolled forward and felt the icy grip of a small piece of metal as she rose to her feet and swung it.

She drove the little silver knife directly into his face; angled up it pierced just under one eye and up into his skull. She would have pushed it straight through, if she could, for what he had made Harkner do. For what he had done to these people - his 'subjects'. For what he had done to the Breachmen - her family.

'Unexpected,' was all Caldor said.

He stumbled back and fell onto the shelf. It tilted, wobbled, and fell. All around, the glass jars smashed and their contents spilled out onto the floor. The soft tissue within scattered or sliced open on the glass, or simply sitting wet on the plain stone.

Flea gagged as the smell hit her in waves, worse and worse. She spun and fled to the door, avoiding as much of the oozing liquid as she could.

'What have I...?' Stirc's eyes were wide as he looked over her head at the carnage beyond. Caldor's body lay face down over the toppled shelving unit, the small steel dagger protruding from it. Flea pushed past him and grabbed Caleb's robe and forced him down the corridor.

She turned back to face Stirc, who was still standing above Caldor's body.

'Come with me.' She pleaded to him. Just as shouts emerged from the tunnels behind at the sound.

Stirc must have dashed to keep up as they reached the unlocked door as he was with them again. Flea grabbed two of the bundles she had stashed by the door and put one into their hands. Caleb got the one meant for Harkner. How could he have turned against the Breachmen? Against Mr. Volchak? After what they'd done? He'd always kept her safe, kept them both safe. If she could speak to him, just let him know she was okay.

Focus

She motioned for them to follow her. The water was ice cold against her skin and dragged at the heavy robe, but washed away the ichor in her eyes and hair. As she clung to her own bundle, acting as a float, she pulled at the rope that lay in the water and disappeared into the darkness, three times. It dragged her out into the bay from the other end. She'd done what she came to do. She had lost a lot in the process. Stirc and Caleb clutched their own bundles behind her, as the water washed away the filth of the place.

The water splashed in her face and washed away the tears there too.

Chapter 38

The blood spat up into Volchak's face as the axe cleaved the man's skull, the hand of the now-lifeless body still gripping the hilt of the sword he hadn't time to pull from the scabbard. Volchak snarled as he knocked the next man aside and then brought the axe down onto his stomach, the woollen blue uniform offering no resistance as the blade bit into the ground. Foot on the chest, he dragged the weapon out in time for the upswing to catch another man, who had been charging at him with a stone hammer, in the chin as he sidestepped the man's swing.

The command staff had been ill-prepared for the charge, even if only the two of them had made it through. Olaf swung his long sword with both hands taking the head off the first, a clerk Volchak had maybe shared a bottle with once on the road, and then stabbed through the second, a snot-nosed lieutenant who had chewed out the Breachmen over their poor attire the day after a charge. Good and bad men died all the same, as the pair carved a route directly to the High Commander's staff. A spear grazed Volchak under the arm and he yanked it forward, smashing the man's face with the head of his axe before chopping down on both arms. The man fell screaming onto the lush grass. Volchak could see Smiele only twenty strides away, shouting at the men around him and pointing to where Volchak and Olaf's trail of dead soldiers ended, with the two of them still advancing. Smiele wore a red cloak that whipped about him in a rage, making him seem twice the size Volchak knew he was. That and the glinting mail made him stand out against the bodies running this way and that. Few seemed to pay any attention - but he made for an obvious target.

Then, a shadow was cast over Volchak as the sun was blotted out. At the last moment he dove aside, as the enormous stone hammer thudded into the earth. Volchak rolled as it hit the floor again behind him, and then struggled to his feet, only to dive backwards again as it pounded the ground a third time. 'Why...' Thud. 'Wont...' Thud – a fourth. 'You.' Thud – a fifth. 'Die?' Harkner screamed as he kept swinging the hammer and Volchak kept scrabbling to get away. He had covered maybe ten paces, and they now seemed alone on the side of the hill - no one else looking to advance on the massive man and the blood-soaked enemy commander now standing opposite him.

Volchak spat to his side, an angry metallic taste telling him, somewhere, he'd lost at least one tooth from a blow to the face.

'I killed you on the wall. We'd be free. That was the deal.' Harkner seemed almost desperate, whether it was anger or fear in his face, Volchak didn't know. He feigned a swing of the axe towards Harkner, who skipped a few steps back.

'I've always been tough to kill, you know that.' Volchak stopped moving. Caught his breath for a moment whilst keeping the axe raised ready. 'That uniform doesn't scream freedom to me.'

'It was the only way. They would not let her go. I had to... to stop you.' There were tears forming in the big man's eyes. He frantically burst forward and swung the hammer down at Volchak, smashing it into the ground as the smaller man stepped aside and smacked Harkner's face with the haft of the axe. He felt the nose crunch under the impact as Harkner shouted in pain. Volchak stepped back, creating more space between them.

'Flea is safe. She is with me, Harkner. At Yrfrite.' Harkner froze. His head turned as his eyes shot back to Smiele.

So, he was lied to then.

'She found me, got me on the boat. You're on the wrong side of this, friend.' As Volchak said the word friend, he swung the axe, but the big man stepped inside it and blocked the haft with the handle of his own hammer. The two weapons cracked against each other hard, and the vibrations made Volchak's shoulder scream. He shoved the man back with his other shoulder.

'You're lying.' Harkner said, no conviction in his voice.

Volchak stood firm, feet planted on the ground. He was uphill slightly of Harkner now and his head almost at the same level.

'I'm many things Harkner, you are right. A killer. A monster. Violent. Bloodthirsty. Guilty for all of this.' Volchak motioned around them, back towards the valley below where the two armies still fought. 'But I'm no liar. Leave now and one day you'll be able to find her again. Fight me, and you won't survive this. You know that.'

'I…' Harkner's eyes were glistening with tears. He looked to Volchak, to where Smiele stood shouting, to the valley and back at Volchak. 'I refuse to die. Caldor, Smiele… damn the lot of them.' Quietly, almost silently. He threw the hammer to the ground in front of him.

At the same moment Olaf's sword penetrated through his chest from behind, rammed by the Duke's over his head.

'No wait!' Volchak tried to stop it, but it was far too late already. The giant body crumpled onto the floor, falling back onto Olaf, who was pinned underneath. The sword was now run through Harkner up the hilt. There was nothing Volchak could do.

'Volchak!'

He immediately knew the voice. High and nasal. He knew to whom it belonged.

He turned and looked up the hill. Two men stood. Smiele in his shimmering plate mail and luxurious long red cloak, and a scared looking clerk, holding a sword out in front of him, the end wavering as his hands trembled.

'Smiele. This is over.' Volchak said.

'Non-sense. Your little rebellion is finished. If I'm not mistaken, we have your Duke pinned over there beneath my most recent recruit's body. And you're outmatched here, Breachman. Your brutal tactics don't work in a civilised fight.' Smiele's tone was familiar, confident. He flourished his sword in front of him in a fencing salute.

'That won't stop me killing you.'

'Perhaps. But until then.' Smiele came at him with his glorious sword. Flashing in the mid-day sun, the man moved far faster than Volchak had expected in his heavy armour. The sword swung down, Volchak knocked it aside, but then it came back from the other side and then jabbed at him twice with incredible speed. One jab caught Volchak's shoulder through his leather armour. Volchak jumped to the side and parried the second with the head of his axe. He stumbled back out of reach, feeling the blood running down the inside of his arm. The clerk just stood where he was, none too keen to get involved.

Smiele stood in an aggressive pose and caught his breath for a moment. Volchak felt his shoulder burn as he lifted his axe, his left arm sluggish where he had been pierced by the tip of the sword.

'Why me?' Volchak was breathing heavy, leaning slightly to one side.

Smiele swung the sword twice more - Volchak side-stepped the first and then parried the second with his axe, pain screaming through his shoulder now. He shoved Smiele back with the haft of the axe.

'What?' Smiele sounded less confident now, but still his voice carried the air of superiority he was accustomed to.

'Why did you choose this for me? Why wouldn't you let me go? What am I to you?' Volchak shouted the last question as he swung the axe towards Smiele. Overhead, missed. Followed through into a wide arch left to right that carried Volchak's whole body round. Smiele put his sword in the way, but the weight of the axe knocked it back into his side and sent him sprawling onto the ground. Volchak went to raise the axe over his left shoulder for a finishing blow, but found his arm simply wouldn't support the weight. He screamed as he dropped to one knee with the pain crawling across his back and neck. The blood was dripping out from his sleeve on one side, the dull ache in the back of his head was exploding across his skull as his other shoulder was on fire. He propped himself up, unsteadily, to standing with the axe under his right arm. The world was a blur in front of him – a shining shape was on the ground nearby, moving.

Smiele rose to his feet. Volchak wobbled on his. 'You? You think I chose you? I couldn't care less about you and your insignificant life. You were just a random act. Plucked from the obscurity of the masses. I expected to have to replace you within months. When you turned out to be a useful, I kept you around. But you were never anything special. Mark my words, you lived longer than anyone planned, but Breachmen are just fodder. I used them to weed out the undesirables, to teach the people their place. You aren't supposed to still be here. You are supposed to die!' Smiele was almost laughing now, bellowing to the sky.

Smiele shot forward with his sword in an enormous lunge, the longsword held out to skewer Volchak. In his rage, Volchak leapt forward into it, felt the steel slide effortlessly through the leather and into his left side, cutting a huge gash across it. He had dropped the axe as he headbutted Smiele square in the jaw, whipping his head back. Volchak used his free hand to seize the cloak from behind Smiele's head and wound it round the man's neck. He pulled it tight so the High Commander's face bulged. Volchak landed hard on the ground, pain searing through his side and shoulder as he dragged at the cloak with all his might. The weight of Smiele's large armoured form on top of him pinned his legs as he cradled the man's head, face snarling and blood flying from his mouth. Volchak cried out for the years wasted by this man for no other reason than he was useful to him. Tighter and tighter, he pulled at the cloak as Smiele's bloodshot eyes protruded further and further from his head. Smiele's teeth gnashed and his arms flailed, but Volchak held him firm, lying underneath him on his back as Smiele's thrashing grew less and less, until finally he was completely still. Volchak rolled the body off him, blood leaking down his face from where he struck Smiele, and from his wounded side. He knelt and picked up the sword, then drove it down into the body, pinning it to the hillside.

Volchak looked up at the clerk, still frozen with the sword out in front of him.

'Sound your retreat. It's over.'

The world spun as he collapsed next to Smiele, lying next to his axe on the ground, as the world turned black.

Chapter 39

Volchak scraped his foot in the dirt, drew a line across in front of himself. *A battle-line*. He stared at it. Looked up. The shield wall was ahead. He gripped his axe tight, felt the leather on the haft digging into his hands, pinching the skin. Any moment a charge. A breach. Would he survive this one? He crossed the line, at a slow walk. Reached the shield wall and smiled, shook his head to himself as he reached behind the shield and undid the leather knot that held it on the log. His arms were still cumbersome, hands clumsy, but recovering. He moved down the line to the next one, axe left on the ground by the first log.

'You can clean my chamber pot when you're done!' Kaelith shouted as he approached, walking alongside Tamryn, still cloaked with her hand bow at her side.

'Not even I would survive that ordeal.' He turned and smiled at the sound. They clasped arms when Kaelith reached him, foot kicking through the small line that Volchak had left on the floor of the Breachmen arena. The sting in his side and shoulder subsided quickly as the man released his grip, beaming.

'You will be staying in the capital Kaelith?'

'Me? Oh no. Far too civilised. I seek a more rustic aesthetic. Why, I will escort the new Duchess of Yrfrite back up north.' He turned and winked to Tamryn, who rolled her eyes.

'Curses. Why did I agree to this?' She asked.

'I couldn't think of a better protector.' Volchak smiled at her, and bowed his head.

'Aye and I couldn't find one.' She half-cocked a smile and stepped away, evidently giving them some space for their own goodbye.

Kaelith grinned. 'Been a pleasure. Couldn't have tried to ambush a nicer man.'

'Thought you weren't trying to get me?'

'That's the thing about a lie, my friend, tell as much of the truth as you can. Keep well.' Kaelith jogged after Tamryn, his ruffled shirt bouncing along as he slipped slightly on the dusty ground and corrected himself. Volchak continued down the line, removing shields.

Once he had them all stacked away, he looked across the empty arena and saw Flea. She was standing at the Eastern door to the arena, next to Olaf. He picked up the axe and walked slowly towards them, his legs tired, his neck aching and the pain in his left side reminding him of the past few months.

'So, your sister then?' Volchak nodded over to behind him, Flea stood up on tiptoe to peer over his shoulder, but Kaelith and Tamryn had long gone.

'Ah. Yes, she will take over as Duchess of Yrfrite. Caleb needs me here. The people are angry and still don't really understand what happened. Stories of the Order Guard and the mounted warriors. It's all a bit messy.' Olaf was smiling. The lines on his heroic face seemed a little deeper, the scar on his cheek a little darker. Seemed a few of his fights were catching up to him as well.

'What will you do with them? The Guards?' Volchak didn't specify which.

'Country needs an army. But I think this will be different. We will strip them back, putting some of that metal to good use. In the fields, in the factories.'

Volchak considered a moment, then replied.

'Good. You'll lead them?'

'Me?' Olaf chuckled. 'Despite what I've been doing for the last few years, no, war isn't for me. I am an administrator, a governor, not a military leader. I'd rather thought you might want the job?'

Volchak shook his head. Doing so sent a spark of pain down his leg - which threatened to buckle. He held his right arm up against the frame of the doorway into the arena; the movement made his shoulder hurt.

'Think I'm about done,' he said.

Olaf nodded.

'Well then, with Klyssa dead, I suppose I'll need to find someone else. Someone experienced, someone clever. Someone who isn't afraid of a fight, but isn't looking for one.'

Volchak smiled. Olaf grinned. They both looked at the girl standing to his right. She was staring up at the stone wall of the Breachmen's arena, where Volchak had lain a few months prior. She seemed a hundred miles away, eyes following a bird flying above the wall.

'Eh, Flea?' Volchak prompted.

She shook her head and looked at him. As if only noticing he was there.

'Eh what?'

Volchak held out the axe, the weight of it now too heavy in his tired arm. The weathered bronze blade caught the last of the afternoon sun, for a moment it seemed clean, polished, fresh and new. He let it go into her hands, which dipped slightly with the weight.

She'd get used to it.

-How It Begins-

Volchak climbed down from the last rung of the wooden ladder, feeling the stabbing in his shoulder as his foot hit the hard ground. He sighed and looked up towards where he had attempted to fix the roof. It didn't look right; boards were slightly askew and one of the thin wooden stakes hadn't gone all the way in. Might work. Probably not. He'd have to climb back up.

'Dammit.'

He tossed the heavy wooden mallet down with a grunt, shrugging his shoulders painfully. He walked back across the yard. He'd lost nearly half of his second harvest because of that hole in the roof, had thought little of it till the rains came.

As he walked, he was careful not to trip over the dry, rutted ground. At this point he had turned his ankle so many times he had run out of curses.

The house before him looked tired, stonework cracked and one window bulging outwards at an alarming angle. Was it going to collapse? Probably not. At least not today. He walked through the open door, damn thing wouldn't close all the way, and into the small kitchen. He was greeted by the familiar warmth from the hearth held in by the thick walls. A draft from that bulging window whipped away the warmth. Volchak glared at it.

Something had caught his eye though, and he bent slightly to look directly through the cloudy glass. In the field on the other side of the collapsed fence, there was a small blur. Volchak stepped back to the sink, well to the pail of water that he had placed in the sink since the drain appeared to leak back onto the floor rather than into the ditch outside. He washed his hands in the cold, clear water, turning it murky with the mud and sweat from the morning's work. He worked the water into his scarred hands, under his chipped nails and leathery wrists.

'No blood today,' he whispered to himself, as he looked around for something to dry them on. Finding nothing, he wiped them on the front of his plain cotton shirt.

The blur had grown closer and, as he stood in the yard, Volchak could now see the man atop of an imposing white horse. He had seen many horses now, of course. Kaelith's during the war, but many more since. They had passed on the road adjacent to his land from their new mine in the West. He suspected the miners had cut right through the mountain range by now and were now bringing them in by the hundreds. There were lots on that side. *Maybe he should get one?* He rubbed at the back of his head, feeling the hairless scar from his first encounter up close with one. *Maybe not.*

He stood still, hands empty at his side, and closed his eyes. He felt the slight winter wind caressing his face. It pulled at his long, curly grey hair and cut at the two wet patches on his chest. As he listened, he could hear only the steady thud of the horse as it approached. His neck ached from the work this morning. His shoulder hurt, as it always did. His legs were tired and his back was sore from the time in the fields, or maybe the time before that. He sighed, and he waited. Hoping it wouldn't slow down and would just ride right over him. Like it should have done the first time.

'Not much of a farmer.'

His eyes opened to see the grinning face of Kaelith, atop his powerful white charger. He had stopped several strides short.

'Well, you make a fine Duke.' Volchak meant it. The breastplate shone, even in the weak sun of winter. The blonde ponytail was radiant, tied with colourful ribbon. The gleaming basket of the curved sword sheathed at his side glinted. And a glorious, pearl-white shirt, with many, many ruffles, swayed in the breeze.

'Duke Consort. I'll never convince her to be a wife, but I daresay nobility agrees with me.' Kaelith beamed at him and looked around. 'Should fix that hole, you know,' he added, nodding at the barn.

Volchak broke into a smile and shook his head.

'Aye, I know. How is Flea?'

'Ah, the Commander of the People's Guard? Fearsome woman, that. You're lucky you ever got to fight with her. A firm but fair commander. Finest the King has ever seen. Saved the realm, she killed most of the treacherous Order council didn't you know?' Kaelith beamed at him. 'Guess it was no surprise who replaced them in charge over there either.' Volchak thought of Stirc. He'd met him off the ship in Yrfrite when Flea returned- a changed man.

'You are happy here?' Kaelith continued. There was no judgement in his voice, but a hint of concern.

'I am alive. Although, I guess I still have to try hard to remain that way. It is peaceful here, but farming isn't as easy as I'd thought.'

'Guess that's why farmers are all so miserable all the time.' Kaelith laughed. The noise caused his horse to jolt against the bridle, making him re-arrange the leather reins in his hand. The horse span on the spot once before he calmed it, the slightest shine taken from his glorious image.

'Damn thing.'

'What does the Duke-Consort of Yrfrite need that would make him ride from his city to speak to a simple farmer?' Volchak asked.

'Your help, Volchak.'

The sun passed behind a cloud, and the glint from Kaelith's breastplate faded. He leant down and retrieved something large from the straps on the back of the horse. It took him a moment to undo the clasps and lift whatever it was into both his hands. He dropped the oil-skin and threw the heavy object towards Volchak.

Volchak caught the haft with his left hand, the pain shooting through his shoulder and down his back as he did so. The familiar pain. His other hand slammed onto the grip and rolled it in his hands. The welcome pain. He instinctively widened his stance, bent his knees and readied himself. *His pain*. He looked the axe up and down, the deep scratches along the shaft from countless impacts were still there. As were the gaps in the leather that pinched his fingers from where the soft leather squeezed against cold bronze. It was still over-sized, heavier than was practical, cumbersome and brutal. He felt its weight, rooting him to the spot - immovable. The blades were dull and weathered, stained from heavy use - as he had always known them, but sharp and ready. The world around him was clearer, brighter. The axe hadn't aged, hadn't changed.

Volchak brandished it in his hands and looked back to Kaelith.

Well...

The End

About the Author

Chris Barker was born a thousand years too late into a world entirely too realistic for his liking.

In his opinion, he should be riding one of Kaelith's horses gloriously into battle. Or sprinting across the open field charging down a shield wall with the Breachman. Or possibly just drinking himself into a stupor in one of the capital's many taverns – one of the seedier ones.

Since he isn't though, you'll maybe find him walking with his ever-patient wife and dog in the woods of Buckinghamshire. When he isn't outdoors, he'll be sat in his study at an antique desk, with his grandfather clock ticking away in the background, flying spaceships in virtual reality.

A self-confessed uber-geek. He studied Criminology at the University of Manchester and became enamoured with the interaction between opposing players, warfare, game theory and the strategy of conflict. After graduation, he joined the financial sector during the spectacular collapse at the beginning of the financial crisis. He has been fighting that battle ever since.

He writes for fun. If someone enjoys one of his stories then it proves he can take 26 letters and put them in an order that makes someone happier. He hopes that someone is you.

contact: info@squidinkpublishing.co.uk

Please help others join the Breachmen

Leave a review

For more information or to get in contact visit:

www.squidinkpublishing.co.uk

info@squidinkpublishing.co.uk

Squid Ink Publishing